THROUGH MANY WATERS

Romaine Manning's only interest had been her career in medicine until the love of two men turns her world upside down. Jeff Elster, a racing driver, is devoted to Romaine, but can't resist other women. Ian Vannery, gentle, artistic, trapped in a nightmare marriage, finds real love for the first time. Romaine buries herself in her work. But her heart aches with loneliness that only a man can heal.

OTHER NETTA MUSKET TITLES IN LARGE PRINT

Cloudbreak

Nor Any Dawn

Through Many Waters

THROUGH MANY WATERS

Through Many Waters

by

NETTA MUSKETT

MAGNA PRINT BOOKS
Bolton-by-Bowland
Lancashire . England

British Library Cataloguing in Publication Data

Muskett, Netta
 Through many waters. – Large print ed.
 I. Title
 823′.912[F]   PR6025.U9T/

 ISBN 0–86009–301–8

First Published in Great Britain by Hutchinson & Co.
(Publishers) Ltd. 1961

Copyright © 1961 by Netta Muskett

Published in Large Print 1981 by arrangement with Hutchinson
Publishing Group London and New York

Printed and bound in Great Britain by
Redwood Burn Limited   Trowbridge and Esher.

Chapter One

ROMAINE sat in front of the fire and felt a long shiver running through her, in spite of the warmth of the room, in spite of the luxurious wrap of quilted satin and swansdown which had been her mother's Christmas present and which she was almost surprised to find herself wearing.

She could not remember taking her dress off. It had been purely automatic though she had not gone so far as to put it on its hanger in the wardrobe. She had flung it across a chair, a gleaming thing of green and bluc brocade, severely cut because that was her style but rich in colour and texture and it had moulded her long limbs and swirled about her feet, and Jeff had told her she looked like a fish in it.

A fish!

It was the recollection of that which had made her shiver, for she had been no fish that evening, the last night of the old year, the first morning of the new year which

7

might mean so many things to her if she let it.

A soft tap at the door disturbed her.

'Come in, Mumsie. I'm not asleep,' she called, and her mother, loving and anxious, came into the room, dressing-gowned, her hair in a neat sleeping-net, obviously just out of her own bed.

'Not even in bed yet, darling? It's three o'clock! Did you have a nice time?'

'Yes. Lovely. Is it really three? Go back to bed, Mumsie. You should have been asleep hours ago. I'll get into bed. Really I will.'

'Well, thank heaven you can lie in as long as you like in the morning and nobody can call you up. I'm so glad you've finished with that dreadful hospital job and you can have a long rest.'

In spite of the hour, she knew that her mother would have liked to stay and talk about that long rest, but Romaine had no intention of getting involved in any such conversation, least of all with her mother. Everything had changed for her – or had it? In any case, she was not ready to talk about it. In her present mood and at three o'clock on New Year's morning, she might say things she would afterwards regret and not be able to unsay.

She rose from her chair and kissed her mother, that in itself rather unusual, for the Mannings were not a demonstrative family though deeply loving.

'Good night, Mumsie,' she said. 'Or rather, good morning. Happy New Year. Go to bed, and I think I will lie in in the morning,' and she led her mother to the door and shut her firmly outside, undressed and began automatically to remove her make-up.

She had not wanted to look at herself in the mirror, for surely she would look different? But she didn't. The same face looked back at her, the same clear grey eyes, the same mouth which had scarcely needed the lipstick which she never wore during the day at the hospital where she had just finished her time as a junior 'houseman'.

Yet her mouth, at least, should have looked different, for Jeff had kissed it long and breathlessly, had called her a fish when both of them had known she was no fish, no cold-blooded creature, but a woman, vital and warm and loving, appalled now to find that she was so.

She had not really wanted to go to the dance at all. She had been tired after her last day at the hospital, with its many details of handing over to the new doctor, last visits to her favourite patients, receiving little gifts from the nurses and the other doctors with whom she had worked, touchingly aware that they had been fond of her even though, as the daughter of a rich man and with no need to earn a living at all, she had always seemed apart from them.

She had intended to have that rest, and then look for a partnership somewhere and go into practice. She had had bitterly to accept the fact that she could not become a surgeon, which had been her ardent desire. She lacked that essential something, and had accepted it and had made up her mind that she would at least be a very good general practitioner.

She had always wanted to be a doctor and not even her mother had been able to deter her.

'Darling child,' Lady Manning had complained, 'there's no need for you to be anything at all. With your looks and your

10

father's position, you'll marry some nice man and then what good will all that work be?'

'Mumsie, it's no good. I can't just be Sir Julius Manning's daughter, the daughter of the house, a deb. dressing up and going to endless parties, finding myself a rich man to marry. I don't want to marry at all! I'm not made that way. Really I'm not. I ought to have been born the daughter of a poor man – though then I suppose I should not have had this expensive education, so called, or be able to go to medical school at all. Don't you see, Mumsie? It's something I *must* do. It's what I've always wanted to do.'

Her father had had the final word. Head of a private banking concern of international repute, a position which he had inherited from his father and which, in his turn, her brother John would inherit, Sir Julius sympathised with his wife's desire to keep Romaine cherished and cosseted and finally married to a suitable husband, but he knew that the girl would not be happy until she had got this 'doctoring thing' out of her system.

So she had her own way. She went

through medical school, worked unbelievably hard (and unnecessarily, her mother thought) to get her degree, and had done her time at one of the women's hospitals and now, at twenty-five, was determined to launch out on her own.

She was too young, of course, much too young to be in practice on her own, but if she could find an older woman, perhaps two of them, willing to take a young partner, she would get the necessary practical experience beyond what she had already had at the hospital, and her father would find whatever money was required.

So, leaving St Faith's on the last day of the year, she had been all set for her future life.

And then, that very night, she had met Jeff Elster!

He had come up to her quite brazenly and taken her from her partner.

'Mine, I think?' he said, and before she could even register her surprise and affront, she had been swept away in his arms.

He was tall, half a head taller than she was, with thick, dark hair several shades darker than her own, which had a chestnut glint in it when it caught the light, and his impudent eyes reminded her of bluebells in a wood, though it was a ridiculous thought to have about a man's eyes. His arms closed about her like a coiled spring and she felt the aliveness in his lean body run through her like an electric current.

'You — you had no business to do that!' she said indignantly.

'Why not? You were the only girl in the room for me as soon as I set eyes on you, and you like it, don't you — Romaine?'

'How do you know my name?'

She tried to keep up the indignation, but could feel it ebbing from her.

'I kept asking people till I found out. You're Romaine Manning, the daughter of the great Sir Julius. I'm Jeff, Jeff Elster. How do you do, Romaine? Now we've been introduced and you can get friendly.'

'Doesn't it occur to you that I may not want to?'

His arms held her even more closely. She could not escape except by making a scene.

'No, because you do,' he said. 'Come on, Romaine. Take off that look you're trying to keep on your face. I chose this waltz. You know what it is?' and he sang the words to her softly, his cheek touching hers so that he whispered them in her ear.

'You're beautiful, you're lovely.
We haven't met by chance.
I've just been waiting for you,
My best, my last romance.

She felt something stir in her which had never stirred before, and with the primitive instinct of the trapped female, she fought against it and yet knew she did not really want to fight at all.

When the dance ended, she tore herself out of his arms and joined the party of her friends, weaving her way frantically towards them and clutching at the arm of her brother, who was the nearest man.

'Have this with me, John. Please dance,' she jerked out breathlessly and with raised eyebrows, he obliged as the music had already started again.

'What's the idea? Run out of partners, or what?' he asked.

He was not a particularly good dancer and since she had no need to be partnered by her brother, they usually avoided each other, good friends though they were. For one thing, John was shorter than she was, a solid and stocky figure.

'I'm being pursued,' she told him. 'Don't look. Just dance. And don't tread on my feet or my dress if you can help it!'

But as soon as the dance ended, *he* was waiting for her and she knew she was lost and did not try to escape him again. She was still in his arms, when, just before midnight struck, the music stopped with a long roll of drums and everybody stood expectantly for the magic moment, the last of the old year.

He had manoeuvred them so that they were near a door, and as the music stopped, he pushed it open and let it close again behind them. They were in a deserted passage. Everybody else was in the dance hall waiting for midnight to strike, and they were quite alone.

She knew what was going to happen and did nothing about it. That stirring within her had become a tumult, a rushing tide that engulfed her, that left her powerless, rendered her blind and dumb and deaf to all but its compulsion.

And Jeff kissed her, holding her closely,

15

and her arms went about him and the roll of the drums and the striking of the hour seemed all a part of that magic moment which heralded not only the birth of a new year but the birth of herself as a woman in love, in love for the first time in her twenty-five years.

When their lips had ceased to cling, he still held her, tilting his head back so that he could see her, his blue eyes dancing points of mischief mingled with a tenderness which had not been in his fiercely compelling lips.

On the other side of the closed door, they were singing 'Auld Lang Syne', but she scarcely heard them.

'It's not auld lang syne for us, my beautiful, is it? There's nothing old about us, nothing to remember, nothing to forget. Aren't you glad we're young together? When shall we get married? Today? Tomorrow?'

That brought her to her senses and she struggled to get free, but he still held her with arms like a vice.

'Don't be absurd,' she said. 'I don't know you. We've only just met.'

'I know. Does that matter? "I've just

been waiting for you, My best, my last romance." Remember? Don't struggle to get away from me, darling. You can't, you know. You don't really want to. You want to stay in my arms for ever, just as I want to hold you – close, very close, closer than this, the closest there is. It's what you want, isn't it? It's what I want too, more than anything in the world. To have and to hold till death us do part. Isn't that the way it goes? But who wants to talk about death? Let's talk about life, and all the fun it's going to be, and all the love. I do love you, Romaine. But you know, don't you?'

'Jeff, be sensible. I'd think you were drunk, if I didn't know you're not.'

'No. I don't drink, or scarcely at all. Can't afford to in my job.'

'What is your job, Jeff?' she asked helplessly.

'I'm a racing motorist, not quite in the top flight, of course, or you'd have heard of me, but I'm going to get there. I've got several things lined up, small things like Goodwood and Brand's Hatch and I'm racing for my firm, but that won't be for long. When I do big things I shall be on my own and we shall go all over the world and

17

have fun—'

She put her hands over her ears, still held fast by his arms.

'Don't! Don't! The whole thing is fantastic – absurd. Of course I can't marry you. I – I'm a doctor!'

He put his head down and pushed one hand away with his lips.

'So what? I know you're a doctor, but don't doctors marry? And you don't have to keep on doctoring if you don't want to. You won't be able to, when we're married.'

She let her hands hang by her sides, knowing she could not get away from him.

'I don't want to give it up. I don't want to marry anyone. I don't want to marry you, Jeff!'

'Who are you trying to convince? Yourself? You won't convince me, you know. We belong. You know that, don't you? There are people in the world that are made for each other, but very few of them have the luck to meet. We have, Romaine. You're not going to let such a wonderful chance slip? Don't you feel in your bones that you belong to me and I belong to you? Darling, you're so beautiful. I love everything about you. The way your hair

18

grows and that reddish light in it,' taking his arms from her so that he could frame her face with his hands, and she no longer tried to escape. 'I love your little nose, and your wide eyes which perhaps, when you're not with me, look serene, like clear, grey pools. I love your long lines and your little breasts and your nice, flat tummy. How wonderful you'll look without all these trimmings! Best of all, just now, I love your mouth, my darling – the way your lips curve – and their warmth,' and he kissed her again and the world spun about her and there was no longer any sense in it, no longer anything but Jeff and his arms and his lips and the warmth of his body against her own.

She had wild thoughts which didn't belong to her at all. She would have given herself to him, freely, ecstatically, had he asked her to and had they been anywhere but in a passage outside a dance hall!

Then she was aware of people laughing and moving about, of the door opening behind them, and she drew back instinctively and he shielded her from curious eyes.

'A happy new year, my darling,' he

19

whispered, but she only shook her head and could not answer.

She was returning to herself even though she knew she would never be that familiar, serene, well-balanced self again.

'I must go back. I must find my friends,' she said, her voice shaken and unfamiliar.

'We won't dance again. It would be anti-climax to have you in my arms again in front of all those people. I'll see you tomorrow, my sweet. I'll ring you up first,' and he stood aside and let her go without touching her again.

She did not know how she got through the rest of the time until her party was ready to leave. She danced automatically and did not even look to see if Jeff's tall figure was there. She still felt lit and warmed by the fire he had kindled but dared not let herself think. When she did, she would not believe that it had really happened.

She had come in John's car, and though she could have had several alternative escorts and guessed that he would have preferred to take somebody else's sister home, she announced her intention of returning with him.

'Anything up, old thing?' he asked her as they drove away.

'No.'

'Who was that tall, dark chap you were dancing with?'

'Jeff Elster.'

'Chap who goes in for motor racing?'

'Yes. Do you know about him?'

'Only by name. Bit of an idiot, but they're all as mad as March hares. Kill himself some day, I suppose. Can't understand what they see in it or what good it does to go faster than anybody else.'

John, two years her senior, was his father's son, serious hard-working and industrious. He was being groomed to take his father's place in the city and asked nothing better. Nobody was less likely to understand and sympathise with the harum-scarum Jeff, and certainly John would never have asked a girl to marry him at their first meeting!

She did not pursue the topic of motor-racing, but John's voice flowed over her unheeded as he explained to her the niceties of the rise or fall of British Bank Rate. Dear John. She was so fond of him,

21

but the fire of Jeff's ardour was still all about her and she could not have cared less about anything as prosaic as the bank rate.

Once in her room, she had nothing to divert her mind from the problem which should have been no problem. She should have been able to cast it aside as she had cast aside the green and blue brocade in which he had told her she was a fish but had already known that she was not.

It was in vain that she told herself the whole thing was fantastic, an episode born of the dancing and the music and the excitement of the last night of the year. She would not have been moved by that. She was too calm and level-headed. But tonight she had been neither, and she was appalled at the discovery of herself as something quite different. Even here, in the room familiar to her since childhood, she could not recapture the girl she had been. She could still feel his arms about her and his mouth bruising her lips, still see the half-mocking, half-tender blueness of his eyes and hear his voice saying those absurd, incredible things to her, sure of the response which had leapt up in her to meet them though she had denied them.

Marry Jeff? *Marry* a man whom she had only just met, of whom she knew nothing except that he was a racing motorist? As if that in itself were not enough!

Whatever would her parents have to say about it, if they knew? She thought of her father, a man of serious affairs whose opinions and advice were sought and highly esteemed; of her mother, proud, gracious and kind to the many whom she considered her inferiors, holding rigidly to a code already outworn and admitting only the chosen few to her friendship.

What would either of them think of a man like Jeff as a husband for their only daughter? What, really, did she think of it herself?

In the end she had recourse to a sleeping pill which drugged her into an unconsciousness from which she was roused by the shrilling of the telephone bell beside her bed.

She had been roused like that many times as houseman at St Faith's, and she started up in bed to pick up the receiver and speak into it with a confused idea that she was still on duty call.

'Yes. Dr Manning here,' she said, and came to full consciousness at the sound of the voice which had pursued her into her dreams.

'My, aren't we formal this morning! Where are you? In bed still? I guessed you'd have a phone by your bedside, even if you hadn't been *Dr Manning!* Did I wake you, darling? If I did, I'm sorry, but I couldn't wait a minute longer. Can I come round? I suppose I shall have to wait for you to get up, though I bet you look delectable at this moment, all rosy and rumpled and dewy-eyed! Never mind. Before long I'll see you like that. How long before you're dressed?'

'Jeff, you mustn't come. You can't. How could I possibly explain you?' she stammered, looking at the door as if she were afraid he might come in that very minute.

'Do you have to? I suppose you will have to, in time. All right. Don't get in a flap. I won't come, but will you meet me? Better say for lunch, as it's after eleven now. Shocking hours you doctors keep!'

'Jeff, I — I can't! Tell me your address

and I'll write . . .'

'No you won't. If you did, it would be to say there's nothing doing and I'm not going to give you that chance. I'll meet you outside Harrod's. You can walk there. Twelve-thirty. I'll wait half an hour and then come to the house,' and he rang off.

She knew he meant it. She would have to go, would have to see him again. She couldn't possibly let him come to the house. Her mother was having a luncheon party and she was expected to be there, but she would have to make some excuse.

Feeling humiliated by the necessity, she sent a message to her mother, who would be still in her room, saying that she had been called to the hospital, dressed quickly and slipped out of the house. It was still too early for her to keep the appointment and she wandered round Harrod's, bought one or two things she didn't want and then, in a panic, went out into the street. It was a quarter to one. What if he hadn't waited, but had gone to the house?

But she saw him at once, in slacks and a leather jacket, his hands stuffed into his pockets.

'Jeff!'

25

'So you've come?' He took her left hand and squeezed it for a moment. 'I had the devil's own job to park. It's round the back somewhere. We shall probably find the majesty of the law standing beside it. It's much easier to rob a bank than to park a car nowadays. I must try it sometimes. Darling, you look ravishing. Is it mink?' touching her fur coat as he let her hand go.

'It was the only thing I could find,' she said crossly. 'You didn't give me much time.'

'An hour and a half? How much time did you want?' he jeered. 'This way, sweet. Ah, no copper, thank goodness,' steering her towards an open sports car that stood by the curb. 'Officer, I'm about to depart,' as the inevitable policeman appeared, note-book in hand. 'You wouldn't arrest me and throw me into your dungeon on the first day of the year, would you?' with an engaging grin.

'Well, sir . . .'

'Good lad. Thanks a million. Hop in, darling. Isn't she a dazzler? I mean the car, of course,' with a wink.

The officer shrugged his shoulders and let them go. He happened to be in love

26

himself.

'Where are we going?' asked Romaine weakly.

She had not got over the thrill of last night. It was still with her. Perhaps it would always be. She snuggled down into the collar of her coat and refused to let her mind dwell on that.

'I really meant to go to a little pub I know where they do a darned good steak, but I can't take you there looking like a million dollars so we'd better find something rather more classy. What about the Mitre at Hampton Court? Know it?'

'I've been there once. It was rather silly of me to wear this. Isn't it – I mean – won't it cost rather a lot there?'

She didn't even know if he could afford it!

'It's all right. It's a celebration. Our first meal together! Lashing of champagne and all that.'

'I don't like champagne.'

'Good. Neither do I. That's the first taste we've found in common – no, the second,' turning to look at her as they pulled up for traffic lights, looking first into her eyes and then at her lips.

27

She flushed and turned her head away, feeling that he had kissed her and he laughed softly and put his hand on hers for a moment.

'You're adorable and I love you even more than I did last night. Isn't it fun to be in love?' moving the gear lever as the lights changed.

She did not answer. What could she have answered? Was she really in love, or was this just a mad frolic that would die as quickly as it had been born?

When he spoke again, it was about cars, which were plainly his chief interest in life. She knew nothing about them, except how to drive her own little Morris, and told him so.

'Never mind. You will, darling. I've been driving a Cooper Climax, but they're going to let me have a go with the new Lotus at Goodwood. You must come down. Monday? I'm taking her out on a trial run, just to see what she'll do and to get the feel of her. There won't be anybody there but the mechanics. I'll let you know what time I can pick you up.'

'You seem to take it for granted that I have no other engagements.'

'Well, the chief one's mine, isn't it?' he asked her with his impish grin. 'You're permanently engaged — until we're married, of course. We'll have to talk about that.'

She could find nothing to say to him that might shake his calm assumption that she loved him, and as the day went on, she lost the wish to tell him so, for it was no longer true. He was the most delightful of companions, gay, amusing, sending her into gales of laughter one moment and turning her heart over with his tenderness the next. They walked in the gardens of Hampton Court Palace, completely deserted on this freezing day, and he took her in his arms and kissed her long and satisfyingly until she no longer tried to resist this insidious thing that was creeping through her to possess her. The thought of marrying Jeff seemed no longer fantastic; he had taken hold of her life and she knew she could not think of it now without him.

And it had happened in two days!

'Jeff,' she said seriously to him when they were on their way back and laughter had fled from them and only quietness remained, 'I can't run away with you. It would hurt the parents too much. I shall have to take you to meet them. I'm afraid you won't like that a bit.'

'No. I know I'm not good enough for you, darling. You could marry a lord, couldn't you? The wonderful thing is that you're going to marry me, aren't you? Just tell me you are, after having said so many times that you aren't, and I'm ready to meet the devil himself!'

She smiled ruefully.

'They aren't that, you know. They're sweet and dear and they want what they *think* is the best for me, as their daughter. I'm a sort of – of – changeling child. It was bad enough when I wanted to be a doctor, but this . . .'

He nodded.

'I know. I know I can't be right for you as far as they're concerned, as far as anybody is concerned but you. *You* know it's all right though, sweetness, and that's the only thing that really matters.'

'If I marry you, I can't follow my profession any more, can I?'

'Not unless I give up mine, and there isn't anything else I want to do or could do. Would you give it up for me, Romaine?'

'I wouldn't have thought I could ever do that for anyone, but – I think I could, Jeff,' she said in a low, shaken voice. 'I could bear anything but to lose you now.'

He heaved a sigh of relief.

'Then the worst is over and I'm ready to tackle anything or anybody now. When shall I come? Tomorrow?'

'Oh, not so soon, Jeff! I – I may be able to talk to them, to – to prepare them a bit.'

'You're still not sure, are you? I'm willing to wait a bit but I've got to see you every day until you say the word. No other dragons to fight, are there? Nobody else in the offing?'

'No. Nobody else. I've never wanted anyone before.'

'Bless you for those kind words, lady. Well, we're nearly there. Have you got to explain where you've been today?'

'No, not really. I said I'd been called to the hospital,' she said in a small, shamed voice. 'I can't do that again. I'm supposed have left my job there.'

'You won't change your mind and have dinner with me? It wouldn't be anything very posh, but I could manage it.'

'No, really, Jeff. We're dining out, and I

31

couldn't be rude enough to get out of it. As it is, I shall have a scramble to change and be ready in time. Stop at the corner and let me get out. I can run the rest of the way.'

He pulled up, but before she could get out of the car, he gave her a bear hug and a quick, fierce kiss.

'Don't forget you're mine,' he said. 'I'll ring you in the morning. I took today off, but there will be some work lined up for me tomorrow and I may not be free before the evening. See you then,' and she ran from him along the street, his final words echoing in her ears.

How could she see him every evening, even most evenings? Now that she was at home, with no immediate plans made for the future, her mother had seized the opportunity of arranging social activities for her in the hope that she would decide to give up what still seemed a ridiculous and unnecessary thing to Lady Manning. She might even meet some nice man and fall in love with him, which would disabuse her mind of any idea of going into practice as a doctor.

Tonight they were dining with friends and going to the ballet; tomorrow a crowd of young people were coming in, and the big drawing-room would be cleared for dancing; the next day something else had been arranged. How could she ever be free to see Jeff?

Yet she knew that somehow she would see him. He was in her heart and in her blood and she could not live without him. In spite of sudden qualms as she thought about the difficulties she would have to face when she told her parents, she was gay and full of fun and life that evening and her mother watched her and thought fondly that already she was beginning to become absorbed in the sort of life that was naturally hers and forgetting that dreary doctoring.

When Jeff rang her up in the morning, she told him she could meet him in the afternoon.

'No good, darling. I shan't be free till six. I'm a working man, remember? See you about six. Say ten past, where I put you down last night.'

'Oh Jeff, it's so difficult! I'm expected to be in. Whatever can I say?'

'That's your funeral, my sweet,' he told her cheerfully. 'See you at ten past six.'

'I won't be able to stay long. I've just got to be in for dinner at seven and I shall have to change.'

He chuckled.

'Just a slave on the treadmill, aren't you? Well, ten past six. Bye, sweetness. You know what this is?' and she heard the kissing sound of lips as she put up the receiver.

For days that ran into weeks it went on like that, and she lived in a fever and knew that with each of those rushed, stolen meetings she was getting deeper and deeper in love with him. The time spent apart from him was wasted time, and she lived only in and for that spent with him. It could not go on. She must tell her parents, or let him do so, and late one evening, when she was alone with them, she told them.

'I've got something to tell you,' she said, trying to remember that she was twenty-five and entitled to make her own life and choose its course. 'You won't like it a bit, but I've met someone, a man, Jeff Elster, and I want to marry him.'

They looked at her in amazement, her mother's eyes quick with fear, her father's stern and ready, she knew, to hear her story and disapprove of it. It was he who spoke first, checking with a gesture his wife's attempt to do so.

'Who is this young man, Romaine? And why do you say we should not like it? Do we know him?'

She had a sincere liking and respect for her father, but he was a reserved and silent man of whom she had always stood a little in awe.

'He – he's Jeff Elster and you don't know him. He's a racing driver.'

'Romaine!' This from her mother, in shocked surprise.

'A racing driver? You mean that that is the way he earns a living? Racing with motor cars?' asked her father's incredulous voice, chilling her with its icy disapproval.

'Yes. People do, you know. He has to do a job as well, for the present, though he won't have to when he has won a big race. He – he works for a garage.'

'A *garage*?' asked Lady Manning, outraged. 'You mean he repairs cars, serves petrol and so on?'

'No, not exactly that, though he does

35

repair cars, racing cars that have to have special treatment, special knowledge.'

'A garage hand! Well, really Romaine! Have you gone mad?' asked her mother.

'I knew you couldn't possibly approve, that you'd be shocked, but I love him and I'm going to marry him.'

'And remain a doctor?' asked her father witheringly.

'No, I shall have to give that up because soon, if Jeff wins his next big race, he'll go abroad. He'll be racing all over the world and I — I shall go with him.'

Her mind shrank from the thought. She had not seen him race, but she remembered that day when he had taken her to Goodwood and she had seen him doing his practice runs on an empty course and had shut her eyes as the car screamed round the bends and in her imagination she had seen other cars competing with his and had visualised the dangers of that terrific speed. She had felt that day that she could never bear to see him in an actual race.

'Have you considered what this means? The sort of man you propose to link your life with? The conditions under which you will be living? I don't know what these men

36

earn, of course, but you will have no settled home, no proper life,' said her father judicially.

Romaine turned from one unyielding face to the other.

'Father — Mumsie — I know I've been a disappointment to you all the time. I've never really fitted. You didn't want me to go in for medicine but you were good about it and let me. I must be a sort of changeling in the family. I don't belong, or see things the way you do, but — I'm very fond of you and I hate to hurt you or — to do anything that would make you cast me off. I'm in love with Jeff. He's become the centre of my life and I want to marry him. I mean to marry him, but — I hope it won't part us. I'm very sorry. That's all I can say.'

'Oh — Romaine, Romaine!' moaned Lady Manning, and she leaned back in her chair and covered her face with her hands.

'You're of age, of course, Romaine,' said Sir Julius, 'and you don't need our consent to your marriage, but you had better bring this young man to see us. Bring him to dinner tomorrow night.'

'We're dining with the Maybury's,' said

his wife faintly.

'We shall have to cancel that, my dear. This affair of Romaine's must be settled.'

'Then you don't — you won't — just throw me out without meeting him?' she asked with the first smile she had been able to conjure up, but there was no reflection to that smile on the faces of either of her parents, and she slipped away to her room with relief that at least she had told them.

When Jeff made his customary telephone call the next morning, she issued the invitation to him rather nervously, and he laughed.

'What are you afraid of, poppet,' he asked. 'That I shall eat peas with my knife or gargle my soup or something? Why, I've even got a dinner jacket! It may be a bit green at the seams, but I don't think it's got the moth in it. If it has, I'll black my shirt where it shows, so cheer up! Love me still?'

'Oh Jeff, so much!'

'Then that's all that matters, isn't it?'

To him perhaps, but not to her, she thought.

She need not have worried, however, for the evening passed off well. Jeff was charming to Lady Manning and deferential to Sir Julius, chose with care subjects for conversation which Romaine would not have supposed he knew anything about and did not talk motor cars nor use the racing slang she had feared, and when the two had been left alone for a few minutes to say good night, Romaine drew a breath of relief. If they did not approve, they were going to accept him.

He snatched her hungrily to him.

'You were wonderful,' she said.

'Gosh, I feel stifled! Kiss me back to life, darling. Is that the sort of rarified atmosphere you live in? It made me want to tear off all my clothes and do a war dance in the nude!'

'Good job you didn't,' laughed Romaine. 'How on earth did you know about some of the things you talked about? Theatres, books and so on?'

'I've read the papers like mad all day and was careful to watch their reactions so that I could change my angle at any moment! Don't let's talk about it, though. Let's talk about us and how soon we can get married now that I've got the chequered flag all right.'

They were married in a month.

Though her parents had agreed to accept Jeff Elster into the family, they had wanted her to wait, hoping, she knew, that she would change her mind, but he would have none of it.

'Look, darling,' he said, wheedling her, 'you know how I feel about you. I'm mad about you, can't think clearly about anything else until I've got you. When I'm racing, I shall see you all the time instead of the track, and you wouldn't want me to have an accident for want of you, would you?'

'But I'll be more to you when I'm your wife – or shan't I?'

'Of course, but I shall know you're mine then and I shan't have this carking fear that some other fellow will step in and get you.'

They wrangled amicably over the date, but in the end decided that they would marry early in June so that she could go to the Dutch Grand Prix with him and make it part of their honeymoon.

'I don't want a lot of fuss, but I'd like to be married in a church,' she said.

'Anywhere you like so long as you

marry me,' he told her blithely.

Her mother insisted on a white wedding.

'You don't want to make a secret affair of it even if it is — well, not quite what we should have chosen for you. You must have at least two bridesmaids and invite our friends. Don't forget that you're our daughter, darling. I take it that Jeffrey has *some* family of his own?'

He obliged by producing for the occasion two irreproachable maiden aunts, whom she discovered afterwards were neither maiden nor aunts, but he had no parents or other family which Lady manning privately thought was as well. Her future son-in-law was presentable and knew how to conduct himself properly, but he was not out of the second nor even the third drawer, had not even been educated at a public school, and it was wiser to draw an obscuring veil over his origin and background.

He had been quite frank with Romaine about it, had told her that his father had been a private in the army and had been on leave when he and Jeff's mother had been killed in an air-raid whilst he himself had been evacuated into the care of a Welsh

41

family who had since emigrated to Australia, leaving him behind. He had had no real claim on them and had chosen to stay in England with foster parents found for him by the council.

'There wasn't any money to educate me or anything,' he said, 'but the Jepsons were very decent people and kept me out of mischief and I suppose I just growed! I'm naturally imitative and I have gradually acquired the right accent and more or less good manners, and there you are. That's what I am. Do you mind?'

'I don't mind anything but that you're yourself,' she told him, 'but I don't think we'll tell the parents! They wouldn't be too pleased, especially my mother, but I don't care two hoots. Her kind of people are dying out, but she doesn't and can't accept it. With her, it is important to have been to the right school.'

'I'm quite willing to have been to Eton or Harrow,' he offered obligingly, and she laughed.

'You'd be found out in no time,' she said. 'We just won't say anything about it.'

She was deliriously happy and seemed to have no regrets about giving up her career. Henceforth her career was to be Jeff's wife, and she wanted nothing else.

Chapter Two

LOOKING back afterwards at the turmoil and confusion of her marriage with Jeff Elster, it seemed to have had all the attributes of the way in which he earned his precarious living. It was a life of excitement and hazard, of living on the high peaks and existing in the corresponding troughs of despair with none of the stability or peaceful humdrum of a normal married life which she longed for.

She had moved into a completely different world from the serious, ordered life of the hospital and the equally well ordered if less serious existence as the daughter of Sir Julius Manning. It was split up into sections by the dates of the races in which Jeff was taking part and during the weeks preceding them, and particularly in the immediate days and nights before them, she seemed to live, move and have her being amidst racing cars and their drivers. No one talked of anything else but speeds, laps and averages and she felt she was married to a racing car. Jeff became nervy and irritable as the time approached and seemed scarcely to know that she existed.

But as soon as the race was over, he became again the lover, eager and passionate and beloved. He was contrite about his neglect of her and, though he laughed it gaily aside, sympathetic over her fear for him which she knew she would never get over.

He even offered, in his contrition, to give up racing.

'We'll get a home and settle down, darling. That's what you want to make you happy, isn't it? I'll get a job at something or other ...'

He was holding her in her arms, all the lover, tender, possessive, and she pressed herself against him and laughed unsteadily.

'It wouldn't make you happy, even if you meant it,' she said.

'I could mean it – or I think I could,' he

insisted, but she knew too well the absorbing passion of his life to try to pin him to it.

'No. You wouldn't be you any more. I married you knowing that I would have to share you with an engine and four wheels, you crazy idiot, and I'm not going to try to turn you into anything else so long as you — come back to me like this,' with a little shiver as she turned in his arms.

She lived for these magic, wonderful interludes when she had him for her own and refused to look ahead.

Some day I'll get to the top. You'll see. Then I shall be satisfied and I'll retire and we'll get a farm or something and dig ourselves in and take root,' he promised her.

But he was a long way from that goal yet, for ill luck seemed to dog him though he laughed at it ruefully and would never admit to bad luck.

'No. I just wasn't good enough,' he would say to people who would have condoned with him. 'I took the bend badly,' or 'I was a chump to do this, or that.'

He was mad with himself for his failures

45

and his breakdowns, but he never tried to put the fault on his cars or on anyone but himself and would cheerfully and generously applaud the winner and was immensely popular both with his fellow competitors and the public.

Romaine endured agonies in Monaco, in Holland and in Belgium, unable to stay away from the course, equally unable to watch as the cars hurtled by at hair-raising speed, sitting or standing with her eyes closed and her ears strained, imagining him in every spill, every time a car ran off the course or turned over or caught fire.

He seemed to bear a charmed life for all the ill luck which kept him from being amongst the first few, or even from finishing the race.

'That's poor old Jeff at the pits again!' she would hear someone say. 'Wonder what it is this time?' and when it became clear he was out of the race, she could open her eyes and feel that profound thankfulness that for this time, at any rate, he was safe.

She knew that her nerves could not stand the strain any longer, and after the Belgian Grand Prix, in which he seemed to have escaped by a miracle from a somersaulting car, she decided that she could not watch any more.

'I'll stay at the hotel, Jeff,' she said. 'I'd rather. I should only make an idiot of myself and I'll get Fred Goby to telephone me when the race is over or if – if anything happens.'

Goby was his chief mechanic and his best friend, a cheerful, matter-of-fact, unimaginative cockney with a deep devotion to Jeff which extended, with an admixture of slight awe, to the girl whom Jeff had married. Thereafter she sat in her hotel bedroom, or close to the telephone if there was one in her room, and all animation seemed to be suspended until she heard the cheerful, cockney voice assuring her that ''e's O.K., Mrs Elster. Bit o' bad luck in the tenth lap jes' when 'e'd got the race all sewed up!' and there would follow something about gears or clutch or some other thing to which she never even listened, so great was her thankfulness. Life had started to go on again. Jeff was safe.

'You know, Mrs. Elster, you worry about 'im too much,' Fred would say when

47

they were all together again afterwards, Jeff talking excitedly and laughing and joking at the bar whilst she sat, limp and exhausted, watching him. 'Jeff's O.K. Nothing's going to 'appen to 'im, 'e's a first-class driver and knows 'ow to get out of a bit o' trouble. Anybody like you oughtn't to 'ave married a racing driver!' with a sympathetic grin on his ugly, kindly face.

She agreed with a wintry smile.

'I couldn't have married anyone but Jeff, Fred,' she said chokily. 'Perhaps I shall get over it and take it all in my stride one of these days.'

But she knew what he had said was true. Her imagination was too vivid and she had given up too much for Jeff, abandoned all that had formerly made up her life and was totally unable to adjust herself to this.

After the French Grand Prix early in July, they were to be in England for some time and if she did not go to Germany or to Portugal with him, they could make some sort of home together instead of living in hotels.

They took a furnished flat near the garage which still ostensibly employed him and for the owner of which he raced until such a time as he could afford to race his own cars.

It was a poor enough place, badly furnished and without any of the comforts of a home, but it was at least something which she could pretend was home.

Lady Manning, whom Romaine had tried to keep away from it, was appalled to find her in the untidy kitchen in the middle of the afternoon washing up. Romaine, though she had longed for a home, had no flair for housework, had never had to do any and had no idea how to set about it.

'It's a dreadful little place, Romaine,' said her mother in shocked disgust. 'And why are you doing all this, and at this hour?'

'I know we're in a mess, Mumsie dear, but we had a party last night and got up late and my woman-who-does doesn't come in on Saturdays. Go and sit down in the sitting-room and I'll leave this and get us some tea. Oh, I forgot!' as she opened the door of the sitting-room and revealed its after-the-party condition, the curtains still drawn across the windows, chairs disarranged, small tables loaded with used glasses and ash-trays, the unaired room filled with the smell of smoke and stale alcohol.

Lady Manning said nothing but waited in icy disapproval whilst her daughter pulled back the curtains, opened the windows and whisked away the glasses and ash-trays. The sunshine only served to show up the general shabbiness and discomfort.

Of course her mother had to come and find them in this state!

Romaine could not help smiling to herself rather guiltily when she thought of what had contributed to the condition of the flat that morning.

She had crawled out of bed first and gone yawningly into the kitchen to make them a cup of tea and had returned to the bedroom with the tray to regale Jeff with a tale of what the kitchen looked like.

'What *did* we have to eat last night?' she asked. 'I didn't think we had anything much, but every pot and pan seems to have been used. What was the mess you and Fred concocted? It tasted frightful.'

'It was meant to be spaghetti bolognaise, darling, but we couldn't find any of the proper tomato stuff, so we had to cook some tomatoes and the spaghetti stuck to the pan, I'm afraid, and we had to do some more, only it wasn't spaghetti but the big stuff that looks like worms, so in the end we used rice but cooked too much of it. Isn't rice the very devil? And I couldn't find any onions but Fred nipped out to that Italian shop and got some garlic. Pretty foul, wasn't it?'

'Indescribable. Here's your tea, darling. Do you mind not having a saucer? They must all have been used for ash-trays or something.'

'I don't mind anything when you look at ravishing as you do in that blue thing. Do you know that I've got the most bee-ootiful wife in the world? Kiss me, darling.'

'No, Jeff! You'll have the tea all over the bed!'

'Blow the tea — *and* the bed except when you're in it!' and he stretched out his long arms and caught her and pulled her down to him and the tea was forgotten and went cold.

'Do you know that it's nearly twelve and we haven't even had breakfast or thought about lunch yet?' she asked presently,

51

flushed and tender-eyed, beautiful from his loving.

'Who cares?'

'Darling, we've got to eat sometime, and we've got to clear up that ghastly kitchen before we can cook anything else.'

'Let's go to the Steering Wheel for lunch and tackle the chores afterwards – but not just yet. We've got the whole week-end to do that in. I don't know that I want to go out to lunch, do you? Let's go and rake out bread and cheese or something and have it in bed.'

'Oh Jeff, it's an awful way to live!'

'I think it's a wonderful way, and who's to bother about what we do in our own time and our own home? You know, you were quite right to insist on us having a place of our own. It quite definitely has its points and I'm liking it. I feel very married this morning, don't you?'

She laughed.

'I ought to! Jeff, we must get up. Have you any idea what the flat is like?'

'Going house-proud on me?'

'Me house-proud? That's just the point. I don't know the first thing about housekeeping!'

He twined his arms about her.

'You know about the only thing that matters, loveliest.'

The only thing that mattered to him? Wasn't it cars and racing?

She caught back the temptation to say so, to spoil the only thing that mattered to *her*, which was that he should love her and need her sometimes and she should be there when he needed her. Had she ever been the serious, dedicated doctor?

In the end, though he had been unwilling to leave her to do the clearing up and all that washing of dishes, she had persuaded him to go out with some friends who had rung up whilst she had set herself distastefully to the hated rask in the kitchen.

And it was there that her mother had found her.

'You really cannot live this, Romaine,' said Lady Manning when they were having tea from the cracked cups that did not match an old brown teapot. She had beautiful china of her own, some of it wedding presents, but there had been no room for it in the flat and it was still at her parents' home with the rest of the wedding

53

presents.

'It's only temporary, Mumsie, and we're making do with it until Jeff is able to settle down in a proper home.'

'You mean give up motor racing? Is he going to do that?'

'Well – not for the present. I know it's hard for you to understand, but he's so keen on it and it really is his life. He wants to make good at it, to reach the top . . .'

'You are right when you say I cannot understand him – or you. To live like this after what you have been used to!'

Romaine smiled determinedly. Whilst she had been making the tea, she had rushed into the bedroom and changed her frock and brushed her hair and put on a little make-up in order to be more presentable in her mother's eyes.

'You know how I've felt about that for a long time, all my life really,' she said. 'I've never wanted to live that sort of life.'

'You prefer this?' with a contemptuous look round the room.

'If it means Jeff, yes, I do. I love him, Mumsie, and that's all that matters really.'

'Even if you do, that's no reason why you should be so uncomfortable and work like a galley slave. This woman who you say works for you is obviously inefficient and unsatisfactory. I must see what I can do to help you.'

'Please, Mumsie, don't. We're not always in this mess, I assure you. It's just that we had a party last night, as I told you, and Mrs Cumins doesn't work here on Saturdays and we — we didn't get up very early. Jeff would have stayed to help me but I wouldn't let him. I don't mind doing it a bit, really.'

'I shall certainly see what I can do for you,' repeated Lady Manning as she sailed out to her waiting car with the liveried chauffeur in attendance.

Jeff came in as soon as she had left.

'Snakes, you've had a visitation, duckie, haven't you?' he asked. 'I saw the car leaving and wondered who was dead until I caught a glimpse of your mother inside and prudently kept out of sight till she had gone. Our stock must have risen considerably! I saw all the curtains on the other side of the road and in the downstairs flat fluttering. Not finished yet? Come on, I'll give you a hand. Or do you think we could leave it till Monday morning and

Mrs Cumins?'

'Oh, we can't, Jeff. She'd pack up on us if she found the place like this! Mumsie was struck with horror. She wants to find someone for us, but we can't let her do that, can we?'

'Why not if it makes her happy? I hate to see you messing about with pots and pans like this.'

She laughed. Even washing pots and pans could be fun with Jeff.

'Who got them into this state, I'd like to know? I think we could put this burnt one under the sink and pretend we forgot it. Or shall we throw it out?'

With a grin, he opened the window and dropped the offending pan with its sticky, nauseous contents down into the yard below where it was lost amongst the rubbish and lumber of many years.

'What about dumping the lot there?' he asked.

'And having to replace every pot and dish in the place? No, let's do it and then go out for a meal. I'm starving, aren't you?'

These were the happy times when she felt he was wholly hers and that the strange tide of events that had caught her and borne her so suddenly and swiftly away from the self she knew would carry her forever, holding and supporting her through storms and tempest to reach for a while this haven of happiness. They belonged to each other, she and Jeff, so utterly different in temperament and purpose yet indissolubly bound by their love.

The comfortless inconvenient little flat took on the semblance of a home. Lady Manning, true to her intent, had found them someone to replace the shiftless Mrs Cumins, an elderly maid retired from her own service and now a widow, who had known Romaine as a child and who lived conveniently near. She made no trouble of their untidy ways and did not expect Miss Romaine to do anything more than get their make-shift, irregular meals. She had a key and came in at all hours to 'tidy them up', did their shopping for them and the only complaint she made was that they wasted good food by preparing a meal and then suddenly going out instead, according to some whim of Jeff's.

'Billy darling, don't worry. Take it away yourself and eat it,' Romaine would say gaily to Mrs Bill.

'I could heat it up for you tomorrow, or make a shepherd's pie, Miss Romaine.'

'Jeff hates left-overs however much they are camouflaged. Besides, we may be out tomorrow. Throw the meat away if you don't want it.'

Mrs Bill tut-tutted about the waste of good food and suspected that Romaine often paid for it out of the allowance she received from her father, horrified now and then to find that she had over-stepped the mark and was 'in the red' at the bank. At such time the Elsters became as wildly economical as they had been extravagant, ate sparingly at home or invited themselves to meals at the houses of friends and managed to eat enough to last them through the next day until Sir Julius's cheque came through again or Jeff got what was left of his heavily mortgaged month's pay.

'Don't worry, sweetest. Some day, when I begin to land the big prizes, we shall be in the money,' he would assure her gaily, 'and we're managing to stay alive, aren't we? Mrs Billy won't let us starve.'

Happy days! Improvident, glorious

days, nights of loving which ironed out all the creases and made everything worth while.

Then there would be another of the big races which would work Jeff up into a fever of nervous irritability so that she was almost glad when the day itself came and the dead weight of fear wiped out all the little squabbles and left her tense as a taut string, waiting for Fred Goby's voice at the end of a telephone wire.

When he came back, love came into its own again and he was the passionate, demanding lover who could satisfy her to the uttermost and make her forget everything that might have spoiled their marriage. She knew how lucky she was in her physical love, how seldom a woman knew such fulfilment, how many marriages went on to the very end, or broke down, without that perfect completion which is the strongest tie in the world between two people in love.

'Oh Jeff, do you know how lucky we are, you and I?' she asked him once, replete with loving, utterly at peace in his arms.

'Of course I do, my darling. To have

found just you out of a world of women! I love you. Or have I mentioned that before?'

'Yes, several times, but tell me again. Kiss me, Jeff. Love me. Love me a lot!'

He kissed her, her lips, her dark rumpled hair damp from her ecstasy of loving, her throat, her smooth bare shoulders against his own, ran his hand caressingly down her long, exquisitely moulded thighs which quivered instantly with the thrill of his touch.

'No one else could make you feel like this, could they, belovedest?' he asked her. 'You couldn't love anybody else?'

'Of course not! How could I? You're my man, my husband, my lover, my other self. Oh Jeff – Jeff . . .'

'And it's worth it? You've forgiven me?'

'Forgiven you? What on earth for?'

'For being such a pig to you before I went away, snapping at you, saying things that I knew were hurting you but which I couldn't stop myself from saying.'

She laughed.

'Oh, that? It's forgotten. I knew you didn't mean it, that it's all part of your incomprehensible make-up, your safety valve.

'It's when you're away that I remember and hope you've forgotten things that I've snapped back in return but never meant. I'm always terrified that – that I shan't get a chance to say I'm sorry – that . . .'

He closed her lips with kisses.

'Poor darling. Do you think I don't know that you didn't mean them any more than I did? That this is what really lasts,' kissing her, 'and this – and this – and this.'

When he went to Morocco in October to race in the Grand Prix, she nearly made up her mind to go with him. The people who had let them the furnished flat had wanted it back and they had had to turn out and she had had to move into a small hotel. It was a cheap, shoddy place because they had run through all their money and she was too proud to ask her father for more and Jeff was in his usual state of irritability and nervous tension when he seemed not to care how or where she would live until after the race.

But she did not go. For one thing she could not face again the agony which, amongst the excited crowds ghoulishly waiting for, almost hoping for, an accident, she would have to conceal under a stoical front. For another she knew she was going to have a baby, had discovered it only a few days before Jeff was due to leave and she dared not tell him. He did not want her to have children yet, nor did she want any herself as things were. She still hoped for that 'settled' time in their marriage which showed no sign of coming yet. After Morocco, Jeff was entering for the American Grand Prix which was only six weeks away and he wanted her to go with him. Before he came back this time, she would have to make up her mind about the baby.

There was no telephone in her bedroom at the hotel so she would have to wait in the dreary, chilly lounge for a message to be brought to her and, as is so often the way in the very early days following conception, she began to feel wretchedly ill and the torturing anxiety over Jeff did not help her.

Finally, learning on enquiry that there had been a breakdown in communications between Morocco and England and that Fred Goby would probably have to resort to cabling, she dragged herself to her room and took a strong dose of a sleeping drug which would give her forgetfulness for at least a few hours.

She was not roused from her deep unconsciousness even by the repeated knocking at the door by the porter with the cable that had come through by telephone, and he came into the room to find her lying on the bed unconscious. When he failed to rouse her, he rushed down the stairs again to tell the manager that she was ill.

'She's sleeping like the dead,' he said, goggle-eyed. 'I can't wake her. I think something ought to be done.'

The manager, who had made it his business to find out who she was, telephoned the Mannings' house and brought Lady Manning to the hotel in a fever of anxiety. She had been with her daughter the day before and had tried to persuade her to go home with her, but Romaine, though looking strained and ill as she always did when Jeff was away, had refused.

'I must be here if there is a message,' she said.

'They would send it on.'

'No, I must stay here. I must wait,' said Romaine feverishly.

Suppose she had found the strain of waiting too much? Suppose she had taken something to end once and for all this repeated, senseless anxiety which had at last become unbearable?

She brought her own doctor with her, the big Rolls causing a stir as it drew up before the hotel, and demanded to be taken to Mrs Elster at once but was infinitely relieved when the doctor assured her that Romaine was only suffering from a slight overdose of a powerful drug and that as soon as she recovered, she could be moved into the comfort of her parents' home.

'This is no place for her at all,' said Lady Manning angrily, looking round at the poor appointments of the room and at the empty grate.

'Put a fire here at once,' she commanded the obsequious manager. 'Bring an electric fire if you have one, and hot-water bottles and some proper blankets. And open the window. Has anyone been into the room today to clean it? It is by no means clean. And bring fresh towels. There is no need to change the bed linen as I shall be removing my daughter as soon as she is sufficiently recovered. Is that supposed to be her lunch?' looking distastefully at the untouched tray, with fat congealing on the stringy-looking meat and grey boiled potatoes and a mess of cabbage.

Romaine had asked for it to be sent up to her but had not attempted to eat it.

They scurried about to do her imperious bidding, flustered manager, curious maid and frightened porter, and after a time, when Romaine had been left alone with her mother, she opened her eyes languidly and then sat upright.

'Mumsie! What are you doing here? What happened? Has there been a message? An accident to Jeff?'

'No. There was a cable from someone called Fred to say that your husband had some sort of trouble and has given up the race but that he is unhurt,' said Lady Manning, tight-lipped.

Romaine lay back on her pillows and closed her eyes again.

'Thank God. Oh, thank God!' she murmured. 'I was so afraid. I always am. But – why are you here?'

The drug was making her drowsy again, but Lady Manning roused her determinedly.

'You've taken something, Romaine. I don't know what it was, but the people here could not wake you and very properly sent for me and I am going to take you home. Sit up. Put your feet to the floor. Where is your coat? You can go in these shoes. The car is outside. There does not appear to be a lift, so you must manage to walk down the stairs. You cannot possibly stay here and now that you have heard that your husband is safe, there is nothing to keep you here.'

Romaine yielded to the comfort of being cared for, of having all responsibility for herself taken from her, and within the hour she was back in her own room that had been hers from childhood, in the soft bed with its satin eiderdown and bedspread, with its delicately perfumed pink sheets and a fire burning cheerfully in the grate. During her childish ailments, she had always had a coal fire in her bedroom instead of the electric one. It had been a special treat to make up for having to stay in bed.

A special treat!

She snuggled down under the bed-clothes and let her mind drift back over a childhood that had been so happy, before she had disrupted the family by wanting to go in for medicine, before she had so greatly and finally disrupted it by marrying Jeff.

She felt calm and at peace now. Jeff was safe and she was at home, surrounded by the luxury and care which had been missing from these months with Jeff, five of them now. Guiltily she enjoyed the luxury, her mother coming in softly, a maid bringing her a daintily laid tea tray with gleaming silver and fragile china on a white cloth, delicate finger-sized sandwiches, hot buttered toast and little sweet cakes.

And then sleep again, deep and dreamless, from which she woke to find the old doctor looking down at her, fingering his lip thoughtfully. She knew him well. He had brought her into the world and was a as much familiar friend as doctor and they were alone in the room.

'Well, young lady?' he asked. 'Now you're awake and in your right mind, what have you got to say for yourself? What did you take to scare us like that?'

She told him.

'Of course I took too much. I was

unhappy and worried stiff about Jeff and I really didn't think.'

'And you a doctor?'

'Yes, I know. Silly, wasn't it?

'Of course you didn't take enough to do yourself any real harm, but it gave your mother a fright, and for some people, it *might* have been too much. Did you mean to take too much, Romaine?'

She sat up with a jerk and stared at him.

'Of course I didn't! Why should I want to? How could anybody possibly think that?' she asked hotly.

'Well — one wonders if your marriage . . .'

'My marriage is perfectly happy and I adore my husband!'

'All right. But don't be so stupid again. You may not be so lucky a second time. Why don't you stay here with your mother for a bit? You can't have been comfortable in that hotel on your own.'

She laughed ruefully.

'Pretty awful, wasn't it? But it's only for a few days. Jeff will be home the day after tomorrow and we can look for something else, a flat or something.'

But when he had gone, she reflected

rather unhappily about the situation. Jeff cared so little for his creature comforts that he could not appreciate how she felt about living under such conditions and after all, was not the main thing to be with him when she could, however they lived? She looked round the luxurious room and ached for his presence, for his arms and his lips and all the joys that no one else in the world, no amount of comfort and ease, could make up.

'Oh Jeff, Jeff,' she whispered into the pillow, 'come back to me soon.'

But the next day a further cable was brought to her, sent on from the hotel. This time from Jeff himself.

DELAYED FEW DAYS ENGINE REPAIRS LOVE JEFF

Something serious must be the matter with the car for Jeff to be staying with it himself. As a rule he left everything to Fred Goby and flew home straight to her after the race. Had they told her the truth, or had Jeff himself been injured in any way? She did not know where he was staying and could not relieve her mind by asking for further news, but as the delay was so indefinite, she yielded to her mother's persuasions to stay.

'You can't go back to that horrid little hotel anyway, darling,' said Lady Manning autocratically, 'so you may as well have your things and Jeffrey's packed and brought here and you can both stay here when he comes back. In fact, I think you should stay here until he has found a proper home for you.'

'I don't think he would agree to that, Mumsie. You know he wouldn't when we had to move from the flat, but I suppose our things may as well be brought here rather than have the hotel bill mounting up,' agreed Romaine reluctantly.

When the trunks and suit-cases had been packed and sent from the hotel and put into a big bedroom on the second floor which Romaine knew her mother intended for her and Jeff, in spite of what she had said, Romaine went up there to sort them out and produce some sort of order in Jeff's odd collection of clothes. She was no needlewoman but it would give her some satisfaction, some sense of his nearness, to go through them and sew on buttons, make a parcel for the cleaners' and throw out the things that were long past their usefulness but which, left to him, would never be discarded.

There was, for instance, the ancient, beloved tweed jacket which he had worn right up to the time he left for Morocco and which surely he could be persuaded to part with?

She held it against her cheek and closed her eyes and seemed to draw his dear presence to her by the very smell of it, of tobacco and oil and petrol. But it was too shabby for repair and indescribably dirty and it would simply have to go!

She went through the pockets, smiling at the conglameration of articles that had accumulated in them. Did he want all these bills for petrol, chits from the garage and miscellaneous papers?

She went through the pockets, smiling at the conglomeraout to see what they were, putting them into neat piles – and suddenly she was transfixed, her attention riveted on a scrap of paper, part of a torn letter.

... luck that she is not going with you, darling, after all! Will she be at the airport

to see you off? If I see her with you, I won't let on that we know each other and we can meet on the plane. Have you booked the room at the hotel or do you want me to do it? Darling, what fun! I can't wait!

Yours till hell freezes.

Lucille

Romaine sat on the floor and stared at the letter. Lucille? Who was Lucille and why should she be writing to Jeff like that? And the 'she' in the letter was, of course, herself! What was she to Jeff, and how long had he known her, and how well, this Lucille?

She could not believe it, cried out to herself that it was impossible, that the letter had been written to somebody else and had somehow got there in his pocket – but in her heart she knew.

She went back over the few days before he had gone. They had quarrelled as they so often did just before a race, said bitter things to each other which they did not mean. He had wanted her to go with him, had begged her to go, had flung away from her in anger when she said she would not and she had not even gone to the airport to see him off, feeling that it would be more

72

than she could bear.

If she had, would she have seen this other woman, this Lucille, who was taking her place, planning to share that hotel bedroom with him, with Jeff, her husband, her own beloved Jeff?

And for Jeff to do that to her, to his wife, to his lover!

She left the jacket and the piles of clothes where they were and went down to her own room, locked herself in and paced the floor in an agony for which she could find no relief in tears, for she never cried. That was not her way. Dry-eyed, but with a choking feeling in her throat and desolation in her heart, she thought of the past and faced the future.

Though she had known from its beginning that in her marriage to Jeff she had stepped right out of character and in maintaining it had thrown aside all her natural inhibitions, her upbringing and her training, she had known a deep happiness in it. Now she had to face the fact that that happiness might have been merely a shell, a façade, a mere screen like the set for a film picture with nothing behind it. It was a bitter reflection, hard to take and to accept.

If there had been nothing solid behind that façade, then Jeff's love had been a sham and all that she had done and suffered for her marriage meaningless.

Her intelligent mind struggled to rise above the enchantment of her love for Jeff and to see it at its true value. Had it really been nothing but physical delight? If he had deceived her consistently throughout their marriage with this Lucille or possibly with a succession of women, there was no escape from the belief that she had loved a myth, been chained by her physical needs to something which had never existed, and the sooner she recognised and accepted that fact, the better.

Time and time again her thoughts turned to the immediate present and the knowledge that whilst she was agonising here, he was with Lucille. She recalled all the tenderness and the fun they had shared, the wild moments of passion and the deep, quiet happiness that had followed fulfilment. Was he sharing those same experiences with this other woman? Uttering the same intimate words of endearment which had been sacred to them and which she had believed were for

74

her ears alone?

It was like a sword plunged into her heart, surely its death agony.

She wondered what she was to do when he returned to her, where and how she was to meet him. Certainly it could not be here in her parents' home. Her pride and dignity revolted against that. They must meet in private and alone, and in the end she took a suite in a London hotel, though it was more than she could afford and she had to humble her pride by asking her father for a loan.

'I hate to ask you,' she said to him, 'but things get a bit disorganised when Jeff is away, and I am not sure yet of his plans.'

Sir Julius shot her a keen look. She was putting on a brave front but he knew that she was worried and not at all well.

'Of course I will let you have it, my dear, and not as a loan which you might find difficult to repay. But I have been wanting to have a talk with you, to put you into a better way of life and make you more secure. You know that I never approved of your marriage, but we won't go back on that now. I do feel, however, that you and Jeffery have given this motor racing a fair trial and that it is time he found a way of earning a living for you and himself which is less precarious. You must forgive me for straight speaking, but it seems obvious to me that he is not making a success of it and is simply spending his time going about the world and enjoying what is only a hobby for a rich young man and which will never earn him a livelihood. I am going to put up a suggestion to you and, if you agree, to Jeffrey. I realise that he has not the temperament nor the ability for a profession or for any good position in the commercial world and that his interest lies wholly in motor cars, and I am therefore prepared to set him up in a good garage concern which will give him both a reasonable livelihood and an interest. It is not at all my idea of a good life for you, with your background and your ability and interests, but it is making the best of what I consider a disaster for you, Romaine.'

She was silent for a few moments. If only Jeff would agree to something of the sort, it might still be possible to save their marriage, to start again with a more normal life and a home and the sense of security and permanence which his present way of life could never bring.

But she knew he would never agree.

'Father, I do appreciate what you say, and your — your wonderful generosity in spite of what I know you feel about my marriage. But Jeff would not agree to it. This passion for motor racing is in his blood, an essential part of life for him. It's a sort of madness that people who haven't got it just can't understand. I don't understand it myself, even though I'm living with it. I suppose some day he'll have to give it up or — or ...'

'Or kill himself,' Sir Julius ended for her grimly.

She nodded and looked away and knew from the quick lurch of her heart that it was not dead.

'I live with that fear,' she said in a low voice.

Sir Julius said no more, but sat down and took out his cheque book and gave her far more than what she had asked for.

'This is all I can do for you then,' he said harshly, and left her.

Chapter Three

ROMAINE was waiting in the hotel suite for Jeff to come to her, mechanically rearranging the flowers she had bought, altering the position of a chair, a small table, restless and unable to settle to the books and magazines she had brought with her, or to do the needlework which she had been trying painstakingly to do.

It was a week since she had received the telegram telling her that he was delayed for a few days for 'engine repairs'.

Engine repairs!

She had left a message with the manager of the hotel where he would be expecting to find her, but had not gone to the airport to meet his plane after receiving the telegram telling her of it. He added 'all my love' and 'longing to see you, darling'.

How much of that was true? All the love that she had had to share with Lucille? And longing to see her because, perhaps, he had had a surfeit of this other woman?

She veered between anger and her own longing to be with him again, not knowing yet how she was to meet him but knowing that there must be complete honesty between them.

She heard the whirr of the lift which stopped at her floor, felt her heart turn over as he made some laughing remark to the lift attendant, and then, after a perfunctory knock at the outer door of the suite, he was in the room, striding across the floor to meet her, catching her in his arms, kissing her unresponsive lips, becoming aware of the stiff lack of response of her whole body.

He held her away from him and looked at her in puzzled concern.

'What's up, darling? Aren't you glad to see me? Not the returning hero, I'm afraid, but at least the returning husband!'

She drew herself away from him and his arms dropped from her. She was pale and shaken, aware that even at that first moment of reunion, the treacherous thing inside her would have leapt in instant reponse to his touch.

'Should I be glad, Jeff?' she asked in a low voice, turning away from the temptation of his arms and his lips but not before she had seen the quick look of alarm in his eyes and heard his caught breath.

So it's true, she thought dully. There's no explanation. I didn't just make it up. He has come to me from *her*.

He put up a hand to rumple his thick hair, a familiar gesture that caught at her foolish heart.

'Darling . . .' he began when a knock at the door of the suite interrupted them, and he went to it to admit a waiter with a trolley which held a bottle of champagne in ice and two glasses.

'Thanks,' he said, 'that's all,' and when the man had gone, he said with attempted lightness, 'I asked them to bring up a celebration.'

'What are we celebrating, Jeff?'

'I thought — my return. What is it, darling? Come on. Out with it, whatever it is.'

'I think you know what it is, don't you? I found — this,' and she took from her pocket the crumpled scrap of letter and laid it on the table, and now her eyes met his proudly, accusingly.

He picked it up and read it, though he had recognised it at once. How had he been such a fool as to let it come into her hands?

'Is it true, Jeff? But of course it must be. Don't try to lie about it or push it aside.

Let's be honest with each other. Who is this woman, this Lucille, who booked a room for you both when I had decided not to go with you?'

'I haven't very much to say. It's no good my denying it. I did go to the hotel with her. I spent one night with her and then left her. I was sick of myself. I couldn't come straight back to you, which is why I stayed away so long.'

'Who is she?' Romaine's attitude was unyielding, her face and voice implacable.

'A girl I met at the club. She was going to Tangier on the same plane. Her people live in the Gambia. She had to break her journey at Tangier.'

'So it was convenient for her to stay there with you, as I did not go? I imagine you have known her for some time. On these terms?'

'No! At least believe that, Romaine. I have known her for some time and I knew that she was – that sort. Easy, you know, and not averse to – to – well, having a good time now and then.'

'And as you were easy, too, you fixed it up. All this at a luncheon date at the club?' asked Romaine contemptuously.

'I know it sounds a rotten thing to say, but you asked me to be honest with you. We didn't exactly fix it up, but I was angry with you for not going and in a moment of – well, madness, I suppose – I rang her up and told her, and she did the rest. If you'd only gone with me to the airport to see me off, I don't think I should have done it. As it was, I still felt sore about your not going and I was sick about being out of the race and – well, it happened, and that was that. It's no earthly use saying I'm sorry, is it?'

'No, not much use.'

'I could kick myself for doing it. I hated every minute of it. It was just one of those things that men do. It didn't mean a thing to me. Do you believe that, darling? Please believe it and forgive me. Can you?'

'I don't know, Jeff. Honestly, I don't know. You say it was just one of those things that men do, some men, perhaps most men. I'm not ignorant about things and I know that men and women are differently constituted, that a man can betray his wife by such little affairs which mean nothing to him whilst a woman in love couldn't possibly do it. I'm trying to sort out what it really means to us and to our marriage, but it's difficult.'

'You're not going to break up our marriage for it, Romaine?'

She heard the pleading note in his voice and recognised the weakness behind it. She might bring herself to forgive this one lapse, but it had done something irreparable to their marriage. She would never be able to forget it. Their love would never have its same completeness because her trust in him had been destroyed. How could she know that it would never happen again, if not with this Lucille then with some other woman?

'I don't want to, Jeff. I still love you, no, don't touch me!' as he made a movement towards her, 'but not in quite the same way. I believe you, I *must* believe you, when you say it meant nothing to you, but that's the difference between men and women when they are truly in love. The woman gives all and demands all, but the man has his reservations. He can love with the mind whilst he regards the body as still his own, not given wholly and for ever to the woman. He reserves the right to such little affairs as you say this has been and the woman must accept that. Forgive me if

I'm being a bit – pompous and pretentious, but I'm thinking aloud and trying to make sense of my thoughts for both of us. I don't want to rush into anything now, or out of it. I don't want to make an irremediable mistake and spoil for ever something which has been – beautiful . . .'

Her voice, which she had kept level and thoughtful broke suddenly and she turned away.

He came behind her and laid his hand on her shoulder. His touch, even through the suit she wore, burnt her, but she did not move or shake it off. This was one of the things that she must meet and bear if they were to come together again, this and much more. Just how much could the physical, her unbearable longing to be in his arms, be made to substitute for the whole love and trust of the mind which he had destroyed?

'Romaine – darling – my love,' he said pleadingly.

She moved to face him and his hand let her go.

'Not yet, Jeff. You must leave me time to get over it. Shall we have the champagne? It may do something for both of us,' and she lifted the bottle from its pail of ice and poured it, but with an unsteady hand, so that it frothed over the side of the glasses and spilled on the floor.

Their love had been like that, she thought. A heady, exciting thing full of froth and bubbles which had spilt over and left so little in the glass still to be drunk!

'Would you like to have dinner here or shall we go out?' he asked warily, with nothing really decided between them.

'Go out, I think,' she said. 'My room is here. Yours is on the other side,' and she walked across the sitting-room to the door of one of the bedrooms that opened out on either side of it and he heard the key turn in the lock.

She was taking no chances, he thought ruefully. What a fool he had been, what a crazy lunatic to risk losing Romaine for that cheap little nobody. As an after-thought, he cursed himself for having left that letter about for Romaine to find.

In the room allotted to him he found only such things as he might need for a few days, another suit, some underthings, his dinner-jacket suit, and he dressed in the last-named with the knowledge that Romaine had not intended this arrangement to be a permanency. It was just as well, he thought, unless her old man had come out strongly and greatly increased the allowance he made her, for he could not possibly have afforded a suite like this! A private bathroom led out of the bedroom, and he presumed she had her own too. Thank heaven he could at least take her out to dinner in style, and he rang down to the reception desk and ordered orchids for her.

She was not wearing them when they met again in the sitting-room. They stood in a tumbler of water on a table there and his eyes went enquiringly to them.

'You're not going to wear them?' he asked.

She shook her head.

'Perhaps they ought to have been lilies. For a dead love,' he said with a vestige of his old, mischievous smile, and she returned it reluctantly.

'This is a palatial place,' he remarked.

'I know. I didn't know where else to

86

go. I've been staying at home, but I didn't think you'd want to come there – in the circumstances. Shall we go?' picking up her wrap. 'I'd like to try that new place, the Cazar, if it's all right with you?'

'If I can afford it, I suppose you mean? Well, I can – just. If I hadn't been able to, I take it your father would have paid? Is he paying for all this magnificence?'

'I borrowed the money from him, yes,' she said serenely. She was poised and confident now, sure of herself and a million miles away.

'It's all part of the scheme to make me feel the low-down hound I am?' he asked savagely.

Her pleading, sorrowful look almost unmanned him.

'Don't let's quarrel now, Jeff. Let's just take this evening and enjoy it.'

He picked up her hand and kissed it.

'I'm a brute,' he said. 'I don't want to quarrel with you, darling. Heaven forbid! Let's go to the Cazar. I'll get a taxi.'

Romaine knew, when they danced together later, that he was breaking down her defences. Her nearness, the close hold of his arms, his cheek against her hair, showed her how vulnerable she was and that she could forget everything, forgive anything, whilst she was with him like this. Was it weakness, the weakness of her sex before the dominant male, or the strength of her love?

They did not speak again of their future or the past, but when they returned to their suite she went from him without a word and he heard the key turn in the lock of her door.

So that was that! He was not to be forgiven.

Behind the locked door, Romaine lay sleepless and tormented and at last she slipped out of bed and gently turned the key in the lock. Jeff had kept his door open and heard the key turn and in an instant was beside her bed, looking down at her with a half-ashamed, half-exultant smile, his eyes pleading for forgiveness.

'Romaine?'

'Oh Jeff – Jeff – I can't forgive you and I don't trust you, but – oh, my darling, I love you so!' and she opened her arms to him.

Jeff, it seemed to Romaine, was like an unpuncturable rubber ball.

As soon as he felt forgiven and restored to favour, he had no fears for their marriage and was on top of the world again, gay, light-hearted, full of plans which had no substance in them. Romaine, more far-sighted and practical, could see them drifting towards the rocks unless he found some stability and some purpose in life other than his craze for speed and for success as a racing driver.

'Jeff,' she said on that first morning after their reconciliation, 'we've got to make plans, sensible and stable plans for a future that includes me as well as you. In the first place, we've got to find a home. We can't go on living here, nor could I ever go back to the insecurity of that wretched little furnished flat, or that even worse hotel.'

'I know, darling, but how and where can we find any place where *you* would care to live? I'm easy. A bed, a table and a chair that holds two are enough for me,' he said blithely.

'You're quite right when you say they're not enough for me. I want a home of our own and I'll learn to manage it and look after it and live within our income. I want to put to you a proposition which Father put to me.'

But when she had told him of it, one glance at his face was enough answer.

'Don't think I don't appreciate the offer, sweet,' he said, 'but it wouldn't work. I'm all set for the World Championship once I get over this bad patch, and then, well, I may think of retiring from racing and I'll have plenty of money of my own to start something without your father's help.'

'Oh Jeff, come down to earth! You'll never win the championship. The papers say it, other drivers say it, even Fred Goby says it. The really top people have a different mentality, a different make-up. You haven't got what it takes.'

His face was angry and mutinous.

'You don't believe in me, do you?'

'Not that way, no. I'm being entirely honest about it, Jeff. You're only playing with life, enjoying a hobby and pretending that it's a job. I know it's fun, something you like doing better than anything in the world, but, darling, you're married to me . . .'

'Are you making an issue of it, Romaine? Putting an ultimatum to me?' His lips set dangerously. 'Because, if you are, I think we've reached breaking point.'

She gave him a speculative look.

'You mean,' she said slowly, 'that I am to do all the giving in this marriage?'

'Giving? Giving money, do you mean?' he asked. 'Are you throwing that up at me?'

She rose from her chair at the breakfast table (they were breakfasting very late in their own suite) and came to him and linked her arms round his neck.

'Darling, no. You know I didn't mean that. What's money compared with our happiness? What I meant was that you want me to go all the way with you over – that affair whilst you are unwilling to come part of the way with me and change your way of life to make me happy.'

For a moment he did not move but sat staring in front of him, a look on his face which she had never seen before and could not understand, a look of dogged determination at variance with his usual nature as presented to her.

Then he slipped an arm round her.

'Romaine, are you asking me to give up racing as a proof that I love you? As a punishment for what I did in Tangier? I could, for you, but you won't ask it of me, will you? It isn't just a hobby, as you and your parents think. It's my life, the only thing I want to do or can do, and I shall get there in the end. I promise you that. I don't think I should make good at anything else because my heart wouldn't be in it. Give me another chance, darling. In six weeks' time there is the American Grand Prix for which Mollers have entered me. If I pulled that off, if I could get even a decent place in it, we should be made. I'm not tied to Mollers. I could race for anybody after that. Name my own terms . . .'

She sighed, kissed him and returned to her own chair.

'If it really means so much to you, I won't insist,' she said, and his face cleared at once.

'Thanks, darling. You won't regret it. You'll see. You'll come with me this time, won't you?'

She shook her head.

'No, I can't. We're going to have a baby, Jeff.'

His eyes widened and his jaw dropped open. 'No!' he cried, so thunderstruck at the idea that she had to laugh.

'Darling, don't you know about the birds and the bees? We've been married nearly six months and it's a wonder it hasn't happened before. We've taken a lot of risks, you know.'

He grinned and pulled a face.

'I know. When you're in love, as we are, you don't think of possible consequences, do you? How do you feel about it?'

'Glad, I think. I'm not sure. I'd like life to have been a bit more settled first. How do you feel?'

'I don't know. I think I'd rather it was just you and me. I can't see myself as a dad, can you?'

'Nor myself as a mum! Still, it's happened, or I think it has, though it's too soon to be sure yet. You see, dear, if it's true, I couldn't go to the States with you. Even in the early days, which it will be, I just couldn't take it, the anxiety, the awful tension even if I didn't watch the race, waiting in the hotel room for Fred or someone to ring me, imagining all sorts of things – Jeff, you don't know what it's like!'

He rumpled his hair and gave her that comical look, part boy, part man, that always tore her heart.

'It's the devil, isn't it? Perhaps I oughtn't to have married you, but I can't imagine life not married to you, can you? If you really feel you couldn't stand it, that's all. What will you do whilst I'm gone? Go home, do you think?'

It was evident that not even her news would move him from his determination to go, and she relinquished with a sigh that last hope.

'We'd better make a real effort to find me somewhere to live,' she said. 'I shouldn't want to go home. Let's start looking right away so that with any luck we can move out of here.'

'Right. Let's go through the adverts,' he said with enthusiasm, picking up the

Telegraph which had been brought up with their breakfast.

Romaine, the practical one, laughed.

'We shan't find anything in our range in the *Telegraph!*' she said. 'They're all superb mansion flats at about a thousand a year which don't even mention such things as mod. cons. They take those for granted! And in duplicate or triplicate probably. All I ask is one, just one, mod. cons. of our own.'

'But at a price! You know what it was before when we were looking for a flat.'

'I know. I want to talk to you about that, Jeff. To get even reasonable comfort, especially with a baby coming, will cost more than we can afford, as things are.'

He shot a suspicious look at her.

'You're not going to ask your father to pay for it? I shouldn't like that any more than I like him paying for this place.'

'Neither should I. We're going to stand on our own feet from now on. I'll get a job, Jeff.'

'What as? And with a baby on the way?'

He frowned.

He's so unpractical, she thought, between irritation and tenderness. He didn't want his wife to work, and yet had not the means to keep her!

'My own real job,' she said. 'Doctoring. I've thought it out and I could get something, not a practice, of course, but there are always jobs going, school work or at a clinic or something. It wouldn't be any handicap that I was going to have a baby. It might be rather the reverse if it were at a baby clinic because I should be going through it myself and other mothers would trust me to know from experience, not just academically. The only trouble would be to find a flat near enough both to my job and to Mollers.'

'It won't matter about Mollers after December.'

'We couldn't count on that.'

'You don't think I can pull it off, do you?' he asked tight-lipped and with that look in his eyes that warned her she was treading on dangerous ground.

'Oh, of course, you may do,' she said quickly. 'It would be grand, wouldn't it?'

He did not reply, except to say that if

he were going to show up at the garage that day, he had better get a move on.

His young pride was hurt, she knew. What she did not know was the extent to which it had been hurt all the way through their marriage by her lack of faith in his ability to succeed and the light way in which she treated what he regarded as his job in life, which he took seriously.

He had always suffered from an inferiority complex. He had been mediocre at school where he would have liked to shine. Even the short space of time during which he had really worked there, he had never succeeded in achieving more than that mediocrity and had soon ceased to apply himself seriously. He was gay, amusing, with a light, facile wit which had attracted the wrong sort of boy. He was a king amongst the non-workers and preferred their admiration to the uncertain approbation of his teachers and largely wasted his time at school.

Speed and its hazards had always attracted him and he had snatched eagerly at the chance of motor racing as the most hazardous and spectacular thing he knew. Dogged by ill luck, which was partly on account of his volatile temperament, his enthusiasm quickened and brought to boiling point by being brought into contact with racing drivers who, as rich men, could afford to do it as a hobby, he had inevitably set his social standards higher and dreamed himself into a world he was never likely to attain – until he met and fell in love with Sir Julius Manning's daughter.

Instead of raising him in his own estimation, marriage with Romaine had increased his depressing sense of inferiority and she had unconsciously added to it by regarding his racing as no more than a hobby, something which he had to get out of his system before he settled down to making a living.

It had been that that had really brought about the affair with Lucille Baynes.

He had never been even remotely in love with Lucille. Romaine still held his heart in the hollow of her hand. But he desperately needed the encouragement of someone's admiration, and Lucille provided that. She was pretty and brainless and, as he had told Romaine, 'easy', and not at all averse to an affair with a man who was young, attractive and doing a dare-devil job. She flattered him and had shown herself more than ready to console him for the refusal of his wife to go with him and in his disappointment and anger over that refusal, he had yielded to the temptation of Lucille.

But it had been Romaine he had wanted, especially after he had found himself out of the race, and he had found Lucille not only a poor substitute but the means of producing in him a disgust of himself so that he had flung himself out of the hotel where they had stayed and had even left her to pay the bill!

Well, after all, it was she who had wanted it and engineered it all, wasn't it? Still, he rather wished he had paid that bill.

And, back in England and in the luxurious hotel suite, he could not have paid the bill, which drove him still further down in his own estimation, for Romaine was his wife, not a casual pick-up.

Now Romaine wanted to get a job and they were going to have a baby and as things were, he could not very well object to her providing for herself what he could not provide. It was better, anyway, than sponging on her father, that pompous, important man who looked down on his son-in-law but would have kept him because he had married his daughter!

It was certainly not the pleasure he had imagined it would be to enter even the fringe of life at that level. Wildly in love with Romaine as he had been and still was, he just could not take her people and their way of life, but he realised that he had dragged her down into poverty and discomfort by his pride and that it could not continue, for Romaine's sake. He would provide for her and the child, he must provide, and he could do it by achieving that success in the American Grand Prix in December.

But he had a bad shock that morning when he reached the garage and strolled in the private office of Mr Dace, the manager, blithe and sure of himself outwardly at least.

'Sorry I paced up in the Moroccan,' he said. 'Damned bad luck, wasn't it?'

Mr Dace gave him a freezing look.

'I could call it something else. Inefficiency,' he snapped. 'I gather that you were not there when the mechanics gave the car a final check-up and their O.K.'

No, he had not been. He had taken Lucille out to dinner, but had been working on the car all the afternoon and had been satisfied with its condition and performance. There had seemed no need at all for any further check-up.

'I – no – that is, it was O.K. when I left in the afternoon,' he said.

'If you had been there yourself, you might have foreseen the clutch trouble. I may as well tell you, Elster, that Mr Moller is not satisfied. He has been on the phone to me this morning. Naturally I defended you, as I have sponsored you all along and I still believe you can do it.'

'Mr Moller doesn't suggest a substitute driver for the American, does he?' asked Jeff, alarmed.

'Not in so many words, but you'd

better watch your step if you want to stay with us. That's all I can say about it,' and he ended the interview by picking up the telephone with a nod of dismissal.

Jeff was nonplussed and not a little disturbed. How was he to know that those damned mechanics, Goby and the others, had had another go at the car after the afternoon's trials? He remembered now that something had been said about the clutch just before the car was wheeled to the starting line, but it had not been said to him and he had not taken much notice. Anyway, it was too late then to do anything about it, and he was always in such a nervous state just before the start of a race that Goby would not disturb him unnecessarily.

Dammit, he must do the American job. Everything depended on it and if he were to be thrown out by Mollers, it wouldn't be easy to find someone else to take him on. He was a first-class mechanic, of course, but he didn't want to come down to tinkering about with cars for someone else to race!

He did not say anything to Romaine about it. He did not want to destroy such confidence as she had in him; neither did he want to have to explain to her what he had been doing that evening and rake all that up again.

It was not too difficult for Romaine to find something to do, for doctors were overworked and there were all too few to take on the additional jobs in the schools and the clinics, and she was appointed to the charge of a post-natal clinic at a newly established health centre in London's East End. It was not a salubrious part in which to live but an old house was found for her which would shortly be condemned to demolition to make way for a new block of flats, but had still a year or two's survival.

Jeff grimaced when she took him to see it. It was in a littered and neglected back street which teemed with children, it badly needed the decorations which they would have to do themselves, and it had all the inconveniences of the Victorian age, without even a bathroom and with the other toilet facilities outside the back door. It had three floors of two rooms each above ground level, and the kitchen was in a dark, damp basement.

'Not much of a place for *you* to live in, is it?' he asked.

'No, but at least it's somewhere to live, not too far from your work or from the clinic, and it has possibilities. I can use the two ground-floor rooms for my private patients, if any, have our living-room, with a kitchen and a bathroom on the first floor, and sleep at the top.'

'You've got it all worked out,' he said, 'but what do we use for money?'

'We can do the decorating ourselves, and Father will lend us the money for the plumbing, which we can't do. Don't be awkward about that, Jeff,' as his brow clouded. 'We can't live here unless we do,' and, reluctantly, he agreed.

They found a 'little builder' who was co-operative, and the painting and papering providing them with a good deal of fun, owing to their complete lack of experience. Romaine consulted books in the free library and was painstaking and careful, whilst Jeff was quick and slap-dash, but time was short, and if he produced some rather bizarre effects, at least they made the house cheerful and habitable.

Rummaging amongst the second-hand shops for furniture, they found a bath which Jeff said only needed a coat of paint.

'You get old Joe to fix it and I'll soon do that,' he said blithely and did so with unfortunate results for Romaine, who took the first bath in it, stuck to the paint and, striped like a zebra, had to get him to scrape it off, to their hysterical amusement.

By the time the work was finished and they had bought the absolute essentials of furniture, some of it on hire-purchase, they were at the end of their resources, even taking into consideration the generous 'loan' from Sir Julius, and though Romaine had confidently expected to be able to employ a woman to do the housework, they decided that they could not afford it.

For Romaine, brought up with the luxury of well-trained servants to wait on her, running her own house and doing all her own work was a nightmare. Jeff carried up the coals and helped with the cooking and the washing up, but he was being kept hard at it at Moller's and was often in too late to help with the accumulation of work.

'Never mind, darling. Leave it. We shan't die if the place is untidy, and we're happy, aren't we?' he said to her cheerfully and settled down to the pools coupons which were going to win them a fortune but never did.

Romaine was busier with her professional work than she had ever thought she would be, for an epidemic of influenza made her services in ever-increasing demand and Jeff would come home to find the little waiting-room crowded with coughing, sneezing patients and Romaine kept busy in her surgery until late in the evening. Upstairs everything was in the sort of muddle she hated but had not had time to do anything about, but Jeff was serenely unconscious of any of it so long as she was there to be made love to when her last patient had gone.

But very soon she was too exhausted for that and the inevitable quarrels ensued, though they were always made up in his arms, for they were still lovers.

She was overworked and her

pregnancy was telling on her even in these early stages and it was a relief to her when he told her that he was definitely going to the States to race one of Moller's cars.

He was jubilant about it.

'It's a big thing for me, darling, the biggest ever! Old Moller never had much faith in me, but after I got the chequered flag at Brand's Hatch last week and came in second at Goodwood, he's had to change his mind. If I have any sort of luck in the American, I shall go on to the Argentine, but I should be able to pop home for Christmas in between.'

She was torn between relief and the fear which never left her whilst he was on the race track. He would be happy, she knew, and when he came back she would have got over the present miserable stage in her pregnancy, a stage in which she would be better without him. She could rest more without the constant need to appear to be quite well when she had to consider Jeff, and once the influenza epidemic abated, she could take more care of herself.

But in this first knowledge of the

coming separation, she clung to him desperately.

'Jeff, you will take care, darling, won't you?' she gulped, her voice stifled against his neck.

'Of course I will, sweetness,' he assured her gaily. He could never believe that anything could happen to him. Perhaps racing drivers had no imagination? Her own was vivid and acute.

'Oh Jeff – if anything happened to you . . .'

'Nothing will happen, I promise. Why, the roads in this country are far more dangerous nowadays than a race track! At least the cars are all going the same way and there are no side turnings for idiots to come out of. And this new modification of Moller's is a beaut. All very hush-hush at the moment, but I had a try-out on her this morning and she goes like a bomb,' and he went into enthusiastic details of which she understood nothing but merely listened to his voice and watched the eagerness of his face and knew that nothing in the world, not even herself, meant more to him than this race.

'So long as you come back to me, Jeff – just come back,' she whispered.

'I shall, my darling. Never fear!' he assured her with that gay self-confidence so typical of his whole attitude to life.

Chapter Four

SINCE Jeff expected to fly home for Christmas, Romaine had been busily preparing for his return and at her mother's insistence, had engaged a daily woman for the housework. With Jeff away, and part of his salary paid to her by arrangement with Mr Moller, she was able to manage better, and life was easier and more smooth-running than it had been at any time since her marriage.

With the epidemic lessening, she was no longer in so much demand by the doctors who had relied upon her to take on the overflow of their patients and she had decided not to continue seeing people at her house for the time being.

The work of the clinic had increased considerably and gave her enough to do so that when Jeff came home, she would have more free time for him and regular hours. Also she had got over the early troubles of her pregnancy and now felt more fit than she had been for a long time. She found that she was enjoying such work as was left to her to do in her own home, and, armed with cookery books, did a good deal of experimental cooking against the time when she would have a husband and a family to cook for.

Now that she was free of the nausea and discomforts consequent on her pregnancy, she could think with joy of the coming of the child who had become an entity to her, a living thing that was part of her and part of Jeff. Jeff wanted a boy and was already making plans to buy him his first car, but she secretly hoped for a girl, who would at least not tear her heart to bits on a racing track! Or would she? She could not imagine that Jeff could be the means of producing the quiet, sweet little stay-at-home for whom she longed. But then she had not been that herself!

As the day of the big race approached, she worked herself into a fever of apprehension and was almost sick with relief when he telephoned her.

'I'm all right, darling, though I came in with the also-rans but not at the tail end. Old Moller didn't expect me to win, of course, but at least I completed all the laps. Pleased with me?'

'Oh Jeff — darling — of course I am,' she said shakily.

'Liar! You'd have been satisfied if I packed up in the first lap so long as I wasn't hurt, wouldn't you?'

'We—ll,' she began, and they both laughed, she in glad relief and he in the wildest of spirits.

'All right. You needn't say any more. You're no wife for a racing driver are you? I expect you've seen me smashed to bits or burnt to death a hundred times during the last few hours. What about you? Are you all right? From the crackles and fizzes on the line, you might have bronchitis with complications or the house might be on fire.'

Their voices rose and fell and almost died away on the trans-Atlantic line but it didn't matter. She knew that he was all right and after all, she reflected somewhat wryly, he knew that she was safe enough and did not need any assurance as to her welfare.

But a few hours later Mr Moller telephone her.

'Mrs Elster? This is Moller. I've just promised your husband that I would speak to you and he wouldn't give me his answer until I could assure him of yours. You know he's done well over there. Very well. He appears to have handled his car superbly and I want to give him a better chance now. I've entered him for the Argentine early in February and am sending over a new car for him to try out and I have suggested him staying out there until after that event and run the car in some of the smaller races. They don't count for the championship, but they will give him good experience on the race tracks over there. Of course, racing drivers shouldn't have wives, should they? He says he wants your consent first. It's a great chance for him, Mrs Elster, so what have you to say about it?'

What could she say? She knew that secretly, in her heart of hearts, she had not wanted Jeff to do well in what might have been his last major race if he had failed badly.

Grudgingly she agreed to his proposal. It would mean that Jeff would not be home for Christmas nor for some weeks afterwards and she would miss him badly, but there was nothing she could reasonably do about it. Mr Moller was right. Racing motorists should not have wives!

Jeff wrote her long, loving letters all about himself and his prospects and little about her and her prospects, but she didn't mind.

She wrote him that as the clinic was closing down for a few days she would spend Christmas with her parents, and it was untold luxury to be pampered and cossetted again, with breakfast in bed and every want foreseen and supplied with loving care, and to have nothing in the world to do.

When the clinic opened again in the New Year, her mother pointed out to her that there was no real need for her to return to the house. Her hours were definite and she could go backwards and forwards in her own car.

'In fact, dear, in the circumstances, there is no reason why you should not have Blosser for the time being. He can easily be spared and it would be safer and less tiring for you as you're going to have this baby.'

Blosser was the second chauffeur and was used almost entirely by Lady Manning, but as Sir Julius did not keep his own car and chauffeur waiting for him in the city, the two chauffeurs were a somewhat unnecessary extravagance, as Romaine knew.

'I couldn't possibly have your Daimler drawing up in front of the clinic,' she protested, laughing. 'They'd think I was at least a funeral or royalty!'

'Well, Blosser can take you in your own little car,' decided Lady Manning in her authoritative fashion, and Romaine at last agreed, though she had not needed much persuasion to remain in her comfortable quarters.

She did not tell Jeff, however, that she was doing so. She felt slightly guilty at abandoning the home on which she had insisted but after all, since he was not there to share it, there was not much point in her remaining alone in it. But as a result of her keeping from him the knowledge of how she was actually living, a slight strain had grown up between them of which he was more aware than she. She was not a good letter-writer and could find little to say that would interest him. She had not the knack of putting over her personality in letters, and they were short and concise and except that she told him she was looking forward to his return, he felt that they might have been written by anyone.

Her pregnancy, without the comfort and support of the one being in the world who could to any extent share it, had driven her into herself. Only a woman understands this feeling of isolation, of being suspended between two worlds, she and the mysterious growth within her. Her longing for him was so intense that she had to restrain herself almost physically from going to Mr Moller and demanding that he be brought back to her, even for a day, but she was incapable of expressing any of this in her letters.

He, on the other hand, wrote in a free and wordy style that brought him vividly to her. Often ungrammatical and illspelt because his thoughts ran faster than his pen, his letters had so much more to say than hers had. He seemed to be on the move all the time, doing a lot of things which her static life could not match.

There came a time when he had not written to her for some days. She was not surprised at that, for the big race in the Argentine which had been his real reason for staying was only a few days off. He would be keyed up, living on his nerves, unable to think of anything else.

It was one of the days when she had not to go to the clinic, but she was too restless and anxious to stay quietly in the house and rest. Her mother was out and had taken Blosser and the Daimler, and Romaine went round to the garage for her own car. It was the quiet time of day when the traffic would not be too bad, and she decided to go to the house and see if there were any letters. There might even be one from Jeff. On the way she stopped to buy an early edition of the evening paper, but she did not look at it until she was in the house, had found no letters of importance waiting for her and had sat down with a cup of coffee to have a rest before the return journey.

Almost immediately she saw his name in a short paragraph in the stop press and was electrified by what it said, her breath catching, her heart racing and then seeming to stop. She had a feeling of suffocation and sat swaying in the chair, staring at the newspaper whose lines danced and ran into a meaningless jumble before her eyes.

Santiago, Chile. Jeff Elster, the British racing driver, was injured in a car accident here today. His wife, who was in the car with him, was also injured.

Romaine's mind whirled in circles that cut into each other and made no recognisable pattern. Chile — how did he come to be there at all? Injured — how badly? And his wife, *his wife*, in the car with him? How could she be? His wife was sitting here trying to grapple with the confusion of her mind and with the sudden sharp pain of her body which presently shut out all other pain.

The telephone bell rang, but during the time, the long time, it took her to drag her contorted body towards it, it was silent. The caller had gone.

She knew by this time what was happening to her. She was losing her baby and she had to have help. She could not think of any other number to dial, not her mother's, not Dr Melby's. She dialled 999 and asked for the police.

'The front door is not locked. I am ill. I need help,' and she managed to gasp her address before another sharp spasm of pain sent her writhing to the floor and into merciful unconsciousness.

She had a confused, disjointed memory of strong arms, of reassuring voices, a journey in an ambulance and finally of hospital bed.

After a welter of pain came blessed oblivion, and she came back to consciousness to find her mother beside her screened bed, a nurse bending over her and adjusting the drip-feed from the bottle of plasma above her head.

'Mother – how – did you – where ...' she asked weakly.

'It's all right, darling. You're in the hospital. Dr Melby was here and sent for me. Don't try to talk now,' said her mother's reassuring voice.

'I've – lost my – baby, haven't I? and then, out of the jumble of returning thought, one emerged clearly. 'Jeff! Jeff's been hurt and – I was with him, but – how could I have been? How could I?' and she tried in a frenzy to sit up.

They pushed her gently down and the doctor came in and the needle in her arm brought oblivion again.

'She seems to think that something has happened to her husband,' said Lady Manning. 'She may have heard something. Were there any letters, do you know? Or a cable?'

'I don't know, but I can find out. She'll be all right for an hour or two now. I am due at my surgery but I'll drop off at her house and will bring any information I can find when I come back. It was lucky that I happened to be in the hospital when they brought her in.

Don't worry, Lady Manning. She's quite strong, you know, but I should say she had some sort of shock to bring this on. It might have been news of her husband, of course, poor girl. I hope nothing's happened to him but all we can do is to keep her quiet. I expect you'd like to stay with her?'

'Of course. Can you put her into a private room?'

Lady Manning was horrified to find her daughter in a public ward, though the screens gave her a certain measure of privacy.

'Later perhaps. It would be inadvisable to move her now. She's in good hands, you know, and she'll have every care.'

Dr Melby was brisk and businesslike and as good as her word. Finding no letter or cable at the house, she did find the number of the garage on the telephone pad, rang up Mr Moller and ascertained that he had received news of Jeff's accident but had failed to get in touch with Romaine.

'Mrs Elster might have seen it in the evening paper,' he said. 'There was an account of it there. I tried several times to get hold of her but got no answer to my telephone calls. I am very sorry, very sorry indeed, but the accident was not a very serious one, though he will be out of racing for some time. I understand that both arms were broken but no other injuries.'

Dr Melby found the crumpled newspaper on the floor and pursed her lips as she read the paragraph which must have given Romaine the information.

'So his "wife" was with him, was she?' she thought. 'I wonder what that young man has been up to? May be just a case of mistaken identity, of course, but I wonder?'

She had no use at all for Jeff Elster and thought that Romaine, with her intelligence and capabilities, had thrown herself away on him. What was he doing rushing about the world enjoying himself, and probably with another woman, whilst Romaine was doing a good and useful job here and carrying his child too? Well, that was finished, anyway. Probably a good job, though Romaine would not think that.

Poor child.

She told Lady Manning what she had found out and left her with the newspaper and no further comment.

Whatever she may have thought, for once Lady Manning kept silent when Romaine had returned, slowly and reluctantly, to consciousness and to life. There might be some quite innocent explanation of the 'mistake' in the newspaper column; on the other hand, there might not, and she felt that unless Romaine herself broached the subject, she could not interfere in any way.

Romaine had been moved into a private room as it was not thought advisable to let her leave the hospital yet, and she lay white-faced and silent, co-operative in all that was being done for her but completely uninterested. The room was filled with flowers, but she had not troubled even to read the cards attached to them nor the letters and telegrams of good wishes which came for her.

'People are so kind,' she said listlessly. 'Will you answer them, Mother, and say the right things?'

'Mother' now, not the old, childish 'Mumsie'. She seemed to have left both her childhood and her girlhood behind.

Mr Moller was amongst those who sent flowers and wrote to her. He told her the latest news of Jeff and the extent of his injuries and that he would be flown home as soon as his arms, in plaster, could take the risk of possible jerks on the plane. This, too, her mother was asked to answer, but Romaine refused to see him or any of the visitors who would have come.

'I don't want to see anyone or talk to them, except you and Father,' she said, though Dr Melby recommended her to do so.'

Until she found out the truth about Jeff's companion on that ill-fated journey and had made up her mind what to do about it, she could not meet the look in the other people's eyes which might betray their thoughts.

But when she was within a few days of going home, she did receive her first visitor, though with shrinking fear.

'He — he's rather a strange visitor for *you*, Mrs Elster,' the nurse said. 'He says his name is Goby.'

Romaine caught her breath sharply. Now she would know. Fred was her friend as well as Jeff's, and not even to save Jeff would he lie to her. He was utterly straightforward and honest, but now that the time had come, she could hardly bear to face it.

'All right, nurse,' she said quietly at last. 'Please ask him to come in.'

He brought her flowers, snowdrops, and laid them on her bed.

'I thought you would have plenty of the grander flowers,' he said.

'Thank you, Fred. I like them so much. They're – rather like you.'

His ugly, square face flushed with embarrassed delight.

'Me? I ain't no snowdrop,' he said, slipping back into his natural speech in spite of his cultivation of Jeff's.

'You're good and simple and – honest,' she said with a quiver in her voice.

'I'm sorry about the baby, Mrs Elster. Jeff was tickled pink about it.'

'Was he? Fred, tell me about Jeff, everything. Not about his injuries. I know about them. But — but the rest of it. I must know, you see. I must know before he comes home. There was a woman in the car with him, wasn't there? What woman, Fred? Who was she and what did she mean to him?'

He shifted his feet uncomfortably. So she knew about that. It was that blasted report in the paper, of course.

'Yes, there was someone, Mrs Elster. Just a friend of Jeff's.'

'A friend? But it happened in Chile, where he had no real business to be according to Mr Moller. He was on his way to the Argentine, and had no need to go to Chile. Where were you?'

'I — I'd taken the car down. I was waiting for him. He just thought he'd take a trip around.'

'With the race only a few days ahead? And with a woman? A woman the newspaper report called his wife? Tell me the truth, Fred. I must know it. Were they living together?'

Her voice and her face were cold and hard. Poor Fred could not know the terrible, searing pain that lay below that surface. He had always admired

Romaine, but stood in awe of her. She was not, he thought to himself, at all the sort of woman who would understand how Jeff could love her and yet have this affair with someone else.

'You — you don't want to think too much about that, Mrs Elster,' he said unhappily. 'She — Mrs Ramsdell — she isn't — I mean, she's a nice girl . . .'

'Nice? To be living with a married man and posing as his wife? All right, Fred. Don't say any more. I understand.'

'I'm going back there, to see Jeff again. Mr Moller's sending me. Is there — can I — what can I say to him?' floundered Fred.

'Nothing.'

The word was sharp and crisp. What was the use of going on? Of trying to make something of her marriage? There had been the woman in Tangier. Probably there had been others. Jeff's idea of marriage and hers was utterly different. She could not trust him, and without trust, how could a marriage continue?

She lay dry-eyed, empty, heart-broken, facing the future?

★ ★ ★

Jeff had not meant it to happen.

With time to spare, he had decided to take a look at fabulous Hollywood but realised when he reached Los Angeles that he could not stay there. He had booked in at a modest-looking hotel but was appalled at the price of even the cheapest room and knew that Mr Moller, generous though he had been in the matter of travelling expenses, would not be likely to look with favour on such expenditure and ruefully decided that must move on without his catching even a glimpse of the fantastic world of stardom.

He was in a drug-store, alone and rather chagrined by not knowing how to spend his one night there, when he caught sight of her. There was something familiar about the shape of her face and her short, dark hair and when she turned fully to him, he realised that though she was a complete stranger to him, she had a look of Romaine about her. She was older, more worldly wise and sophisticated, but the look was there, and when she gave him a half-smile from grey eyes so much like Romaine's, he returned the smile almost unconsciously.

'English and far from home, aren't you?' she asked in a friendly fashion without coquetry across the space between them at the bar.

'How did you know?' he returned. 'You're English too, aren't you?'

She laughed.

'It sticks out a mile. The uniform, you know,' her glance travelling over the inevitable sports jacket and grey slacks. 'Do you mind if I talk to you? It'll be nice to hear my own language again. What are you doing here?'

He moved nearer to her, sliding his stool towards hers.

'I'm on my way south but thought I'd have a look at Hollywood whilst I had the chance, but it's not for me, I'm afraid. Too expensive!'

'You'll find it even more so if you go around with that look of the wandering sheep waiting to be shorn! There are plenty of shearers. Where are you staying?' and when he told her, she made a grimace.

'I can do better for you than that,' she said. 'Don't be alarmed. I'm not one of the shearers waiting for your fleece! You'd better check out of there and let me find you a place. There's an empty room where I'm staying if you can trust me. Can you?'

He looked into the grey eyes so like Romaine's and decided that he could.

'Why should you bother about me?' he asked.

'No reason except that you're a fellow countryman with that look of a lost sheep. It's all right, you know. I'm not one of those and I'm not going to take you to a haunt of vice. I'm Elinor Ramsdell, not that that means a thing to you. I'm one of the thousands of hangers-on waiting for crowd parts but temporarily sick of the game as I know I shall never get anywhere, not even a bit part and I was just deciding to get out. If you're thinking of gate crashing Hollywood, don't. It's not worth it. See all these people round here? That's what they're doing, most of them.'

'No, I wasn't thinking of it,' he said, and he told her what he was doing in

America, looking at her as he talked and realising that the resemblance to Romaine was only superficial. There was a hard look about her, the look of disillusionment and experience, and on closer inspection, he saw that she was considerably older, probably in her late thirties.

Still, she was someone in this city of strangers to talk to, and it seemed a long time since he had heard his own tongue.

'Come on,' she said at last. 'Let's go. Have you got a car?'

'It's at the hotel. As I didn't know where to go and you're not given a chance to look round and think, I decided to foot it for once.'

'You'd better come and have a look at my place first and assure yourself that I'm no female wolf! We take a street car from here.'

He always maintained that what followed was due entirely to Elinor's fugitive likeness to Romaine, though that was only superficial and she soon lost that vivacious hold on him in revealing herself as a woman of charm and a careless enjoyment of life which could never be Romaine's.

'I'm not out for romance or anything like that,' she told him with a keen, bright look at him as he went rather hesitantly into the big, shabby lounge of the hostel where she lived. 'It's on the level, and so am I. I didn't want a fellow countryman to be thrown to the wolves, that's all. Oh, Nobby,' to the elderly man behind the reception desk, 'this is Mr Elster, a friend of mine just out from England. Is No. 64 still free? If so, take him to have a look at it, will you? And don't forget that I know the price of it! I'll wait down here, Jeff.'

He saw at once that the small, single room was much more within his reach, arranged to remove his possessions to it and returned to find Elinor the centre of a small crowd of unpretentious men and girls who accepted him as casually as she had done, talking with engaging frankness about their work, or lack of it. Most of them seemed to be on the struggling fringe of the great film industry, their phraseology a meaningless jargon to the Englishman. He never learned the surnames of any of them, and he was simply 'Jeff' to them and regarded as Elinor's perquisite.

'We can eat here after a fashion, if you like,' she told him, but as he had to find his way back to the hotel where he had left his belongings, she went with him, got him out of the obligation to pay for his room and let him take her out to supper at a small, cheap bar he would never have found for himself.

Undoubtedly at that stage, she was good for him. She was no gold-digger even if he had had the money to spend, showed no inclination for having an affair with him and was, as she had said, 'on the level' with him.

During the few days at his disposal, she showed him how to make the most of them without spending a fabulous amount of money, even managed to get him past the well-guarded gates into one of the big film studios and smuggled him into one of the crowd scenes where he enjoyed himself hugely but was exhausted by the experience which the rest of them took in their stride.

Under her guidance, they made a tour of such famous places as Sunset

Boulevard and Beverly Hills where the great stars have their huge, luxurious houses and from afar caught a glimpse of these legendary beings themselves, though she laughed at his disillusionment at seeing them in the flesh.

By the end of the fourth day, he felt he had known her for years, though she had told him little about herself except that she had been married but that her marriage had broken up.

'That's how I came to be out here. Married a G.I., and lived to regret it, fancied myself as a film star but can't even make a living in crowd scenes. That's Elinor Ramsdell for you!'

She was cheerful and uncomplaining, however, an endearing quality, and possessed of a lively sense of hunour which made her companionship doubly to be enjoyed; but when on his last evening he discovered that she was flat broke, he was appalled for her. She had made another attempt to get crowd work that morning without success and he realised when they met later in the day that she had not eaten since the night before!

'I didn't mean to let that out,' she said, laughing ruefully at his startled expression.

She wore good clothes, was always well groomed, *soignée* to the last detail.

'But . . .'

His eyes travelled over her well-cut suit, went from her burnished head to her expensive shoes.

'You suggest by that look that I haven't the appearance of being broke!' she said. 'You can always pick up the stars' cast-offs for next to nothing if you know where to go, and I can't afford to get fat.'

'But your husband, your ex-husband if he is that — I thought out here women live on alimony.'

'Only the famous ones who makes a business of it! Opportunity is a fine thing, and I haven't seen or heard of Eddie for years. Never mind. Don't let's talk about me. Now I've admitted that I'm hungry, let's go and eat! Boy, could I eat a hamburger right now!'

When the time came for them to part, he was reluctant to leave her. He was going the next morning and she had said she would be at the studios early in the hope of finding work at least for the day.

'Elinor — come with me,' he said impulsively, not looking towards her future but desperate for her immediate present. She was so gay and gallant and had suddenly, with his discovery of the way she lived, become so pitiful.

They were sitting in his car outside the hostel. Though it was late, there would be no chance of their being alone once they had gone inside and the rules were inflexible about visiting each other's rooms. It was to be their last goodbye.

To his dismay, the eyes that were so like Romaine's filled with tears, but he was not thinking about Romaine just now. In fact he had scarcely thought of her at all during the last four days.

She blinked them away and smiled.

'Idiot!' she said. 'You as well as me. What would you do with me?'

'I shall be able to draw enough money after the race at least to pay your passage back to England. Haven't you got friends there? A home?'

'Yes. Both. But I couldn't let you do that. I've told you, and shown you, that

I'm no sponger. I don't take anything for nothing, and I probably could never pay you back.'

He had caught the note of longing in her voice, seen the flash of it momentarily in her eyes and knew that she wanted to go home.

'You know that I wouldn't ask it or want it, Elinor. Come with me. Come to Buenos Aires where I've arranged to meet Goby and the car. We'll fix something.'

She hesitated.

'Could we — would it be taking you too much out of your way to go to Chile instead of directly to Buenos? I've got friends in Valparaiso. If I saw them, they would probably lend me enough to get home from there. They're shipping people. But it would take you too far out of your way.'

'I think I could manage it,' he said recklessly, impulsive as ever and obsessed by now with the idea of getting her away from Los Angeles, and he began to reckon up distances and times until in the end it was agreed that she should go, starting before daylight the next morning and travelling hard and fast to make the long journey in the shortest possible time.

They covered the allotted mileage the following day and pulled up at a small motel for the night where there was only one room available.

'You have it, dear,' he said. 'Of course you must. You're dead tired. I'll sleep in the car — or anywhere . . .'

They were standing in the doorway of the room to which the clerk had given them the key and had left them with a shrug to their own devices. As long as it had been paid for, they could do as they liked. It was no concern of his.

The two beds looked inviting to the exhausted travellers, as did also the sight of the shower in its screened-off cubicle, and there were cooking facilities in the room which was one of a long series of bungalows leading off an outside, covered passage.

She looked at him with candid eyes.

'Does it matter?' she asked. 'Who is there to consider but ourselves? Don't be idiotic, Jeff. There's room for both of us and you're even more in need of a good night's sleep than I am. Bring in the rest of the luggage whilst I take a shower, and when you're having yours, I can rustle up a meal for us out of the tins we've got. I saw some bread in that office place where you paid. They might have butter too.'

He was too tired to argue. Also he saw the sense in what she said, and by the time he had bought necessities from the man in the office, she was out of the shower, clean and refreshed and in a dressing-gown over her pyjamas.

She fried sausages and eggs whilst he had his shower and she unpacked his case for him, putting the things outside the cubicle.

'Your packing's awful,' she said, 'and I can't find a pyjama jacket without diving to the bottom of the case, but here are the trousers and a dressing-gown. You'll have to make do with them. Do you want to shave?'

'I'd better. It'll save time in the morning.'

It was all so easy and natural.

'We might have been married for years,' he chuckled as he splashed.

If she replied, he did not hear her, but when he came out of the shower, she had the meal ready, the two chairs drawn companionably up to the table and the electric fire burning.

'I tried it and found that the last occupant had obligingly left some juice in it so it isn't costing us anything,' she said, but before they had finished their meal the fire had died on them and she gave a little shiver as the room grew cold.

'Better get into bed,' he said. 'Let's leave the clearing up till the morning. Romaine and I . . .'

He stopped.

'Romaine's your wife?'

He had told her he was married.

'Yes.'

'Are you in love with her?'

'I — yes,' he said again, abruptly, but both of them were aware of that slight pause and of the over-emphasis of the affirmative.

Neither of them spoke again and when she had got into bed, he did not look at her and he turned out the light, but a flashing light illuminated the room at regular intervals and he could see the narrow outline of her body beneath the bedclothes and he was no longer thinking of Romaine.

Presently he got out of bed to see if there were any way of darkening the window to shut out that tantalising sight. He managed to fix a towel over it and when he turned back again, she was sitting up in bed looking at him.

'That infernal sign,' he muttered.

'Jeff!'

He had to pass her bed in the small room to reach his own. Her hand was stretched out for his and he stumbled to his knees and she caught his head between warm arms and drew it to her breast.

'It isn't just the sign, is it? It's me. You and me. Why do we have to fight against it? Two lonely people millions of miles away from home. It doesn't matter to anyone. Kiss me, Jeff. Call it anything you like — love, if you like.'

He lifted his face to meet her lips in the darkness, and knew that, whatever it might be to him, to her it was love.

They stayed in the motel for two more

days and nights, not leaving their room except to buy necessities from the office, absorbed in each other and in the discovery of personalities which they had hidden under the guise of mere companionship, oblivious of time until he realised how little of it remained if he were to take her to Valparaiso and still reach Buenos Aires to link up with Goby and his car.

'Darling, don't take me to Valparaiso,' she said. 'Just dump me near the railroad. I can get there on my own.'

'No, I'll take you. I can't leave you stranded like that. Besides . . .'

'Yes, Jeff?'

'I don't want to leave you at all,' he said in a strangled voice.

'But you'll have to some day, won't you?'

'Shall I? Must I? Elinor . . .'

She put her arms round him and held him tightly. He belonged to her, not to that shadowy woman at the other side of the world who had let him leave her as she, Elinor, would never have done. She had found him and if she could, she would keep him.

To Jeff she was an entirely new experience, a girl absolutely alone, without ties or even a home or any sort of security, yet courageous and uncomplaining and not embittered by her lack of success over either her broken marriage or her inability even to make a living. He felt convinced, too, that he was the first lover she had taken, and knowing that gave him a feeling of responsibility for her. How could he now just abandon her to the off chance that her friends in Chile could and would help her? She was not sure of that herself, and he could not leave her until he knew that she was safe.

The past two days as her lover had revealed to him unsuspected depths in her which he could not take lightly. She was curiously dependent on him without ever admitting it or laying claim to him, whereas Romaine had never been actually dependent on him and he realised now that that fact had irked him. To Elinor he was a man to be admired and looked up to, whereas Romaine he had always been a boy, immature, half-grown, idling away his time with what was to her a hobby whilst she herself worked at a serious job. Though she was his wife, he had never even kept her nor made a home for her, for always there had been her parents' home as a permanent background, her father's money which had helped them out of difficulties. He had never been able to adapt himself to the environment of wealth which was naturally hers, whereas he had been the provider for himself and Elinor and even in these few days had grown in mental stature by so doing.

For the first time he began to see his marriage to Romaine in a different light, possibly a mistake. Did they really love each other with a love that would last? He had felt no responsibility for her and she had placed none upon him. He had not even sent her money and she had not asked for or expected it. He was outside her life and, as he was beginning to see it, he was just a plaything to her, someone to share the transports and raptures of physical loving but in no other way a husband. He was not really necessary to her. The thought struck him forcibly for the first time.

What if he had been free for Elinor?

The thought shook him, standing there with her arms about him and her lips warm against his own, and he had a sudden revulsion of feeling, remembering the love that he and Romaine had shared, the laughter and fun of their physical relationship and her thoughtful, intelligent mind which had met and overcome their difficulties and helped to set at its real value the problem created by their vastly different backgrounds. There was no one like Romaine. There never would be.

He released himself from Elinor's arms and whilst she waited in sudden hope for him to finish his uncompleted sentence said almost harshly, 'I shall go back, of course. This is just an interlude which we shall both forget. Can you be ready to leave in half-an-hour? If I drive fast, we should be able to reach Santiago tonight and with an early start, I can put you down in Valparaiso and go on. I'll go and see about the bill whilst you pack.'

She felt defeated after that one magic moment when it had seemed that he might remain hers. But she had taken a good many knocks in life and never expected that there would be anything else for her, and when he came back, he merely picked up the packed cases and carried them out to the car without looking at her. How had he been so mad as to think for a moment that she could replace Romaine in his heart and his life? Once the Argentine Grand Prix was over, nothing would induce him to stay away from her any longer and until she could and would go with him, he would not go away again, even if that meant the end of big racing for him.

When they reached Santiago, late at night, they encountered one of the difficulties which, small in itself, had such far-reaching effects, for there was only one room available at the hotel and Jeff, after a moment's hesitation, agreed to take it. After all, it was only for one night, their last night together, and he was not proof against the appealing glance which Elinor gave him.

'What's this all about?' he asked, looking at the form he was given to fill in, which was in Spanish. 'You do it, will you?'

He did not notice a man who was standing by and watching Elinor as she filled up the form, but when he returned from seeing about their luggage, he found him in conversation with her.

'Hello, Jeff,' he said with a friendly smile. 'I thought I recognised you but I hadn't met your wife. Remember me? We met in Rome. I'm with the *Augury*, covering the Argentine Grand Prix. Come and have a drink, you and Mrs Elster.'

There was nothing for it but to agree. Afterwards, when he and Elinor had parted company, he could explain, man to man, but at the moment such explanation would be invidious. It was annoying, though. Who would have expected that he would meet someone in Santiago who knew him?

In the morning the two cars left together.

'I'm dropping my wife in Valparaiso with friends,' Jeff said in an effort to shake the other man off.

'That's O.K. by me, old man. It's a better road anyway. Not up to seeing Jeff race, eh, Mrs Elster?' with a chuckle, and his car followed the other closely.

Jeff, anxious now to put an end to this association with Elinor and also to get rid, if possible, of this importunate newspaper man, drove too fast on the unfamiliar road, took a corner too quickly, skidded on the newly wet surface to avoid another car and crashed.

When he regained consciousness, he was back in Santiago in the hospital, his head injured and both arms immobilised in plaster, but it was some time before he was fully conscious, remembered all the circumstances and asked, with some difficulty, after Elinor.

The nurse spoke soothingly to him, but neither could understand the other and it was not until an English-speaking doctor came to him that he was able to get any information.

'Your wife was also injured, but she is in our care and her life is in no danger, Mr Elster. Don't worry. She'll be all right.'

His wife. So that was what they thought. He remembered Barnett, who had been following them and who must have given them the information. Of all the damned things to happen!

If only his head did not ache so infernally, he might be able to think, to see his way through this mess! He thought of Romaine. Did she know about him? Could she possibly know by now what had happened?

'My head,' he muttered, trying restlessly to turn it, to clear his brain. 'I can't think.'

'Don't try to yet,' said the doctor. 'We're going to give you something. When you wake up, you will feel better, but I assure you there's nothing to worry about. Your wife is quite safe and being looked after.'

They gave him an injection and blessed oblivion again and the next time he became conscious, he found Fred Goby beside him.

'Fred? Thank God you've come,' he said weakly. 'How long have I been here?'

'Just over a week, old man. How are you feeling?'

'Like death. All in. Did they – send for you?'

'Yes. Barnett wired the news to the race committee and of course I came at once.'

'The race. That's off, of course. Sorry. What happened? I can't remember a thing.'

'You skidded off the road to avoid another car, but don't worry about that now. Nobody in the other car was hurt.'

Then he remembered Elinor and tried to sit up but collapsed weakly again.

'Fred – the woman. There was a woman in the car. Mrs Ramsdell. What happened to her? They told me she is all right, but is it true?'

'Well, she's hurt a bit, but not dangerously.'

'They think she's – my wife, Fred.'

'I know, but don't worry about that. It'll sort itself out,' said Fred uncomfortably.

He did not tell Jeff that he had been flown to England and back again and that he had seen Romaine and knew that she was aware of the existence of Elinor Ramsdell and had taken it badly.

'Does Romaine know about the accident?'

'Yes. I — I cabled her as soon as I knew that you'd bought it.'

'Tell me the truth about the damage, Fred. Have I had it as far as racing goes?'

'Dunno, old man, but probably not. You've smashed up both arms and bashed your head, but they don't think there are any internal injuries. Nothing's happened to the old brain, anyway!' with a desperate effort of cheerfulness.

Jeff managed a weak, fleeting smile.

'Skull's too thick, I suppose. Damned nuisance, though. Do you think Romaine could possibly know about — about Elinor?'

Fred was saved from having to make a reply by the entrance of the nurse to cut short the interview.

'See you again tomorrow, old man,' he said and took a hasty departure.

On the following day when Fred came to see him, Jeff dictated a letter to Romaine.

'It's damned awkward,' he said. 'They all think Elinor is my wife and I'm in the devil of a mess. I can't ask anyone here to write, not a proper letter anyway. If

150

only they'd let me go home! Hasn't there been anything at all from her? Not even a cable?'

''Fraid not,' Fred had to admit.

'Of course if she's heard about Elinor, it would make her mad. Will you write to her for me, Fred? Just say — say — "Darling, I'm not too badly messed up so don't worry too much about me. I'm longing to come home to you. Do hope all is well with you and the baby. I love you very much. I think of you and want you all the time. All my love, my own darling, Jeff." My head's aching so infernally that I can't think of anything else to say, but get that off to her right away, will you?'

Fred nodded. The Elinor business would take the devil of a lot of explaining, he thought, especially as no denial had been published and he wondered whether or not he himself should publish one.

In the end he decided that he must leave Jeff to deal with this himself, and he sent the letter to Romaine without comment.

By the time the letter arrived,

Romaine had been taken home, still weak from the miscarriage and needing care and rest, of which she was certainly assured in her mother's home. White-faced, large-eyed and silent, she was submissive to all that was done for her but refused to see any of her friends or to enter into any conversation about her husband.

'Mother, do you mind if we don't talk about it just yet? He's not too badly injured and I daresay he will be home soon. I'd rather wait.'

Lady Manning could get no inkling of her thoughts, though privately she hoped that this would be the end of her daughter's unfortunate marriage, and when the letter came bearing the Santiago postmark and addressed in Fred Goby's somewhat illiterate handwriting, she had no scruples about opening it and retaining it.

'All his love' indeed! And careering about the country with another woman! Anyway, the letter did not tell them anything which they did not already know, and his explanations could wait.

Romaine was eating her heart out for

that letter, or for some word from Jeff. When the cable had come from Fred, she had been too ill to care, too bitter about the loss of her baby, but as the weeks went by without word from him, she searched her heart to get matters into their true perspective and found that above and beyond all other feelings was the love for Jeff which could forgive him everything but this final neglect of her.

Many times she started to write to him but her expressions were either too stilted and sounded unreal even to her, or else she found herself pleading with him, begging for his love, and in the end it was to Goby that she wrote, formally and giving him no indication of the agony of her mind but she hoped Jeff's condition was improving. It was, she felt, a poor effort, but until she heard from Jeff, what else could she say or do?

Fred carried the letter to Jeff. From its tone, curt and cold and giving no indication of how deeply she was suffering, it seemed obvious that she knew about Elinor and that her principal reaction to it was an unforgiving anger. It reduced Jeff's mercurial temperament to despair. For the first time in his gay, uncaring life, something was hitting him really hard and though he could not believe that Romaine, of all people, was taking a serious view of an episode which had meant so little to him, it brought him up with a jerk.

'She knows, doesn't she, about this other woman?' he asked Fred wretchedly. 'Who told her? Not you?'

'I wouldn't do that, Jeff, though you've been a bit of a stinker,' said Fred in his honest way, and he told him about the reports in the newspapers which Mr Moller, as disgusted as he, had confirmed.

Jeff moved restlessly. He was up and about, his arms still rigidly encased in plaster, though a minor injury to one foot kept him hobbling and it was thought advisable by Mr Moller, who was paying his hospital expenses for him, to remain where he was for the time being rather than risk any jolting in the plane to England.

'I wish I could get home. If only I could see her – explain ...'

The expression on Fred's face cut him

short.

'It's not my business, Jeff, but it'll take some explaining, won't it? I don't wonder she's sore with you, specially after that first business with that dame in Tangier. Dammit, when you've got a wife like Romaine ...'

'I know. I know. You needn't rub it in. Being a bachelor and not having much use for women, you don't understand what it's like to be parted from your wife for months at a time, and it isn't as if these other affairs really mean a thing to me.'

'Wouldn't it mean a thing if she did the same thing, had other men on the side?' asked Fred uncompromisingly. 'And what about Mrs Ramsdell? Are you just going to ditch her, just like that? Have you seen her?'

'No,' said Jeff uncomfortably. 'Have you?'

'Yes. I had to. They all think she's your wife, and − she's never denied it. Don't ask me why. I don't know anything about women, but she's in a spot as well, you know, and I daresay she's left it up to you to get her out of it.

She'll have to leave the hospital soon because they want the bed, and who's going to pay the bill? You can't expect Moller to and she hasn't any money.'

Jeff got up and hobbled to the window and stood staring out of it. For the first time in his life he had come face to face with himself and he was not liking what he saw. From time to time he found himself still making mental excuses for himself, a man young and full of natural vigour, with the woman he loved far away and another woman close at hand and willing − then he wrenched his thoughts back to the uncompromising and unpalatable truth. What if Elinor had been available and easy? Should not the memory of Romaine have been enough to sustain him and keep him true to her? Elinor had meant nothing to him and now she was hideously tangled up in his life and he was morally responsible for at least her immediate well-being. He could not just cast her off.

When he turned back to Fred, there was a look of desperation in his eyes.

'I've been a fool, Fred, worse than a fool − a low skunk. Of course I've got to do something about Elinor, but in heaven's name what? She's not the sort I can just leave, but how can I take her with me? Yet in a way I'm responsible for her. I can't even give her enough to live on until she can get a job. What about these people she hoped to find in Valparaiso?'

'She wrote to them but the letter came back. They've gone away.'

'God, what a mess!'

There was a long pause and then Fred, who knew Jeff probably better than anyone else in the world did, including his wife, spoke quietly.

He did not excuse him, and he had seen enough of Elinor Ramsdell to feel an overwhelming pity for her and a fierce anger towards Jeff, but he realised that this was a time when mere words were not enough and that it might be a turning point in the life of the two people for whom he cared most in the world, and of a third who had come to matter to him more than at the moment he cared to think.

'She wants to get back to her own country where at least she'll be looked after and given a chance, Jeff, so I'll take her,' he said. 'I'll see she's O.K. until you see what you're going to do about her.'

Jeff stared at him in surprise and relief and some discomfort.

'You will Fred? But how – where . . .'

The thought of old Fred with a woman attached to him in any capacity was fantastic.

'I don't know how or where, or even if she'll go with me, but someone's got to look after her and it don't look as if you can,' said Fred, slipping up in his grammar as he sometimes did for all his care when something touched him deeply. 'You know me. I don't spend much and I got a bit put by and – I can afford it and – it's the best thing I can think of.'

'You're a pal, Fred. If you'll do that – if she'll go – I'll just take it as a loan and pay you back as soon as I get to work again . . .'

Jeff was finding it difficult to express himself, but something of the old optimism was coming back, the immediate obstacle the only one that counted. The farther distant future could be left as usual to look after itself and his spirits rose.

'I'm not lending you the money for her,' interrupted Fred brusquely. 'I'm giving it to you as the only decent thing to do, and by the time you get back you'll have enough on your plate. You don't know what's going to happen yet, how your wife's going to take this, or whether you'll even have a job with Moller. You may be out on your ear seeing as you've got no business to be in Chile at all. I'll go and see Mrs Ramsdell,' and he turned and left Jeff with his thoughts, which he knew would be none too pleasant.

Chapter Five

ELINOR sat in a sheltered corner of the deserted deck and surveyed the wreck she had made of her life and wondered which of the broken pieces she could put together again. She was sad and bitter. Nothing had gone right for her, and this latest misfortune had been largely her own fault. There had been no excuse for it. Had she ever really been in love with Jeff Elster?

She had not seen him in the hospital though he had sent her a note by Fred Goby suggesting that she should do so but the look of her still marred face in the mirror had made her refuse. No one but Fred and the people at the hospital had seen it, but she had been assured that time and expert attention from a plastic surgeon would heal the deep scars which fortunately had not touched her eyes or her mouth.

'I can't let him see me like this,' she had said again and again to the sympathetic nurses who had urged her to visit her 'husband'.

Fred Goby was different. For one thing, he had never seen her as she had been before the accident so that he was pitiful but not shocked, and during the weeks in the hospital a strange friendship had grown between her and this man who was her only link with the outside world; and when, rather diffidently, Fred had told her that Jeff had asked him to take her back to England, she had been quite willing to go and to let Jeff, as she believed, pay her fare. She was at her wits' end to know what she was going to do if she remained in South America, friendless and penniless and needing expensive treatment which she could not possibly afford to pay for and now she was on her way to England with Fred as her watchdog and constant companion. She had come to depend on him in a way she would not have thought possible in the days of her happy-go-lucky freedom, living from hand to mouth.

But what was going to happen to her now? She had been surprised and touched by Jeff's seeming generosity and care for her. What did he mean the end of this to be?

She saw Fred's familiar figure coming towards her, small, compact, purposeful, and the friendly grin on his plain, honest face as he caught sight of her and waved a hand as he came.

'Phew, what a morning!' he said, battling with a gust of rainy wind as he slipped into the chair beside her. 'Sure you wouldn't rather be inside?'

'No. The saloons are so noisy and crowded that you can't even think.'

'Do you have to do that?' he asked gently.

He was so careful now with his aspirates and his grammar though his voice would never acquire a cultured accent and he did not strive for one. He was just himself, a man of the people, with no particular aspirations but to work at his job and to put enough by for a rainy day.

'I shall have to, shan't I? What's going to happen to me, Fred? I was in desperate straits before I left and couldn't think of anything but getting home but – what am I going to do when I get to England? Did Jeff say anything about me? About his plans?'

She had not been able to bring herself to asking that question before, but now it had to be asked.

'Well – not exactly,' said Fred awkwardly. 'Still, he had to get you home, hadn't he? We – he – couldn't just leave you stranded, could he?'

'Why not?' she asked with a touch of contempt for herself. 'Most men would have.'

'Not Jeff,' said Fred loyally.

'Do you know his wife? What is she like?'

'She's a grand person, a doctor, and I don't just mean grand as far as that goes. She's – fine in herself, good, if you know what I mean,' he said, floundering helplessly in his attempt to describe Romaine.

'Good? Yes, I know what you mean,' said Elinor grimly. 'Not like me, though I'm not as casual as you may have thought. It's the first time I've done anything like that, and of course this had to happen!'

'I didn't think you were what you call casual, Elinor. May I call you that?' for it was the first time he had ventured to call her by her name.

'Of course. I'm glad you didn't think I was just – rotten. Are they in love, do you think?'

He hesitated.

'Jeff is,' he said at last, 'but I don't know Mrs Elster well enough to say how she has taken this. I think – once they meet . . .'

He stopped, feeling that he could not discuss the private affairs of Romaine and Jeff with anyone and yet knowing pityingly, that it might matter a great deal to Elinor what Romaine's attitude was and what would be the outcome of all this. He suddenly disliked very much any idea of an ultimate marriage between Jeff and this woman so strangely in his care. It could not bring them happiness and he found himself wanting beyond everything, happiness for her. He had cared for many lost dogs, frightened children, injured kittens, and to him Elinor was all those.

She was silent, her mind worried by confused thoughts. If this Romaine were so high and mighty as to be unforgiving of Jeff, he might in the end feel that he had to marry her, Elinor, but was that what either of them would want? If she married again, it would have to be to a man not in love with another woman, and her mind took a startling turn as her eyes met the steady, honest ones of Fred Goby and looked away again.

Was it possible? This odd little man with his selfless kindness, a quality which had come to mean more to her than any other in life?

She thrust the extraordinary idea away into the back of her mind and rose precipitately.

'It's too cold out here,' she said. 'Let's go in, shall we? I'll teach you to play canasta.'

When they reached England, he made all the plans for her and she left herself in his hands with a feeling of comfort such as she had never known. She would let the future take care of itself. It was bliss not to have to think or worry, though there was no reason on earth why he should be doing all this for her. They kept up the pretence that he was carrying out Jeff's instructions though the pretence wore very thin. He found a room for her near his own bachelor flat, took her to a doctor, arranged for her to be treated by a plastic surgeon, cared for her in every way and knew she had come to mean more to him than anyone in the world and by the time Jeff was able to fly back to England, he had told her so, amazed at his own temerity.

They were in his flat and she was

making the tea for him. He had given her a key and had become accustomed to finding her there when he came in from work, the meal daintily prepared and set, instead of his former scratch meal on a corner of the table and as it was an interminably cold spring, there was a small fire burning before which a thin, nondescript stray cat was curled round. When he was in England he always kept a window open for them to come in over the tiles. They were many and various.

He gave her a smile of contented welcome and bent to stroke the cat.

'Poor pussy. Has she had a saucer of milk?' he asked.

Elinor laughed.

'We really ought to keep a cow. Do you know how much milk they have, not to mention the tins of cat-food and sardines I give them?'

'Poor things, it isn't much to do for them, is it? I hate having to turn them out again but at least they've had a bit of food and comfort. This one's got something the matter with her ear. I'll see what I can do for it before she has to go out the way she came and get on with the battle for existence again.'

Elinor's eyes rested on him for a moment as he bent down to change into the slippers she had set ready for him. Dear Fred.

'You take in all the lost and helpless and broken things, don't you?' she asked in a low voice. 'Me too.'

He dropped his second shoe and straightened himself to look at her, caught by the tone of her voice.

'You're not a stray cat,' he said.

'No, but I was lost and helpless and — broken until you found me. Why have you done all this for me, Fred dear? Let's be honest. I know that it isn't Jeff who is doing it. It's you, isn't it? Why should you?'

He shifted his feet on the rug and looked down at them.

'I — well — I'm doing it for Jeff — or at least that was the way it started,' he said.

'And now? You know that Jeff and I don't mean a thing to each other, that his wife will take him back and forgive him if she has any sense and that that will be the end, for me.'

'Yes. Yes, that is what ought to

happen, of course,' he muttered awkwardly, still not daring to look at her, and she came to him and laid a hand on his arm.

'Are you fond of me, Fred? This is all the wrong way round, and I'm being very bold, idiotic perhaps, but – somehow I don't think you'll say it unless I say it first. Are you fond enough of me to marry me, Because I am – of you.'

He turned to her at that and looked at her, his plain face transfigured with wonder and incredulous joy.

'Do you mean that? Because of course I am. I've – fallen in love with you, Elinor, but – you couldn't ever think of me like that, not enough to marry me.'

She gave a shaky little laugh and put her arms round his neck.

'Suppose you kiss me and find out,' she said and for the first time in his life he found a woman's lips on his own.

'But I'm not your sort,' he stammered when she set him free again. 'I'm not good enough, an ugly old codger like me, and you so – so beautiful . . .'

She laughed again, but this time with

triumph and happiness.

'Beautiful? Me? Oh Fred, you idiot. You're the kindest, most generous and unselfish man in the world, and I love your ugly old mug, and I love you. I've made all the running so far, so how about you having a go? Say "I love you, Elinor, and I want to marry you".'

And still bewildered, amazed at himself and this flood of undreamed-of happiness, he said it.

But he still had to tell Jeff, and though he was pretty sure that Jeff and Romaine would 'make it up' and that Elinor meant nothing to him, he would have to be quite sure. It was so unbelievable that Elinor really wanted him, Fred, and that he was not merely a make-shift if she could not have Jeff.

He had no opportunity for private conversation when he met Jeff at the airport and Jeff, anxious to make his peace with Romaine, went straight to the home of her parents where she was still living.

Apart from writing him a brief note, telling him where she was and expressing regret for his accident, Romaine had not been able to bring herself to contact him again or to answer the letters which one of the nurses at the hospital had written for him. These could not express in any way his real thoughts and he had been in the uncomfortable position of not being able to reveal the fact that she was his wife whilst Elinor was in the same hospital. He had got Fred to address the envelopes and Romaine's heart had always missed a beat when she saw the uniformed, schoolboy writing on them. Though she knew that he could not write himself but had had to dictate the letters to a comparative stranger, their tone only served to increase her unhappiness. Surely, even to a stranger, he could have dictated some loving expression, shown some anxiety for her welfare? There was not even a mention of the baby she had lost, the child that was his as well as hers.

And the iron entered into her soul.

She felt, for the first time, that she had made an irreparable mistake in marrying Jeff, whose ideas, whose way of life, whose very love, were so different from hers. This was not the first time he had

170

been unfaithful to her and probably not the second either. It seemed that as soon as he was away from her, he felt no bond of loyalty to her but behaved as if he were single and free, and the whole idea disgusted and sickened her, for what sort of life could they ever make together if he regarded so lightly the bond of their marriage which had been so sacred a thing to her?

Many were the sleepless, tormented nights she spent thinking of their future, agonised at the thought of life without him and of life with him. How could they possibly go on together, with no trust on her side and no love, as she understood it, on his? She tried to face the facts of her marriage dispassionately. She had given more than her body to Jeff. She had given all there was of herself, mind, body and soul, to her marriage and had enjoyed the physical ecstasy shared with her husband as the ultimate fulfilment, the outward expression of the inner, deeper love of the spirit and as such in itself a precious and holy thing, the perfect fusion of the bodies when the spirits were already one.

But Jeff? What had it meant to him when any light and trivial affair of the moment could take place? There could have been little or nothing beneath and beyond it if he could so easily betray her with another woman. She shrank at the thought of physical contact with Jeff again, Jeff who had not regarded his body as the sacred vehicle for their love, as hers only. How could marriage continue when she felt that she could never bear to let him touch her again, when he had reduced the act of supreme love to the level of the beasts in the field?

He cabled that he was flying home. She would have to see him just once and not again. She wished she could die, had no longer any desire to go on living without him, but if people could die just when they wanted to, there would be few people, wives anyway she thought bitterly, who would be left to grow to old age.

Her mother came into her room as she waited for Jeff, her heart stricken at sight of Romaine's white face and the eyes that told of yet another sleepless night.

'Darling, I don't feel you should see

him when he comes,' she said.

'I must, Mother.'

'Surely you're not going to have him back, after this disgraceful episode about which everyone knows?'

Romaine bristled at her mother's words and once again her mind veered as it had done countless times during the last few weeks and she found herself making excuses for Jeff.

'Probably only our friends know. We're not such important people that it has made headlines, and the main issue is personal to me and Jeff, and other people's opinions don't count,' she said.

'I know, dear, but isn't that personal issue enough? How can you ever be happy with a man who has shown that he has no moral values and no sense of responsibility?'

'Mother, you must leave me to decide on this for myself. I know you've never liked Jeff nor approved of our marriage, but I was deeply in love with him and he is my husband and I have my sense of responsibility, after all. Please leave me to work it out for myself.'

'You know that all I care for is your

happiness, my darling.'

'I know, Mother, and I'm truly grateful, but I've got to work this out for myself, make my own decisions, my own life.'

'I know that, my dear, but . . .'

'Please, Mother. I don't want to talk any more about it until I have seen Jeff. I don't want to seem ungrateful to you and Father, but you can't do anything to help me to make up my mind. I must see Jeff first.'

Lady Manning had reluctantly to leave her to her troubled thoughts. It was too late now for her to produce the letter which she had withheld, and in any case she had destroyed it. Besides, of what real value to Romaine were these empty expressions of love from a man who had treated her as Jeff had done?

When Jeff arrived and was actually in the house and Romaine was going slowly down to see him, she still did not know what she was going to do, but at the sight of him, his face expressing all the old cheerfulness and *bonhomie* and no sort of contrition, her heart hardened. Was that the measure of his love for her?

'Hullo, my sweet. Here's your bad penny turning up again, slightly the worse for wear. Arms not quite up to their usual standard yet, as you see!'

They were still in the plaster which had protected them on the flight, and his eyes went to them and back to her ruefully.

'I am sorry you have not completely recovered,' she said stiffly.

'Oh, merely a matter of time. They wanted me to stay on longer at the hospital but all I wanted was to get back to you, darling. It's been a beastly nuisance, of course, the whole thing, having to scratch from the race and everything, and I bet old Moller's mad, though he's been very decent about it.'

His tone was jaunty and confident, apologetic towards Moller but not in the least towards her, she thought. She could not know that it was a façade and that beneath it he was feeling sick with shame. She had imagined this interview many times but never that he would adopt this care-free, untroubled attitude towards her.

As she made no reply, he spoke again, this time with rather less ease.

'How are you, darling? You don't look too fit.'

His concern for her, which she felt was belated and insincere, deepened her resentment. She had told him in her letter, coldly and formally, that she had lost the baby, but in his own dictated reply he had not referred to it. She had not known that the nurse who had written the letter was not aware that she was his wife.

'You would hardly expect me to be in robust health yet,' she said icily.

'Oh − you mean − the baby and all that. Sorry about it, of course, but there's plenty of time,' he assured her cheerfully.

'You really think that, Jeff?'

'What do you mean, darling? Of course there is. My injury is only temporary . . .'

'And what about mine, Jeff? Hasn't it occurred to you that I also have suffered an injury? One that a hospital and doctors are not likely to be able to mend?'

Now at last the jauntiness left him and he looked crestfallen, but still the small boy caught out in a peccadillo.

'You — you know about it, Romaine?'

'About this other woman. Yes. I've known from the beginning. You must have realised that.'

'You surely don't think there was anything in that?'

'I'm afraid I do, Jeff.'

'It was rotten luck it getting into the papers.'

'Meaning that otherwise I should not have known? You would not have told me?'

'Well . . .'

He was at a loss for words. How could he explain to her that there had been nothing in it? Didn't she know that there could not have been?

'Jeff, we've got to talk this thing out. It isn't a case of whether it got into the papers or not, and probably few people read about it. The important thing is that it happened, and that it matters to us, anyway. It isn't as if it were even the first time that you've been unfaithful to me. There was the other time, with the girl in

177

Tangier, and there may have been more. The fact is, I can't trust you any more, and without trust how can a marriage go on? It strikes at its very foundation.'

Now he was really startled. He had never seriously believed that this could break up their marriage, that she would make such an issue of it.

'You can't mean that, Romaine? That you'd let a little thing like that make you leave me?' he asked increduously. 'You must know that it didn't mean a thing to me? You're the only woman that matters to me.'

'Obviously unfaithfulness doesn't mean anything to you, Jeff, but it does to me. It shatters the very conception of love between husband and wife.'

'But every man has these little affairs.'

'Not every man, Jeff. I know that many men regard it as a little thing and have numerous extra-marital relations with other women which, according to them, don't matter, but to me they do matter. You took me, as I took you, as the one woman, the one man, "forsaking all others". And it isn't as if I have been an unsatisfactory wife to you, a cold wife, which may excuse some men for seeking in another woman what they looked for in marriage but failed to find. I know now you were away from me, but couldn't our close relationship, our *perfect* relationship as it seemed to be, keep you from wanting and taking another woman just to fill in the gap? Especially when I was carrying your child, Jeff?'

He realised how deeply in earnest she was. Her voice was clear and ice-cold, her attitude so utterly unyielding that he employed the only tactics he could in the attempt to break the barrier she had set up between them. Moving towards her, he attempted to stretch out his stiff, bandaged arms, his eyes and his lips enticing, her voice cajoling.

'Darling heart, I'm sorry. I can't say more than that, and that I feel a skunk for behaving like that, but if only I could take you in my arms properly, you'd just know how sorry I am. Gosh, if ever a man wanted his arms, I do at this moment!'

But she drew back and held her head proudly, an inflexible look in her eyes.

'No, Jeff. That isn't the solution now. I don't want you to touch me. I don't want you to touch me — ever again. It's finished between us.'

Incredibly she heard herself saying it. That gesture of his towards her, suggesting that it could all be forgiven and forgotten in a kiss, had frightened her because, for the moment, she had wanted to yield to the mere physical temptation of him. But to what end? What good would it do either of them?

He let his arms drop to the bent position in which the plaster held them and she looked away from the despair in his eyes. She could not go through this again. It must be the end. She could not suffer like this again. She must learn to live her life without him. Love, to be lasting, must be deep and true and mutual in its strength, and his had proved itself to be only a superficial thing. She could live without what it meant to him. She must. Just this agony of parting and then it would be over for ever.

'Romaine, you don't mean that? You can't. After all we've been to each other

– all the fun we've had . . .'

The word struck at her heart.

'Fun? Yes, that's all it's been to you, hasn't it?' she interrupted him bitterly. 'I do mean what I say, Jeff. It's over. Our marriage is at an end. I'm going to – divorce you.'

It was said now, that final thing which so far she had not put into words even to herself. She would not take back either the word or the intent. She did not want her freedom. There would never be another man for her. But she would not remain bound to him, held by just the legal cords of which she would always be aware. She still had her profession which, until Jeff's intrusion into her life, had been its dominant interest. She must make it fill her life again, and if her heart remained empty, for ever unsatisfied, would it matter? Many women had to go through life without the love of a man, fine, splendid, useful women; and at least she had known its mirage.

Jeff went quite white.

'Divorce me?' he echoed. 'For *Elinor?* But we don't mean a thing to each other! She wouldn't want to marry me any

181

more than I want to marry her!'

'That's a matter entirely for yourselves. It isn't because of this woman or any particular woman. It's just — convenient, unless you prefer to give me some other grounds. I believe these things can be arranged so as to satisfy our English law. I have no wish to force you into the position of having to marry this woman.'

'I can't persuade you to change your mind, Romaine?'

'No.'

'Then — I suppose it's good'bye?' he asked bleakly.

'Yes,' said Romaine and turned away from him and left him and locked herself into her room with the storm of tears which she could no longer deny to her woman's body but which brought her no relief. For good or ill, she had changed the whole course of her life and sent from her the source of its happiness.

White as death, stoical, unmoved of face and voice, she went through the martyrdom of the divorce court in which sensation-seeking spectators, and not even her parents who went with her, had

182

any idea how deeply it affected her. Calmly and coldly she answered the few hateful questions put to her and in a matter of minutes it was over, and she left the court no longer the wife of the man she still loved but in whom she had no longer any faith.

It was not Elinor Ramsdell who was cited. Fred, alarmed and disturbed, had revealed to Jeff the amazing fact that he was going to marry her and Jeff, caring nothing any longer since Romaine had made up her mind and could not, he knew, be dissuaded, had gone through the farce required by the respectable English law to provide the evidence. One woman or another, what did it matter to him since he had lost Romaine?

'I hope you'll be happy with Fred,' he said to Elinor, formal and tight-lipped. 'He's one of the best.'

'Do you think I don't know that?' she said softly, a woman transfigured by happiness. 'I'm sorry, Jeff. About how things have turned out for you, I mean. You — you wouldn't have wanted to marry me in any case, would you?'

'No,' he said curtly and went away.

He also was a man transformed, a man she had never known, no longer nor perhaps ever to be again the blithe, care-free companion of those fateful days and nights. He had grown immeasurably older, the gay spirit quenched, his eyes remote and unfathomable, his mouth bitter.

'I can't forgive Romaine,' she told Fred afterwards.

'Don't be too hard on her, love. She's fine and loyal and it isn't the first time with Jeff. Perhaps they would never have made a go of it. They're as different as chalk and cheese. I'm as sorry for her as I am for Jeff.'

'I'm not. If you love truly, you can forgive everything – as you have, Fred darling,' she added tremulously.

He gave her one of his inexperienced, awkward kisses.

'You didn't even know me then, but don't let's ever speak of that again,' and they never did.

Once the divorce was over, Romaine set herself the difficult task of forgetting her married life and going back to the profession which she must henceforth

184

make her whole existence. She had given up her work at the clinic and had been replaced, but in any case she could not have endured the constant reminders of Jeff which a return to it would have entailed. She must cut loose from all such associations and start afresh.

She knew that her mother would have been glad for her to become just the daughter of the house, going about with her and interesting herself in a dignified, ladylike way in such social services as were left to kindly, generous-hearted people by the Welfare State, but such a life could not be hers.

'I'm sorry, Mother,' she said with real contrition, 'but I could never settle down to that. I belong to the next generation, you see, and I've got to work and make something of my life and justify my existence. Besides, think of all the years of work I should be throwing away and – work is all I have left now.'

There was resolution in her voice and no self-pity and her mother sighed. At least, she thought, she was not grieving over the divorce about which Lady Manning had been secretly glad, especially as the baby had not lived. In time Romaine would get over it completely and would then be ready for marriage with some really nice, suitable man, by which she meant a man of their own social class and preferably with money.

It was not easy for Romaine to find the sort of work she wanted and could do, with her knowledge but limited experience, but at last she heard of a small and almost defunct practice in a Hampshire village at present being more or less maintained by a sick, elderly woman doctor.

Romaine went to Worbury to see this Dr Eastcote.

'It isn't even a living now, my dear,' she was told. 'I've had such bad health that it's run to seed lately and such patients as I've had are drifting away to the two men doctors in Greatborough, who run a surgery in the village twice a week but don't really want to. Why not go and see them? They might be willing to take you on as a partner if you did the Worbury work.'

Romaine went to see them and if she

needed anything to strengthen her determination, their hostile attitude supplied it. Drs Heath and Dewey were both elderly men of the old school, who still resented the incursion of her sex into their profession and had a prosperous practice amongst the local bigwigs who preferred to dispense with the benefits of the Health Service. They made full use of the hospital service as far as their panel patients were concerned, and of its private wards where necessary for patients who could pay the bills and between them managed to run a lucrative practice without giving too much time and thought to their non-paying patients. Their twice-weekly visits to the room which they rented in Worbury did not produce very much, but they kept them in touch with the few big houses who were still able to maintain a depleted staff of servants and who could be relied upon for hospitality from time to time.

Though they could not prevent Romaine from buying what was left of Dr Eastcote's practice, they did their best to discourage her, thus stiffening her resolution. She was spoiling for a fight.

'It's a poor district, of course. Dr er – Elster, but a healthy one. Most of the villagers are National Health patients, and those who are not naturally come to us, or rather we go to them. Worbury really has no need of a doctor of its own and we have managed without difficulty to take over Dr Eastcote's patients – at her request, of course. The two surgeries which we hold there weekly are quite adequate in conjunction with Greatborough Hospital.'

'But I take it you would have no professional objection to my taking over such of Dr Eastcote's patients as are actually her own, even if you have been kind enough to help her out during her illness?' asked Romaine briskly.

'Oh, of course none at all, none at all. What we want to make clear to you, my dear young lady, is that there is no actual living to be made in Worbury – except from the private patients, who, of course, are ours.'

'Naturally I should not infringe the accepted medical etiquette,' she assured them and went away thoughtfully.

Perhaps they were right and there was

not a living for her in Worbury, but not only would she be glad to meet difficulties, but also she had gathered from Dr Eastcote that the National Health patients were neglected. Also the old doctor, through being perfectly frank with her, would be glad of any such small amount as her dwindling practice might bring.

'The only thing I really want,' she said, 'is to have enough to buy this cottage and to stay in it for what remains of life to me. If you could find something more convenient . . .'

It was not much of a place, merely a cottage of which the front rooms had been used as a surgery whilst the doctor had muddled along with the kitchen and the two upstairs rooms, and Romaine had no wish to take it on.

'I shouldn't dream of turning you out, Dr Eastcote,' she said, and she was able, through the generosity willingly extended to her by her father, to settle the purchase of the practice on terms gratefully accepted by the ailing doctor.

It was quite another thing, however, to find a place where she could live and practice. Worbury was still almost feudal and most of the houses and cottages belonged to the lord of the manor and were not available for professional occupation. There was only one house not tied in that way, and it was a large one, conveniently placed right in the village but much too large for the occupation of one woman.

To her amazement, Sir Julius offered a solution.

'I've been thinking for some time of retiring, my dear,' he said. 'I'm not getting any younger and John is now quite capable of taking over, and this place, Worbury, is not too far for me to come in once or twice a week if necessary. Let your mother take a look at this place, this Glen House, and if it is suitable, we could no doubt adapt it to your purposes and live there ourselves.'

'Father, would you really do that?' she asked.

She could see the advantages at once, not only to her own comfort but also as far as the practice was concerned. Though she could certainly not do anything which might offend against medical etiquette, it would be perfectly reasonable and permissible for at least a few of the owners of the big houses, whose servants already ostensibly went to Dr Eastcote's surgery, to call her in or let her attend their children, as she would be on the spot and more easily and readily available than the two doctors who were five miles away in Greatborough. They had been so unfriendly and unco-operative with her that she would feel no compunction about it.

She took her mother to see Glen House.

It was old and neglected and the owner wanted more for it than it was worth, but it had distinct possibilities if Sir Julius were prepared to spend money on it, which he was. A surgery and consulting room could be built on to it conveniently, with private rooms for Romaine over them since she felt that she did not want her life to become an integral life with that of her parents, and, again to her surprise, Sir Julius, when he went down to see it, revealed himself as a man who had always wanted a garden, and Glen House had a large and neglected one which could almost be referred to as 'grounds', as indeed it was by the house agent who waxed eloquent about them to an unexpected, likely purchaser.

But it would all cost a great deal of money, as Lady Manning also had wide-reaching plans for the house itself.

'Father, are you sure that you and Mother want to do this? Will you be happy in a village after living in the heart of London? You're not doing this only for me, are you?'

'No, my dear, though what will make you happy will also make us happy. You are all we've got now that John is married, and it is very much to our satisfaction to see you settled comfortably in what we realise is still your chosen career and yet not lose you.'

Romaine was deeply grateful though she was still not sure that they were not making such an upheaval of their lives solely for her. She was conscious as she had never been before of their deep love for her, and was determined to repay it in the only way she could. She was even prepared to fall in with her mother's plans for the social life which would be made possible by their name and position since it would certainly not have a deleterious effect on her as a professional woman; quite the contrary, she thought with a secret smile, remembering the two pompous, self-important doctors at Greatborough who would possibly bitterly regret that they had not accepted her tentative offer of herself as a partner!

She moved down to the local inn to take over Dr Eastcote's practice, using her cottage surgery for the time being, and also to superintend the alterations and additions to Glen House. An army of workmen were already in occupation, the building of her own wing their first job, and she had found a local nurseryman, a Mr Vannery, to undertake the reconditioning and reconstruction of the grounds.

His nursery and market garden were some mile and a half from Worbury, and Sir Julius had found him a man of understanding and vision, to be trusted to carry through the general plan to which he added, with some diffidence and due deference to his employer, some excellent ideas of his own.

'He's a good man, this Vannery,' said Sir Julius approvingly. 'Knows what he's about, does a fine job and does not overcharge. In fact, he is not a good businessman and could charge a lot more, which is probably the reason why he still has only a small nursery at Worbury instead of launching out into something bigger. Still, it suits me!'

Romaine came early into contact with the nurseryman, a taciturn, reserved man in his forties whose skill and devotion to his work struck an answering chord in her. She soon became used to his sturdy, thick-set figure moving about the place amongst the men he was employing there, never interfering as long as they were doing their job but with a keen eye for slackness or shoddy work. Progress was slow but every job, large or small, was done with a thoroughness of which both she and Sir Julius, on his short, hurried visits, approved. He was able to leave more and more to Vannery's judgment, and it was Romaine to whom

194

he referred such matters as needed personal authority though she admitted frankly that she knew very little about them. 'You do what you think best, Mr Vannery. I am sure my father will approve,' she would say and receive in return his slow, grave smile of pleasure.

He pleased her particularly by making narrow beds of old-fashioned, sweet-smelling flowers at either side of the path by which patients would come to her surgery, stocks and Mrs Sinkins pinks, and lavender and night-scented tobacco plant.

'People may be sick or only sorry for themselves,' he said with his quiet smile, 'but they can't be quite so sick or sorry when they're smelling those, and if they pick a few — well, what does it matter if it does them good. They'll all be free-flowering when they get established and will be all the better for being picked.'

'That's a nice thought, Mr Vannery, to put something lovely for them to smell on the *via dolorosa*,' and she saw by his deepened smile that he understood. 'It will make me happy too.'

It was not long after that that she

came into contact with his wife, whom once or twice he had referred to as his 'business manager', saying that he was no good at all on the business side. All he could do was to plan gardens and to grow and love flowers.

Romaine had had to call on a patient, an old woman who was dying of cancer but refused to end her days in hospital and as her way back passed close to the nursery, she had an impulse to go in. There was something restful in Ian Vannery, who always saw death as the prelude to new life.

She had an excuse in having been asked by her father to choose a specimen tree for the corner of one of the lawns.

Mr Vannery was nowhere to be seen amongst the orderly rows of plants and bushes, nor in the long line of glass-houses where several men were at work, but one of them told her that he was up in the office, indicating a collection of buildings near the house. She glanced at the small, grey-faced house which had a prim air with its uncompromising but spotless curtains and its close-shut windows, though the day had been warm and sunny. Somehow it did not seem to belong to him, for he was an open-air man with an objection to stiff formality and any prim arrangement.

A painted board directed her to the office but she came to a halt uncertainly as she heard voices inside, a woman's voice, metallic and censorious, above Vannery's slower, quieter tones.

'Do you mean to say that that is all you are charging Sir Julius Manning for those shrubs? They should be far more than that even if he is buying them by the dozen, and he can afford it.'

'That's not the point. It's too late to move them and they may not do well.'

'Whose fault is that, yours or his?' she demanded.

'He knows he may lose some of them but is prepared to take the risk,' said Vannery mildly.

'And if they die, I suppose you'll replace them free?' she asked scornfully. 'Fat lot of risk he's taking!'

'My dear, I have some advantage from it as I shall be glad to have that patch of ground cleared and he is taking them as they are without specifying named

197

varieties.'

'Well, you're mad to charge him so little. He can afford it, can't he? I shall charge him at least a pound a dozen more.'

'You can't do that, Marion. I've quoted him a price.'

'You make me sick. I don't wonder we're always scraping and screwing if that's the way you go on behind my back, and with a big job like this which you can charge what you like for. You're to ask me, mind, before you give any more firm quotations.'

'It will put me in a very awkward position, Marion.'

'Awkward or not, you must put up with it. Who got you out of the mess you were in over the new recreation ground? We'd have been ruined if I'd let you put all our best stuff in at the price they wanted to pay. This is a business not a charitable organisation.'

'I was only going to put the expensive stuff in that little corner for the blind, sweet-scented things that they could smell.'

'Huh! And have the villagers rooting

them up for their own gardens! And I suppose you would have replaced *them?* Don't sell any more of those lilies. I want them for the church,' and coming out at that moment, she saw Romaine preparing to retreat.

'Yes? Oh − it's Dr Elster, isn't it?' making an effort to change her tone to an ingratiating one.

She was a good-looking woman in her way, but hard-featured, her brown hair in a tight plait on top of her head, her china blue eyes like steel, her lips thin, her face devoid of the make-up which might have softened it.

Ian Vannery was close behind her.

'Oh − Dr Elster. You don't know my wife, do you?' in nervous apology.

Romaine put out her hand, rather in answer to that apology than with any friendly feeling towards Marion Vannery.

'No, we haven't met yet, but I think I know your two little girls. They're having polio injections at the school, aren't they?' remembering the two prim, mouse-like little things. She didn't wonder that they were scared, though it was not of the needle.

'Are you doing those? I thought it was Dr Heath's job.'

'I've been asked to take them over.'

'I'm glad. I never liked that man. We never need a doctor here, but as we've got to pay National Health in any case, you may as well take us on your panel.'

'You and the children certainly. I have come to an arrangement to that effect with Dr Heath, but I'm afraid your husband will have to stay with him as I don't take men patients.'

'Oh, Ian is never ill,' said Mrs Vannery with a shrug. 'Did you come to ask about something?'

'Yes, a specimen tree for the corner of the lower lawn. My father says he spoke to you on the telephone about it, Mr Vannery, and you suggested a deodar, but that's something out of Gilbert and Sullivan opera, isn't it?' with a friendly smile at him.

'There really is a deodar, a lovely tree, one of the blue cypresses. Shall I show them to you?'

'They're expensive but I don't suppose that matters to Sir Julius,' put in Mrs Vannery.

'He is willing to pay a fair price if it is what he wants. May I see them, Mr Vannery?' excluding the woman with a definite snub, but without rudeness.

'Perhaps you would like a cup of coffee when you have seen the trees, Dr Elster?' Mrs Vannery asked, undaunted, and at the look of appeal in Ian Vannery's eyes, Romaine accepted the invitation which she would otherwise have refused.

She was already on good terms with most of the village people, but she could not see herself as ever getting on the same terms with this particular one.

After she had selected the tree, she went to the house with him and realised that Mrs Vannery had made an occasion of it, a well-ironed white cloth on a table in what was evidently the little-used 'parlour', with thin china and plates of home-made cakes and biscuits set on it. The room was shining with polish and spotless, the three-piece suite in green plush obviously almost unused, prim, hard little cushions placed exactly in the corners and nothing for comfort and relaxation after a hard day's work. Even in the short time she was obliged to stay there, Romaine felt stiff and unnatural, matching the surroundings, and when the two little girls came home from school and peeped, goggle-eyed into the room, their mother ordered them curtly into the kitchen.

'I like to keep this room nice, and you can't do it where there are children,' she explained. 'Their bedroom is like a pigsty, or it would be if I didn't keep on at them,' though Romaine thought she had never seen anything less like contented, busy little pigs than the two Vannery children. They had looked, in that brief moment, over-anxious and even scared, and were only too glad to scuttle away at their mother's behest. Possibly they had not seen the inside of the 'parlour' before, and certainly not with a visitor being entertained in it!

Mrs Vannery conducted a stilted conversation in a voice over-careful of her vowels, asking after the health of Sir Julius and Lady Manning and interlarding her speech with the names of the local famous (that is, titled) people who patronised the nursery, and her own personal success in dealing with them.

'Have you always been interested in growing things, Mrs Vannery?' asked Romaine to keep the polite conversation going and to get away from the boring and ill-chosen subject of the titles.

'Oh no. I ran quite a different business, a food shop, during the war. I didn't *own* the business but I think I may say that Mr Blosser could not have run it without me, what with the rationing and the coupons and people trying to fiddle all the time. Not that they could get past my eagle eye!' with a little satisfied laugh. 'I could have owned the business after the war, but with Mr Vannery coming home with no prospect of a job and no particular bent, as you might say, and him having to be in the open air for a time (at least, that is what he *said*),' with a slightly contemptuous glance at the silent Ian, 'of course I had to think of something else, so when this nursery was going cheap, I got it for him — not that he was ever a business man, of course. I have to supply the brains and he the brawn,' with a laugh that made Romaine flush with discomfort. 'We'd soon have been in the poor-house if he hadn't had me at the back of him!'

Romaine rose thankfully to go, shaking hands with a conventional word of thanks for her hostess and making a pointed remark, with a warm and friendly smile, to Ian Vannery.

'I'm sure my father will be delighted with the deodar, Mr Vannery, as he has been with the way you've planned and worked on the garden. It's going to be really delightful, with such fresh ideas and unusual features. I understand you have some rather remarkable orchids, too, in which my mother would be most interested. I'm sure she would like to see them.'

'I should be delighted to show them to her, Dr Elster. Perhaps you would like to look at them now?'

Marion Vannery interposed before Romaine could reply. 'Not now, Ian. There's that order to put up for Cedar House. I suppose you've forgotten that? Any other day will do for your precious orchids, and it is Lady Manning who is interested in them, not Dr Elster. Perhaps you will ask her ladyship to ring up and make an appointment? Though no one can ever persuade my husband to part with any! It is actually a waste of time and of a good hothouse where we could grow something profitable.'

'But I don't think a hobby is ever a waste of time, Mrs Vannery, do you? Especially anything as rare and beautiful as orchids,' and Romaine escaped to her car and a thoughtful drive home.

She felt sorry for Ian Vannery. How had the gentle, quiet-mannered man, his soul steeped in the love of beauty, his life dedicated to its creation, ever chosen for his mate this hard-faced, hard-voiced woman whose god seemed to be money and success? It was easier to see why she had married him, for she must be a good many years his senior and the chance of marriage might have appeared to be passing her by when she snatched at him and caught him.

Inevitably her thoughts went to her own marriage. There had been no 'last-hope' set-up between her and Jeff, yet it had been just as ill-assorted a union. She caught her breath in a half-sob as her mind, never far away from him even now, returned to the agonising decision she had made when she parted from him. She had closed that door but she could not lock it and the lightest touch on it could make it swing wide open again. Jeff — Jeff — she mourned. Wouldn't anything have been better than this bitter sense of loss and loneliness?

Chapter Six

BY the autumn the Manning family had become firmly established in Worbury, and the thing that Romaine had feared most had not come about for Lady Manning seemed to have made the transition from London life to life in a little village with ease and even satisfaction. Whilst Sir Julius divided his time between the garden, in which he discovered a surprising interest, and his twice-weekly visits to his London office, his wife threw herself with zest into the various village activities and Romaine's popularity grew to such an extent that

206

the Greatborough doctors surrendered to her with a good grace their former rather haphazard interest in their female patients in Worbury.

Romaine was at least not unhappy now, but she had lost the blithe joy of living with love as its fount. She took little active interest in anything but her work, but for her mother's sake, and in gratitude for the sacrifices she had made for her daughter's comfort and well-being, she entered, as far as her work allowed, into the social life of the various big houses in and around the still unspoilt village.

Inevitably such activities as the Women's Institute, the sports club and the annual horticultural show had brought Lady Manning into close contact with Marion Vannery, who was an energetic organiser and was flattered by the friendly association with Lady Manning, and was able to assist her in various personal ways. She had, for instance, been able to find her an additional maid in the village who, though surly and not very efficient, at least filled the gap left when the housemaid left to return to London. Romaine, who could get on with most people, disliked and distrusted Gertrude, whose manner often bordered on rudeness, but she felt that the house servants were her mother's affair. She had her own part of the house, her surgery, dispensary and a small kitchen, with her bedroom and bathroom above them, though she took her meals with her parents and another maid was deputed to look after her rooms when the mutual dislike between her and the village maid became apparent.

Jeff and the broken marriage were never mentioned and Lady Manning remarked to her husband with satisfaction that Romaine appeared to have 'got over it'.

'I'm very glad that we came here,' she said. 'It has made a complete break for Romaine and I don't think she even thinks now of that man. In time she will marry again, of course. Young Richard Delmain seems interested and when his father dies . . .'

'Now, Lydia!' warned Sir Julius, smiling.

'Well, Richard is very attractive and quite suitable and it's not natural at her age with her looks that she should spend her life as a doctor. I shall ask Richard and his sister . . .'

'I wouldn't try to encourage anything at the moment, my dear. Romaine is busy and, I think, happy with her work and she doesn't want to be involved in any more sentimental business just now. I should leave her alone and let matters take their course. She'll do what she wants to do in any case.'

Lady Manning sighed.

'Yes, I suppose so, but it's so *unnatural*,' she said.

She was not really deeply concerned over the growing friendship between her daughter and Ian Vannery, but she felt that that again was 'unnatural'. The Vannerys were not of their social class and Lady Manning did not count them amongst their personal friends nor include them in invitations which did not embrace the whole of the village, but she often saw Romaine and Ian together, walking through the extensive grounds of Glen House which were still being laid out by him, or poring over plans spread out on the table in a room, hitherto unused, which now housed the grand piano and had come to be referred to as 'the music-room'.

It was the creation of that music-room which somewhat disturbed Lady Manning.

It had all begun with a day preceding the Flower Show when Lady Manning who with Marion Vannery had undertaken the final arrangements, had been pressed for time and had asked Romaine to call at the nursery to choose some plants which Ian was lending for decoration. As a professional he did not compete with the villagers but always took an active interest in the show.

When they had decided on the plants, Ian took her through his small orchid house to show her a plant which rarely bloomed but which this year was in full flower.

'But, Ian, it's lovely!' she said and did not realise that she had used his name until it was too late. 'It's a pity it has to bloom here, almost unseen. Couldn't you have it in the house in this hot weather, where you can enjoy it?'

He had noticed her use of his name and smiled his approval though she knew he would never use hers.

'I don't think Marion would approve,' he said. 'It has an untidy growth and refuses to be kept in order. What she really admires is the neat, compact growth of the cauliflower!'

She joined in his laughter.

'Well, she keeps the house beautifully even if she doesn't like flowers about. She is a very busy person and I suppose they do make a mess and extra work. I've never seen such a tidy house,' she said.

'Yes, she's very efficient, which is a good thing. Without Marion to keep me in order, I should never be able to find anything.'

'Don't you have any corner where you can make a mess if you want to?'

He gave her a rather sheepish grin.

'Well – yes, I have. It isn't in the house, though. It's here, tucked away behind the compost heaps. Marion knows about it, of course, but she tries to forget its existence. Shall I show it to you?' and he led her to the shed, it was little more than that, where to her surprise she saw a piano amongst the litter of oddments with which the place was filled.

'You see why I can't have a place like this in the house,' laughed Ian. 'I always dread the day when Marion decides to make a raid on it and tidy it up.'

There was certainly no sort of order here but it did not look as though the business of the nursery had overflowed into it. Rather there were books and music and (this was pathetic, she thought) broken and battered toys and children's story books which had been read to a state of dilapidation which would have brought them a ruthless throwing-out from the tidy house.

'The kids like to sneak down here sometimes to play with their old things,' he said with an apologetic smile, 'and I never get around to having a tidy-up.'

'But the piano!' said Romaine. 'Who plays it?'

'Well — as a matter of fact, I do. I always keep the door shut though and play softly and the kids don't mind, but my fingers have got stiff and clumsy with the work in the nursery. I wanted to take it up as a boy, but I wasn't good enough, and then the war came and that finished it. I bought the old piano some years ago at an auction sale and had it put in here. There wasn't room for it in the house, and Marion would think it a waste of time, which of course it is.'

He had opened the lid and was fingering the keys lovingly, softly.

'Play something for me,' she said on an impulse. 'It's all right. Mrs Vannery and my mother will be busy in the show tents for hours.'

He hesitated, flushing under his deep tan, and then closed the door and pushed some music off a chair for her and sat down on a music-piled box before the instrument and played a few tentative chords until, encouraged by her silent attention, he began the slow movement of the Moonlight Sonata.

His fingers were, as he had said, stiff and awkward and his hands lacked practice, but Romaine recognised, if not a master, a player who had sympathy and feeling and an intense love for the music he played.

Romaine sat spell-bound, rather by the surprising revelation of the man himself than by his actual performance. He had unimagined depths, lived a secret life beneath the work in which she had already recognised his love of beauty, seen his gentle touch of some small, difficult plant which needed extra care and his wider vision of a landscape garden such as the one he was developing for her father.

He ended suddenly on a discord.

'I'm not much good now, I'm afraid,' he apologised. 'I used to dream of some day playing on a really good piano, a Bechstein perhaps, but that dream has long gone by and I make do with this poor old thing when there's no one about to hear!'

'Nobody ever plays our Bechstein but the piano-tuner. Why shouldn't you come and play it sometimes? It would be a charity to a dumb instrument.'

He flushed with embarrassment.

'I couldn't do that,' he said.

'Well, some day there'll be an opportunity. I'll make one,' she promised but he did not reply.

Instead he let his fingers run idly over the keys, picking out a tune here, the fragment of another there, until inadvertently he strayed into one which riveted her attention and made her grip the arms of the old wooden chair in an agony of memory.

She heard Jeff's voice again, singing softly, close to her ear, his lips almost brushing her cheek as they danced.

'I've just been waiting for you,
My best, my last romance.'

'No. No!' she cried, not really aware that she spoke, the words forced out of her suddenly white lips. 'Not that. Anything but that,' and she leaned forward in the chair and turned her face away so that he should not see what she knew it must reveal.

He stopped playing at once and closed the lid of the piano.

'I'm sorry,' he said. 'I'm terribly sorry.'

For a few moments there was a painful silence. Then she got up and looked at him with a determined, wavering smile.

'Silly of me,' she said. 'How – how poignant some of those stupid dance numbers can be, can't they? I must go now. It's nearly time for my surgery. Thank you for playing to me. If you are going to the Manor, can I give you a lift?'

'I've got some things to take. I'll take them in the truck, but thank you for the offer, Dr Elster. I'll leave the orchids till the last thing and hope there will be enough sun to warm the tent.'

'The good weather looks as if it's settled for a few days, doesn't it?' and, talking of nothing, they walked together to her car and he watched her drive away.

He knew that she had divorced her husband earlier in the year. Most people in the village knew of Jeff's name, and that of Sir Julius Manning had given it a certain amount of publicity, and he had wondered whether it had caused her any real grief or pain. Now he knew that it had done. He did not know the details, never concerning himself with gossip about such things, but now he found himself wondering painfully about it and about what might have caused the break-up of the marriage.

It could not have been her fault, he thought, and, bending down to replace the stick supporting the heavy head of a carnation in one of the beds, he suddenly pushed it into the ground with a force that snapped it in two.

Nothing more was said for a few days about the unused grand piano that stood in the big drawing-room of Glen House. The Flower Show occupied all their time and thoughts, but a few days after it was over, Romaine saw Ian Vannery superintending some work in the gardens and called him into the house to look at some of her mother's cherished indoor plants which were not doing well.

'My mother and father are staying with friends in town for a day or two and I'm left in charge,' she said. 'The house, of course, runs on its own wheels and I'm not bothered about it, but the servants don't consider the plants to be any concern of theirs so I've had to take them on and my medical training didn't include the care of a sick cactus!'

He soon diagnosed the complaint and suggested the remedy, and they stood talking for a moment in the drawing-room.

'Well, there's the Bechstein,' she said. 'You haven't been to play on it yet. Why not do so now?' opening the lid of the fine instrument invitingly.

Hesitatingly, he ran his fingers over the keys. This was a very different thing from his old piano which, in the draughty shed, he could not even keep in tune.

'How beautiful it is!' he said softly.

'Well, go on. Try it. Play something for me, anything,' and at last he sat down and experienced the hitherto only imagined joy of playing on a perfect instrument.

After that he came several times, but always with a diffident nervousness until she had the piano moved into the other room, which adjoined her part of the house and was never used.

It was after a conversation with her mother that she did so.

'You know, my dear, it isn't *quite* the

thing to have Vannery playing the piano in our drawing-room,' Lady Manning said. 'After all, though I know he isn't really a gardener, not in the ordinary sense of the word, he does work for your father and it would be difficult to explain if anyone called — I mean, one couldn't exactly introduce him . . .'

Romaine laughed.

'He'd run like a hare from the very idea,' she said, 'but you know, Mother dear, you're trying to live in an age that is over for ever. There aren't any classes any more, as you knew them. There are only rich and poor, and the values don't fall into either category yet, and after all, what is there in his playing our piano? It does it good and nobody else can play it. I've long gone past my days with The Merry Peasant, and what with television and radio and superlative gramophone records, a grand piano, even a Bechstein, is only a useless ornament in an ordinary home and takes up wanted space as you've said yourself. What about the room along the hall that isn't used for anything but the storage of a table and a few chairs? We could have the piano moved into that and then it wouldn't bother anyone, not even chance callers or Ian himself!'

'Ian? Should you call him by his Christian name, Romaine? I should never dream of calling Mrs Vannery by hers. I hope he doesn't call you Romaine?'

'Oh no. He's always most correct and calls me Dr Elster when he has to call me anything at all,' laughed Romaine, 'and somehow one wouldn't call Mrs Vannery anything but that. I suppose I just slipped into it and he doesn't seem to mind. Anyway, I think it's a good idea about the piano. I'll get it moved,' and did so.

She had no idea what her friendship was doing to the lonely man shut in his solitude by the ruthless ambition and determination of the woman whom he had married nearly twenty years ago. Perhaps he had loved her once. He supposed he must have done since he had married her, but whatever there had been of love between them had been swallowed up in the years of her dominance. He had been sick in mind and heart rather than in body, and her strength had seemed the only sure and purposeful thing in a world given over to the war which his whole soul abhorred. She had been a rock to which he had clung, a sure defence, the one thing which had brought order out of chaos. Though caught up against his will in the mighty war machine, he had never been a fighter, had hated the senseless destruction to which he had to contribute and the end of the war had left him almost prostrate in body and mind and ready thankfully to lean on her strength and to let her fight for them both.

The out-door work, growing living things instead of destroying them, had gradually healed him physically and mentally, and, always with Marion's astute mind and hard-headedness to let him expand and to hold him in check, he had turned the smallholding into the market garden, and that into the present nursery. He had supplied the labour of his hands, the thought and the imagination; Marion had supplied the business instinct, looked after the finances and kept a tight rein to prevent him from launching out in enterprises which might have been disastrous.

The children had been born, Joan who was now thirteen and Connie two years later, but they too had come under her tight control and he felt that Marion held him unreasonably to blame that neither of them had been a son.

'What do you know about bringing up girls, or boys either, come to that?' she had asked him contemptuously when he had attempted to exercise not his authority but his love and pride in them. 'You leave them to me and get on with your work. That's your job. Leave the girls to me,' and after Connie's birth they had somehow never resumed the relationship that could not have been called love-making, though they still shared the same double bed.

The suspicious mind, the watchful eye ever on the look-out for the smallest peccadillo, had turned the children into the quiet, mouse-like little girls they had become. Amongst their earliest recollections was her shrill voice commanding instant obedience.

'Don't play in the nurseries. You'll

damage things.'

'Don't worry your father. He's got quite enough to do without having to look after you.'

'Don't chatter so much. How do you think I can do my books with all that racket going on?'

'Find something useful to do or I'll find it for you.'

Occasionally, when they felt themselves to be unobserved or when their mother was out, they would sneak down to their father's shed behind the compost heaps and play in whispers with beloved old toys which their mother had cast out or given to the Jumble Sale and which he or they had managed to rescue, and these times were perhaps the happiest for them and for him. Sometimes, the door firmly shut, he would play to them on the old piano, and they would listen, huddled on the floor, and sometimes sing the songs they had learnt at school, in voices that were low and muted and more than a little scared, their eyes constantly on the door in fear that their mother might find them there and be angry.

She was angry with them at most things, and her tongue was sharp and her hand heavy and merciless. Marion never turned a blind eye or a deaf ear and they were afraid of almost everything.

Romaine's easy friendship and her whole personality were a revelation to him. She provided him with the outlet he had lacked, her lively and well-informed mind striking new and unexpected sparks from his so that, in her company, he became an individual and not just a shadow and an echo of his dominant wife. She asked his opinions on other matters than his work, and respected his views even if she disagreed with them. They discussed every subject under the sun, sometimes gravely, sometimes with laughter. He had almost forgotten how to laugh until she evoked his dry sense of humour and showed that she enjoyed it.

Gradually they made Wednesday afternoons a regular occasion for his visits to the music-room at Glen House, for it was her one free afternoon in the week, when she made only emergency visits, and it was also Marion's afternoon at the Women's Institute Library, which kept her occupied until six o'clock. The children got their own tea when they came in from school, and Ian waited to have his with Marion.

'You know, it's a great pity that you had to give it up, Ian,' Romaine said to him one afternoon when, curled up in a chair, she had been listening dreamily to Chopin in contrast to the sonorous eloquence and thunder of Beethoven.

'I should never have become a great player or even a really good one,' he said. 'I should probably have ended up in a rock-'n'-roll band!'

'Perish the thought!' she laughed, and he broke their mood by changing into popular dance tunes, but not the one which had had such an effect on her the first time he had played for her.

She was able to speak of it, though. It hurt, but she wanted to plunge the knife in so deeply that it would never be able to hurt again.

'Do you remember a tune you once played? On your own piano? It was called, I think, "Last and Best". Play it for me now.'

He gave her a quick look.

'Are you sure you want me to?'

'Yes,' and he played it but hated doing so as he watched her flinch and withdraw into herself.

'Why did you want me to play it when it — hurts so much?' he asked her gently.

'Because it hurts. I want to get rid of the things that can still do that, all of them. The knife rather than the long, slow process of drugs. You know that it reminds me of my husband, of Jeff, don't you?' she asked in a low voice, not looking at him. 'The band played it the first time we met. We danced to it and he sang the words to me. "My best, my last romance." It was neither, as it happened. The only thing that made it any different from the others, for him, was that he married me but it was — my first and last.'

'Don't, Romaine. Please don't. You're hurting yourself too much by remembering.'

It was the first time he had used her name.

'I want to. I meant to. It was like lancing a festering sore which will never be better until the poison is let out.

Forget it. It's over now anyway. Yes? Come in,' as a knock at the door interrupted them.

It was Gertrude, and she gave an insolent stare at them both before she spoke.

'Your telephone's ringin' like mad, doctor,' she said.

'Very well. I'll come,' said Romaine, getting up from the chair. 'I've told you before that there is no need for you to knock at any of the sitting-room doors.'

'I thought I'd better,' said the girl with unmistakable meaning, and Romaine, angry, could find nothing to say.

It was soon after that that Mrs Vannery rang up to say that Connie had spots.

'Oh dear,' said Romaine. 'I'm afraid that's measles. I've had two other cases today. Keep her in bed and warm and I'll come.'

She was right. There was an epidemic of it in Greatborough, and it had reached Worbury.

'It's all these pictures they're always crowding into,' said Marion angrily. 'I don't let my two go, of course, but there

227

are plenty that do and so I have to suffer.'

Romaine reflected that it was poor Connie who was suffering, but she did not say so.

'There's probably no point in keeping Joan away from her as they've been sleeping in the same room,' she said, 'but you had better keep her away from school.'

'I should in any case. She'll have to look after her sister. I can't spare the time. Of all annoying things, with the summer bedding orders coming in . . .'

'I don't expect the child got ill on purpose, Mrs Vannery,' said Romaine curtly.

The other woman shot her a look of actual dislike but said no more, and Romaine wrote out a prescription, gave some instructions and left the house. A really unpleasant woman, she thought, and immediately 'Poor Ian!'

Connie had only a mild attack but a week later Joan went down with a more serious one, and the doctor called at the house daily and even, on one occasion, looked in one evening as well.

Ian opened the door to her and looked surprised but pleased.

'Romaine! Marion's down at the church, some saint's day or other tomorrow and she's doing the flowers,' with a touch of contempt in his voice which Romaine thought she understood. Mrs Vannery ought to have been looking after her own child instead of some long-dead saint. Her predilection for church work was a strange facet of her character.

'I hope the saint appreciates the attention,' she said drily. 'I called to have another look at Joan. May I go up? If they are asleep, I won't wake them.'

He followed her upstairs. Joan was sleeping peacefully but little Connie was awake and watchful.

'I took her temperature again the way you showed me, doctor,' she whispered, 'and I've written it down, and then I gave her some hot milk and she went to sleep.'

Romaine nodded and smiled, bending over the sleeping child to take her pulse and lightly touch her forehead without disturbing her. She was touched, and a little angry, to see the arrangements which one child had made for the other, the tray by the bed with its carefully covered jug of water, the thermometer in its disinfectant solution, the small shaded light kept away from her eyes, the little hand-bell within reach. It was the mother who ought to be doing these things.

She went back to the other bed.

'She's a lot better,' she said in a whisper. 'You've arranged things very well, almost like a hospital nurse. Now you settle down and go to sleep, dear. She'll be quite all right, and I'll look in again in the morning.'

Connie gave her a timid smile.

'I'd like to be a nurse,' she said.

'Well, why not, some day? It's a wonderful thing to be and you've certainly got the makings of one,' whispered Romaine brightly.

'I don't suppose Mother will let me be. She says nurses don't make any money and anyway I'll have to be something else when I leave school.'

'Oh well, plenty of time yet. Go to sleep, dear. If Joan wakes I expect she'll call you, but she'll probably sleep till the morning. Good night, nurse,' with a smile, as she tucked in the bed-clothes and was rewarded by another of those shy smiles.

Downstairs, Ian made tea in the kitchen and they were sitting there drinking it companionably when Marion returned. She gave them a quick look, not too well pleased.

'I shouldn't have thought a second visit was necessary, doctor,' she said. 'Joan's perfectly all right.'

'Happily she is, Mrs Vannery, but I was passing and looked in to make sure. She's had a bad attack, you know, but Connie has been looking after her very well.'

'I've made the children useful. If the doctor wanted tea, Ian, you should have given it to her in the other room, not in the kitchen.'

'It's my fault, Mrs Vannery,' said Romaine quickly, 'and it's cosier in here and such a nice kitchen.'

Good heavens, she thought, why am I defending him against her? Why should there be any need?

'It's not bad,' agreed Marion looking round to find something wrong and snatching up the open tin of biscuits to put some of them on a plate. 'My husband would never think of using a plate, of course! Fancy putting the *tin* on the table, Ian! We don't have to live like pigs. And there are saucers that match the cups, you know.'

Romaine rose to go. Mrs Vannery had destroyed the quiet peace she had always felt when she was with Ian. What did the wrong saucers and a biscuit tin matter? Or a cup of tea in the kitchen after a busy day?

'Please don't trouble, Mrs Vannery,' she said, as Marion fussed with the saucers. 'I was just going in any case. I think Joan is better, but she will need care and nursing for several days yet. Also Connie ought to get out in the air. After all, she's been ill, too.'

'Nothing to stop her going out and she's only had measles, nothing to make a fuss about.'

'Even a slight attack can sometimes leave unpleasant consequences, you know,' said Romaine with a note of acerbity in her voice. 'I'll come in again in the morning, and as soon as Joan is well enough, I think both of them ought to go away, to the sea preferably.'

'And who's going to take them? *I* haven't got time. Someone's got to do the work here with my husband always gallivanting about, spending all his time out. At Glen House, I suppose?' shooting an acid glance at him.

'If the doctor thinks the children should go away, my dear, it can be arranged,' said Ian, bold for once. 'Sir Julius is not pressing me and I could leave the work there for the time being so that you can take them away.'

'And a fine mess things would get into here with me away! Who's going to do the books and the time sheets? Keep a check on the orders? Watch the outgoings? See to it that . . .'

Hot and embarrassed at the humiliating position in which Ian was placed and in being made a party to what should have been a purely domestic affair, Romaine made her escape with a murmured good night. How could he live in such an atmosphere? Share his life with this bitter-tongued, carping woman always seeking an opportunity to belittle him?

'Better a dinner of herbs where love is
...' she thought. How did it go on?
Something about a stalled ox and hatred.

Could there ever have been love
between these two? But probably Ian
had no choice now, since 'the stalled ox'
included his two little girls.

She paid only a few more perfunctory
visits to the children now that the real
need for them had ceased and rather
feared the Wednesday afternoon which
would have meant being alone with him
at Glen House and stopped at the
nursery in the morning in the hope of
seeing him and pleading an excess of
work. It was Marion she saw, however.

'Oh, doctor, I was just going to send
for you,' she said. 'It's too annoying, but
I think my husband's down with it.
There was no need for him to go near
the children, but I suppose he did as
soon as my back was turned. You'd
better have a look at him.'

'I can't do that, Mrs Vannery. He isn't
my patient. I don't take men on my
panel, as I told you.'

'Oh, if it's a matter of money, I'll pay

your bill, of course,' snapped Marion offensively and Romaine flushed.

'It isn't a question of money. I am a doctor and if it were a case of emergency, of course I would attend to Mr Vannery until his own doctor could be sent for. You had better ring up Dr Heath.'

'Fat lot of good that would be! He doesn't come all this way unless someone's dying or has money. It's only a matter of saying whether he has or hasn't got measles. Surely that wouldn't hurt you? I'm not going to send for Dr Heath anyway. If you won't have a look at him, he won't have a doctor.' and she turned and went back into the house, Romaine following uncertainly.

After all, what harm was there in making a simple diagnosis if it proved to be measles?

She went up into the bedroom with Marion and it needed no more than a cursory glance at Ian for her to be able to say that he had definitely taken the complaint.

'It's too silly,' he said. 'Measles at my age!'

'I'm afraid it's no respecter of age,' she said smiling sympathetically. 'Well, the rash has come out early so I don't suppose you'll be too bad with it, but you must stay in bed, of course, and I've told Mrs Vannery that she should send for Dr Heath.'

'There won't be any need for that,' put in Marion tartly. 'You can repeat the prescription you gave for the children and Connie will know what to do for him.'

Reluctantly Romaine wrote out the prescription, well aware that unless it were made extremely urgent, Dr Heath was not likely to come out from Greatborough and she would take an early opportunity of telling him what she had done.

'I suppose that is what you charge a private patient?' asked Mrs Vannery, holding out a pound note and a shilling in exchange for the prescription.

'There is no charge, Mrs Vannery,' said Romaine coldly.

'We don't take anything for nothing, so take it,' and, much against her will, Romaine did so rather than pursue the altercation. At least she would not visit Ian again in her professional capacity.

She did not know how Dr Heath knew, unless Marion herself had told him, but the next day he rang her up.

'I hear that you've been treating one of my patients, Dr Elster. I understood that you were not taking male patients, other than children.'

'Oh – oh, you mean Mr Vannery? I didn't exactly treat him, Dr Heath, but I've been visiting the children for measles and Mrs Vannery put me in a difficult position by insisting on my seeing her husband. I was in the house, so I saw him and recommended them to notify you. That was all.'

'I gather that you gave a prescription and accepted a private patient's fee.'

Romaine felt annoyed at the undignified position in which she was placed.

'I merely repeated, at Mrs Vannery's request, the prescription I had given her for the children, and the fee was thrust upon me against my will. I will send it to you, of course.'

'There's no need for you to do that,

237

but I shall be glad if you will not attend a patient of mine again. That is all, Dr Elster,' and he put down the telephone.

Angrily Romaine sat down and wrote out her cheque for a guinea and posted it to Dr Heath. What he did with it was his affair.

She did not go near the Merridew Nurseries again, but a fortnight later she heard in the village that Mrs Vannery had taken the children to the seaside, so obviously she had decided that the business would not collapse without her for a fortnight! It was a pity that the weather had turned very wet so that the children would not get much benefit from the change. She thought grimly of what it would mean for them to be shut indoors in a strange house with only their mother for company!

Late that night, as she was getting into bed, her telephone rang and she picked up the receiver rather wearily. The epidemic was now over, but she had had a good many bad cases and she had been looking forward to an undisturbed night for once.

Ian's voice answered her. It was low

and urgent.

'Could you possibly come? Something's happened and I need you desperately.'

'At this hour? What is it? Are you ill? If so . . .'

'No, it's not me. It's — someone else. I wouldn't bother you if I could think of anything else to do. Do please come, but don't drive up to the house. Park it at the little gate in the lane where it won't be seen, the gate into the orchard. Please come, Romaine. I'll be waiting for you there as there's no proper path and it's very dark. You will come?'

It was an extraordinary request at this time of night, almost eleven o'clock, and with his wife and children away, he was surely alone in the house? But he had made such an urgent request that she could not very well refuse.

'Yes. All right,' she said, and dressed again hurriedly and got out her car, for which a small garage had been built where her comings and goings would not disturb her parents.

It was Gertrude's night off and she was cycling back from the village when she saw and recognised the car as it passed her.

'Wonder where she's going in such a hurry?' she speculated, and being of an intensely curious nature, she got off her bicycle and stared after the lights of the car and saw them, to her interested surprise, turn into the lane which led past the Merridew orchard. There were no more houses beyond it, and it would have been much simpler and easier to go on to the main entrance leading to the house.

'Golly!' she thought with spiteful glee. 'And his missus and the kids away! That's a fine how-d'ye-do and no mistake!' and she got on her machine and rode back to Glen House but made it her business to stay awake until she heard the car return. It was then the early hours of the morning! She had been there nearly all night!

Ian came out of the shadow of the trees as Romaine stopped the car. It was pouring with rain and he was very wet, but she was wearing her waterproof and hood.

'Whatever's happened?' she asked as

he opened the gate for her and splashed through the mud. 'And why this gate?'

'It's a girl. I think she's very ill. I'll tell you later, but please hurry,' and he went in front of her amongst the fruit trees and in through the kitchen door of the house.

In the sitting-room, lying back in a chair with her eyes closed was a girl whose beauty struck Romaine even then as exceptional, though she looked spent and clearly exhausted. Her breath was coming in painful gasps and she was struggling for air, but she was conscious and opened her great dark eyes to seek Romaine's imploringly.

There was no time for questions.

'There's an oxygen cylinder in the back of the car,' she told Ian. 'Get it, will you?' and whilst he was gone she put another cushion behind the girl's head and put a match to the fire.

After Ian had come back with the oxygen, the girl could breath more easily but was clearly very ill.

'I'll have to get her to the hospital,' said Romaine. 'Who is she, Ian? What is she doing here?'

The mere mention of the hospital had set the girl gasping and shivering again.

'No,' she said. 'No. Not the hospital. I want to stay here. Don't make me go!'

He went down on his knees at her side and put his arm about her.

'All right, darling,' he said. 'You shan't go. You can stay here and I'll look after you.'

Romaine looked at the two in amazement. What was this? Who was this lovely, ravaged girl whom he called 'darling'? And now he kissed her cheek softly and smoothed back the fair, tumbled hair. She looked about nineteen but might have been older or even younger, surely an extraordinary adjunct to the life of Ian Vannery?

'That's out of the question, Ian,' she said sharply. 'The girl is ill, though just how ill I can't tell but she has a high temperature and must be got into hospital,' and she moved towards the telephone.

His hand shot out to prevent her from using it.

'No, Romaine. I implore you. Let her stay here at least until the morning. We can put her to bed. She can use the children's room.'

'Ian, don't you see that I can't accept the consequences of not sending her to the hospital?'

'Please, Romaine. I beg of you,' he said, whilst the girl herself struggled to her feet, swaying as she did so, and reached in a dazed way for her handbag, which, like her coat, was wet through. Her thin little shoes were also sodden with water and mud.

'We'll get those wet things off and put her to bed, anyway,' said Romaine in a quandary. 'Then you must tell me what it's all about. Meantime I'll do what I can. Can you light a fire and get the bed ready whilst I get her upstairs?'

'You're not going to send me away?' gasped the girl, her teeth beginning to chatter.

'Not at the moment, anyway,' said Romaine with a worried frown. 'Come along,' and she put an arm about the girl and half-carried her upstairs.

'Give me a nightdress or something,' she told Ian, 'and when the fire's alight, go down and make some milk hot. I'll give her something to settle her down.'

When the girl, dressed in a prim cotton nightdress which Romaine guessed was Marion's, was in the warmed bed and lay in a drug-induced sleep, she and Ian went down to the sitting-room.

'Now,' she said. 'You'd better tell me what it's all about and who she is. Has she run away from home, or is she in trouble with the police, and what has she to do with you, Ian?'

'No. Neither at the moment, though she may be,' he said ignoring the last part of Romaine's question. 'I don't know. She couldn't tell me the whole story. She said she hadn't done anything wrong, but she's afraid – desperately afraid – and I am the only person she could come to.'

'You? But who is she, Ian? You're not – mixed up with her in any way? Have you been having an affair with her? I think you'd better tell me if you've got me embroiled in it.'

'She's – she's my daughter, Romaine.'

'Your *daughter!* But Marion – how can she be, Ian?' asked Romaine, stunned.

'Marion doesn't know about her. Her mother and I were never married. I was very young at the time and I had no money. It was in the war and I was in the army. I think perhaps I would have married the mother, though she was years older than I and – not the sort – one marries. When I came home on leave, she had disappeared and I've never seen her again but she wrote and told me – about Gwen. She'd put her in a home and I – I was glad – to have got rid of the whole affair, as I thought. Then – years afterwards, after I had married Marion, the people at the home traced me. She, the woman, had told them about me. She was dying and – I don't know why she told them. She'd never troubled about the child, but – I don't know. It may have been remorse, wanting to make some reparation or – just to get her own back on me. I shall never know. Anyway, they wrote to me, the people at the home, and I went to see Gwen and – I could see that she was mine. I had a sister just like her and – I agreed to do something for her and look after her. I – love her, Romaine. Maybe because I was very fond of my sister, who is dead, but — she belonged to me and she had nobody else and — she was a loving little thing, quite different from Joan and Connie, who are like their mother. I know they're fond of me in their own way, in Marion's way, but — Gwen loved me and clung to me in — in an appealing sort of way. I used to go to see her and take her presents and one day I told her, told her that she was really mine. I've never told Marion about her. How could I? She'd never understand and she would have turned against me, thrown it up at me, and I'd have been obliged to promise not to see Gwen again. I was able to arrange for her to stay in the home until she left school, but I had to pay for her and — I really wanted to, but it's meant keeping a lot from Marion, doing all sorts of things she must not know about in order to find the money, and when she left school, I paid for her to learn shorthand and typewriting but she could not stay on at the home and she — got into bad company. She's so pretty, you see, and — it nearly broke my heart when she — she

246

went on the streets,' and suddenly his voice broke and he laid his arms on the table and rested his head on them whilst great, tearless sobs shook his body.

Romaine had listened to the story in silence, feeling that she had never really known him before. All this time, behind that quite, serious façade, he had carried this secret sorrow and anxiety. She was bewildered, confused, intensely sorry for him, but there seemed nothing she could say. Standing beside him, she placed a hand on his shoulder and pressed it and presently he lifted his own hand to take hers in a firm grip that seemed to give him comfort.

'Yes, Ian,' she prompted him gently at last. 'What happened now, to bring her here like this?'

He lifted his head. His face was strained and tense and he was suffering.

'As I said, she had got into bad company and — went wrong. I tried to help her, to get her a job, to lead a decent life, but — it wasn't any good. She's got her mother's blood in her, I suppose. She was mixed up in a jewel robbery some weeks ago, but managed to keep out of the police proceedings. Then, yesterday, this morning — I seemed to have lost count of time — these men she's mixed up with did something, robbed a shop or something and she was with them but she swears she had nothing to do with it and I believe her but the police won't if they get on her tracks. She managed to get away but — she didn't know where to go and — so she came here — to me, to her father, Romaine! She's ill and frightened and — I still believe she'll go straight if she's given the chance, but — you know what chance she has if the police get hold of her, even if they can't prove anything against her. You see, they know — about her, that she's not a good girl, and it'll go against her, brand her even if they can't prove that she had anything to do with this hold up. I must help her, Romaine. I must protect her if I can. That's why she won't go to the hospital and why I can't make her go. She's — they'll recognise her. Nobody could pass her by without a second look and she thinks the police are trying to find her.'

'Yes,' said Romaine slowly. 'Yes, I

see, but you had no right to involve me in this, Ian.'

'What else could I do? She's ill, perhaps desperately ill, Romaine, and I had no one else to turn to. Forgive me and try to understand. She's like this through me, because she ought never to have been born, because I could never give her a home or proper care . . .'

'It may be so, Ian. I don't know. Who can say? But the whole thing's tragic for both of you. But what's going to be the end of it? If she gets out of this, if you help her this time, what more can you do for her than you've already done, or with any different result? She's got no home and no background, and you can't give her either now, can you? You can scarcely introduce her into your own home, can you?'

'No. I've thought and thought over any way in which I could protect her and provide her with a real home and people who would care for her but I can't see any way. If — if Marion were a different sort of woman, soft-hearted, understanding — but — well, you know what she is.'

Romaine nodded. She did know, to a certain extent. The girl, even if she were not Ian's daughter, would have short shrift with Marion Vannery.

Right or wrong, she ranged herself on the side of Ian and this frail, lost girl. Whatever the outcome of it, she was not going to rob her of this last chance, if chance it was, to mend her broken life. Also she was someone whom Ian loved and who loved him, and heaven knew he needed love in his life.

'You won't insist on sending her to the hospital, Romaine?'

'No. No, I suppose not. Not, that is, unless she is beyond my care. She *is* ill, Ian, but probably more frightened and exhausted than anything specific. It's pneumonia I'm afraid of, but we'll see how she is when the first effects of the drug I've given her wear off. That'll be in about an hour's time.'

'You won't leave her, Romaine?' he pleaded.

'No, not till I see how she is. I don't know what you would have done if Marion had been here, do you?'

'No, I don't, but as she isn't, we need

not think of that and they won't be back for a week at least.'

'Have you got anybody in to look after you whilst she's away?'

'No. Fortunately she decided I could look after myself. She's left me tins of stuff and I can always make tea. Would you like some now?'

'You sit in a comfortable chair and rest a bit, and keep your ears open for any sound upstairs. I left the bedroom door open and when I've put the kettle on, I'll pop up and see that she's all right. That chair's in a bit of a mess! You'll have to do something about that, or have a good story ready, before Marion comes back!'

He nodded with an attempt at a smile, but went with her into the kitchen to help her with the tea, refusing to sit down until she did so as well.

When they had had the tea and washed up, they went upstairs again and found the girl still in an uneasy sleep, and Romaine decided that she could not leave her yet.

'I'll stay with her a bit longer,' she said, 'and you had better get some sleep.

I'll call you when I feel she can be left. It's going to be difficult for me to come in tomorrow you know, because if anybody sees me — and with your wife away ...'

'I know,' he said humbly. 'I ought not to have involved you in it.'

'Well, we'll see what happens tomorrow. You're too tired to worry about it now. Get some sleep.'

He caught her hand and held it for a moment and then let it go.

'I can't thank you, Romaine,' he said and turned away from her and stumbled into the room he shared with Marion and closed the door.

He was filled with the knowledge that on the other side of the thin wall was a helpless dependant girl, and the woman whom he now knew he loved with all the love of his starved heart.

Romaine watched him go. She could feel the brief, convulsive pressure of his hand. She hoped uncomfortably that he was not getting fond of her, fonder, that is, than a friend should be. It was the last thing she wanted from any man, least of all from one with a wife. She had been foolish to come, but now that she had done so, she would see the thing through until the girl could be got away somewhere.

She bent over the bed, touched again by the girl's astonishing beauty and the look of innocence on the sleeping face which it ought not to be wearing at all. Surely it was not too late to reclaim her and give her a decent life? She thought of her own guarded and cherished existence when she had been this girl's age, still at school, knowing nothing of the world's rough places and her eyes were filled with tender pity. She bent and laid a soft kiss on the girl's smooth forehead and then settled down on the other bed to take what rest she could, rising every now and then to assure herself as to the girl's condition.

When she felt it was safe to leave her, as she had now fallen into a natural sleep, she went to knock softly at Ian's door, but, receiving no answer, opened it and went in.

He had not even taken his jacket off but lay, fully dressed, on one side of the old-fashioned double bed. He looked younger and somehow defenceless and that feeling of tenderness strangely remained. He as well as Gwen had the look of a lost and helpless child. His mouth drooped a little and had lost the firm, rather hard line which she realised was not natural to it, and now she saw the long lashes so much like Gwen's lying in semi-circles against the leathery cheeks, tanned by wind and sun.

His eyes opened suddenly and he woke with a start and became his familiar self again.

'Gwen?' he asked.

'No, she's all right. Better, I think, but I shall have to go now. Can you manage?'

'Yes, of course. Thank you for coming, Romaine, and for – everything,' he said, getting off the bed with an embarrassed look at her.

'I've left some tablets with directions, and I'll get some medicine I want her to take, and bring it. It's better for you not to have to go to the chemist's for it. I'll take a look at her then and I'll come in again this evening after surgery.'

'I don't know how to thank you,

Romaine. I don't know who else would have done what you have done.'

Driving back in the first light of dawn, Romaine reflected wryly that she didn't know either. Was she being a complete idiot to run the risk of getting mixed up with whatever this was? She had had no clear account of what had really happened and she found herself wondering whether she would have done it for anyone but Ian. Their friendship, she knew, had taken an unexpected turn that night, had become closer and more personal.

She ran her car as quietly as possible into the garage, and was asleep when the maid came in to draw the curtains and bring her her early tea.

A quick glance at the morning newspaper told her the tale of a robbery the day before in which the night watchman had been beaten up and a considerable sum of money stolen by thieves who got away.

'A girl is believed to have been driving the stolen car which was later found abandoned,' the report added. The description of the girl might have fitted any girl; it also fitted Gwen.

Romaine felt her mouth go dry. It was unbelievable in the sober light of day that she, Dr Elster, was mixed up in this, and on the wrong side of the law, but she knew that she was not going to do what she ought to do and go to the police. For Ian's sake and the girl's sake, she was not going to give her up.

As soon as she was able to do so, she went to the house, going openly to the nursery as if on business and then, at a suitable moment, slipping away to the house. She found father and daughter together, she fully conscious now and touchingly devoted to him. She was better, but her temperature was still high and her pulse rapid and there could be no thought of getting her away yet.

She wanted to talk, however, and Romaine felt that it was better to let her do so if it would relieve her mind. She sat down on the side of the bed and took the girl's hand in hers.

'Now, dear, perhaps you had better tell us about it,' she said. 'Was it that affair at Bournemouth? Were you driving that car?'

Gwen shivered and clung to Romaine's hand.

'I didn't know. Honestly I didn't. Fred asked me if I would like to go for a drive with them and drive the car. I like driving and I'd never driven a big Jag before and when he told me to go up a side street and turn round, I thought he was just seeing how I managed it. Then suddenly I knew and I got out of the car and ran. I knew I was near Worbury and all I could think of was getting to Ian. I saw a bus and jumped on it and then changed on to a Worbury bus, but it took me a long time to find the nursery because I didn't know where it was, and it was raining and I hid when anyone was coming and didn't dare ask anybody and suddenly I saw him, Ian I mean, and I ran to him and he brought me here, and I felt so ill but I knew I was safe.'

She was becoming excited and incoherent again, and Romaine thought she had talked enough. She calmed her down and reassured her and presently was able to leave her and go down with Ian to the kitchen. She felt that they were both more at ease there than in Marion's cherished parlour.

'Whatever you have in mind to do for her, she certainly can't leave yet,' she said, worried. 'I ought to see her again tonight and I'll contrive to come, but it may be very late. My mother is giving a dinner party at which, barring emergencies, I have promised to appear, and Anita Balcome, who was at school with me and is playing at the Bournemouth Theatre, is coming over after the show and I shall be expected to stay to meet her. Ring me if Gwen is worse and you really need me, but if I don't hear, I will come over – well, probably not before midnight! The village will be quieter then anyway.'

She did not at all like the scheming and secrecy, which were foreign to her nature, but since she had taken on the case her professional interest was involved and she had no alternative.

'Better come through the orchard,' suggested Ian. 'I'll wait for you at the gate.'

'No, don't do that. I don't know what time it will be, and I'll bring a torch and come in at the kitchen door.'

She thought wryly what a funny business the whole thing was, for as 'the doctor' she was usually received into a village home at the front door and conducted in state to the parlour before being ushered into the patient's room. But everything about her friendship with Ian Vannery was unusual and this last affair of Gwen had drawn them very close together.

Gertrude, who had been on duty until the last of the visitors had gone, had just gone to her room when she heard Romaine's car go out. She could be fairly sure that no calls had come for her, as the telephone had been switched through to the main part of the house. What was taking the doctor out so late then?

Her avid curiosity overcame her tiredness and she slipped downstairs to watch the lights of the car turn in the direction of the village and got her bicycle out and followed it. As there was no street lighting, it was not difficult, and by the time she reached the lane leading to the Merridew orchard, she saw to her

259

satisfaction the dark shape of the car parked under the trees.

There was definitely something going on between the doctor and Mr Vannery, him alone in the house, with his wife and children away and she driving there at this time of night. Gertrude resented the fact that she had 'gone into service' instead of into one of the new factories in Greatborough where most of the Worbury girls went, but had not dared to defy her parents, who impressed on her her good luck at being able to live at Glen House, with her own bedroom and good conditions. She bitterly resented, however, being 'looked down on' by the Mannings, especially by Dr Elster and having to say 'my lady' and 'madam' to them, and the idea of Romaine 'carrying on' with Mr Vannery behind his wife's back was exhilarating. And she so stuck-up and hoity-toity that she, Gertrude, was not good enough to answer her door and the telephone!

Filled with ghoulish glee, she went round to the front of the house, hid her bicycle behind the hedge and tiptoed across the lawn. As she did so, a light went on in one of the bedrooms upstairs! They had not wasted much time! Then a figure, Ian Vannery's appeared at the window and the curtains were drawn more closely together. They were not taking any chances!

Cold and tired though she was, excited anticipation kept her there to watch the proceedings as closely as she could, and after a time the light in the bedroom was extinguished and one in the kitchen put on. This window was uncurtained, and creeping silently towards it, Gertrude could see all that was going on.

★ ★ ★

'How is she?' asked Romaine anxiously when she had opened the kitchen door to find Ian bent over the account books.

He jumped up at once.

'Asleep and much better, I think,' he said. 'She's had the tablets you left her and she's been quite quiet and sensible and her temperature is down. I didn't like to ring you up and tell you not to come.'

Actually he had been unable to deny

himself the joy (it might be the last time) of having Romaine in his home again. These two nights might be all he would have to remember for the rest of his life.

'I'd better go up and have a look at her,' said Romaine, but when they had reached the bedroom, Gwen was awake and greeted her with a shy, loving smile.

'I feel so much better,' she said, struggling up into a sitting position.

Romaine pushed her gently down again.

'Pull the curtains closer, Ian,' she said. 'The moonlight is right in her eyes,' and whilst he did so, she took the temperature and pulse and listened to the less-distressed breathing.

'Much better,' she said. 'I think you'll do now, but you gave us a fright, young lady,' with a friendly smile. 'Now you stay there and do all you're told to do, and we'll soon have you on your feet. I'm going to give you something to make you sleep again and I'll pop in and see how you are tomorrow.'

When she had done everything possible for her, they left her to sleep.

'Will you put the light out?' she asked.

'I'd rather be in the dark,' and it was switched off and Romaine and Ian went downstairs again.

'Don't go yet,' he begged. 'It's so wonderful having you here and – I've never seen you dressed like that before,' for she had not stopped to change and was wearing the rather formal dinner gown she had put on for her mother's party, long and of a filmy black material through which her arms and shoulders showed pearly white. Her hair, too, was dressed in a looser, softer style than the usual smooth cap, and curled engagingly round her ears and against her temples. She looked younger and sweeter and he felt his heart beating unevenly.

She laughed a little.

'I don't usually visit my patients got up like a dog's dinner,' she said, 'but it was so late I came as I was.'

'Let me get you some tea or something.'

'I really don't want it, but I think you ought to have something. I suggest hot milk or cocoa rather than tea,' for he looked white and strained and it struck her that he was too thin. 'Sit down and

I'll get it for you. I know where everything is.'

'I can't let you wait on me, Romaine,' he said and put a hand on her to stop her, and at the feel of her warm flesh beneath the flimsy covering, his control of himself gave way and his other hand came out to hold her.

'Romaine – Romaine . . .'

She stood quite still and stared at him, wondering, aware of the leap of her senses beneath his touch. It was so long since she had known the touch of love and seen a man look at her like that, with adoration and longing in his eyes and she knew that there was more than friendship between them. It was not love on her part. For her there would never be anyone but Jeff, but her body responded instinctively to the desire of his and she could not draw herself away though aware of the futility and the danger.

'Why – Ian . . .' she whispered, half fascinated, half repelled.

'Forgive me, Romaine. Forgive me. But I must tell you. I love you. I've loved you for a long time, from the first moment I saw you, I think. You're beautiful and sweet and — oh everything I've ever dreamed of and you've filled my life. Just to know you're here — to see you sometimes — I love you, Romaine. I love you.'

He had drawn her to him, diffidently and nervously at first, but the feel of her body in his arms, her perfume, the sheer feminity of her quickened in him the longing which could only be appeased against her lips.

As in a dream, she offered no resistance and as their lips met, her arms came about him and she surrendered herself wholly to the unforgettable surge of desire.

Then, trembling, she let her arms fall and drew herself away and covered her eyes with her hand.

'That was madness, Ian,' she said in a shaken whisper. 'It mustn't happen again, ever.'

'I know. I know, my darling. But to have held you — to have kissed you this once — was heaven. You're not angry?'

'How could I be? I kissed you.'

'Do you love me, Romaine? Is it

possible?'

She turned away and did not speak for a moment, and when she turned her face towards him again, it was pale and a little sad.

'No,' she said. 'I haven't even that excuse for what I did,' her voice low and pitying. 'I loved my husband. I still love him. I don't think I shall ever know love again for any man. I think he took all that from me and left me — empty. I like you, Ian. I like you very much. You have all the endearing qualities any woman could want but ...'

'But it isn't love. I know that now and — in the circumstances, it's the best thing, isn't it? I have nothing to offer you, not even myself. I belong to Marion,' and his voice, in which she had never heard anything but kindness and gentleness, had a bitter flavour which hurt her.

'Don't think of her like that, dear,' she said. 'She's your wife and the mother of your children.'

'I don't know how that happened, even now,' he said, the bitterness increasing. 'She's never loved me. She doesn't know the meaning of the word. I

266

don't know why she married me, except that she wanted a home and the married state. She isn't even fond of the girls. All she cares about is money, getting on, improving our position – oh, I know I ought not to talk like this. I never have before. But – it's opened the floodgates, being with you like this, kissing you, thinking how different life might have been. I know I could never have married you, even if we had met when you were young and free. You're too far above me. But though I could never have found anyone like you, it might have been some sweet gentle girl who would have cared for me just as I am, not particularly ambitious or much good at making money . . .'

Her compassion brought her to him again, her arm about his shoulders, her cheek pressed to his.

'Don't Ian,' she said. 'You're only making it worse for yourself. It never does any good to go back over the past and think what we might have done if we had only known. Perhaps I wouldn't have married Jeff if I had known the agony, the sheer agony, of losing him, of having to pick up the broken threads and made some sort of pattern out of them. I'm going now, dear. Perhaps I ought not to come again. Gwen's going to be all right in a few days if you go on with the treatment I've prescribed. Start her on solid food tomorrow, light things like milk puddings and steamed fish. Do you know how to do them?'

Telling him what to do, speaking normally and naturally, she gradually restored the position to what it was before that shattering confession of his love and presently, thankfully, she slipped out into the moonlit darkness and refused to let him go with her to her car.

She did not go to his house again.

Chapter Seven

ONE morning, some three weeks later, when Romaine had had to return to the house for something she had forgotten, she was surprised to find Gertrude going through the drawers of her desk, which it had never occurred to her to keep locked. Papers and letters were scattered on the top in confusion and the girl was evidently not expecting any interruption once Romaine had started on her rounds of visits.

'Gertrude! What on earth are you doing in here?' she asked angrily.

Caught red-handed, the girl could only stare and stammer something about 'looking for something'.

'In my consulting room, and my desk?' asked Romaine. 'You can pack your things and go. Go at once. Your money will be sent on to you.'

She knew that Lady Manning was wanting to get rid of the girl, having found her very unsatisfactory, so she had no hesitation at taking matters into her own hands.

The girl gave her a nasty look.

'You'll be sorry,' she said insolently.

'That will do. I have nothing more to say to you. No doubt Lady Manning will give you as good a reference as she can if you want one, but I suggest that you do not go into private domestic service again,' said Romaine sharply.

'I'm not going to be spoken to like that by the likes of you,' said Gertrude rudely. 'You'll be sorry,' and she took herself off with another baleful glance.

Romaine shrugged, put the papers back in the drawer to be sorted out presently and left again. The days of the courteous, well-trained maid seemed to be over, but at least it had been she who was the recipient of the girl's truculence and not her mother. She scribbled a note to Lady Manning to tell her what she had done and thought, distastefully, that she would probably have to consult Mrs Vannery about a replacement for the girl. No one else was likely to know of one.

Late that night, Ian rang her up.

'Romaine? I'm speaking from the phone box in the village. I must see you. It's urgent.'

He sounded distraught.

'Oh Ian, not Gwen again?' she asked in dismay.

She had not seen him, save in the distance, for the past three weeks.

'No. Gwen went. It's something quite different. Can you meet me? I can't come to your house. Will you meet me outside? I wouldn't ask you if I weren't desperate. You know that.'

'All right. I'll come to the gate and walk towards the moor,' she said, disturbed. What else could it be if it were not Gwen?

He caught her up when she had walked a little way. The moor was a lonely place and there were only a few courting couples about, absorbed in one another.

'Whatever is the matter?' she asked at once.

'Something dreadful. I don't know how to tell you, but Marion's found out. About you and me, I mean.'

Romaine felt a shock run through. She had tried to forget those few extraordinary minutes in the Vannerys' kitchen when Ian had been so transformed and she so compliant. In time no doubt she would have forgotten the whole episode, but his words and his appearance brought it vividly back to her mind. His eyes were anguished.

'Found out? But what was there to find out, Ian? Only as regards Gwen.'

'No, it's not that. Gwen left — nearly a

fortnight ago, before Marion came back. I don't know where she went nor who helped her to get away, but the other day I had a letter from her, posted in France, saying she was all right but not giving any address. She covered her tracks completely, as if she had never been. But – somebody must have spied on us – must have seen us – that night – in the kitchen . . .'

His stammering voice could not go on, but there was no need for more words. Romaine's memory mirrored the scene completely, those few wild moments in his arms, their kisses against which she had not struggled nor made any attempt to escape. The apparent significance of the affair and its actual duration and importance were so at variance as to be ludicrous but there was certainly no laughter in his tragic face and horrified eyes.

'But, Ian, there was nothing really . . .'

She could not go on. She was trying to assess the gravity of the situation and the source of his distress.

'I know. I know there was nothing on your part. It was all my fault, but she –

Marion — believes there was. She believes that I — we — have been having an affair, that sort of affair, I mean.'

'But it's fantastic! There was nothing. Nothing actual or serious, I mean.'

Romaine felt herself grow hot and cold.

'I cannot make her believe that. She says she has undisputable evidence that — that you were in my house two nights running. That you spent almost the whole of one night here with your car hidden in the lane and that you left secretly in the early hours of the morning.'

'But who told her? Who could have seen me?' asked Romaine, appalled as she recalled the circumstances and realised that they could be damning evidence without Gwen's testimony.

'I don't know. She refused to say but someone must have been watching. She says we were seen — in the bedroom together — oh, Romaine, can you ever forgive me?'

'But we were upstairs with Gwen. I only came because she was ill.'

'I told her about Gwen but she

wouldn't believe me. Said it was a tale I had made up and challenged me to produce her and — of course I couldn't. There was no evidence that anybody had ever been there and — and it all sounds like a story I had made up. When I told her that Gwen was my daughter, she only laughed.'

Romaine realised that it must have seemed a fantastic tale, and that it had only been produced after all his protestations and denials had failed. And Ian would have been a bad liar in those denials.

'Well, I don't see what she can do,' she said at last, uncertainly.

'But she has. Has done something, I mean. She's left me. She's taken the children and gone away and — and she says she is going to see a lawyer and — and take out a case against me for — for adultery.'

Romaine stared at him, appalled.

'Citing *me?* Me, Ian?'

He nodded miserably and turned away from her, standing with his back to her so that he should not see her face as she took in the full horror of the position.

'You mean — divorce? But she can't. Surely there is not enough evidence? Ian, there can't be!'

'There probably isn't. She couldn't establish in a court of law something that never happened, but she says she will try. She knows now about those Wednesday afternoons too, when I was with you.'

'Playing the piano!' said Romaine derisively, and then she remembered the girl Gertrude and the way she had found her only that afternoon rifling her desk, and her threat that 'she would be sorry'.

She felt sick. What if it had been Gertrude who had spied on her and seen her and Ian in each other's arms, and seen the light in the bedroom of what was supposedly an empty house except for the two of them? She did not know how much that evidence would be worth in a court of law but she remembered on what flimsy, faked evidence she had got her own divorce from Jeff; and poor Ian stumbling through a maze of lying to which he was unaccustomed, would have given himself away a dozen times to the jealous, angry woman who was nothing

275

if not possessive. He had probably admitted his love for Romaine.

'It will ruin me, quite apart from what it will do to you,' she said desperately. 'You know what a village is for gossip. There's no smoke without fire, they will say, even if she cannot win a case against you. What are we going to do about it?'

'I don't know. It happened two or three hours ago and I've just been walking about desperately, afraid to tell you. I daren't even ring you up from the house in case she found out. It's a party line, you know.'

'How long is it since you left the house?'

'Two hours. Three. I don't know.'

'She may have come back, after having frightened you into thinking she had gone.'

He shook his head.

'I don't think so. She isn't like that. It's no good saying that I'm sorry, Romaine. It makes me absolutely miserable to realise the harm it may do you...'

'I was selfish, thinking of myself first,

Ian. It isn't only I who will suffer.'

'It'll be far worse for you. I think that is why she has done it. She knows it is the best way of paying me out – not that she really cares for me any more, if she ever did. I'd do anything, anything at all, if I could only think what to do. I love you so, Romaine, and all I have done for you is to harm you. If – if you cared for me at all . . .'

Her silence gave him the answer to that if he needed it.

She could think of nothing to say, standing there looking into the darkness, her hands thrust deep into the pockets of her coat, her face like carved marble, cold and still. She was thinking not only of herself and the ruin of her career but also of her parents, who had done so much for her, given up their home and their own way of life for her, stood by her in love and loyalty when, against their will, she had studied medicine, had not been able to prevent her precipitate marriage, and when disaster had come of that, had never even reproached her but had set to work to enable her to remake her life with dignity and courage.

And now there was this horrible thing which Marion and village gossip would make cheap and nasty.

'I don't see that we can do anything about it,' she said at last. 'We must not see each other again, of course, and Marion may think better of it and come back. After all, it is the break-up of her home and marriage as well, and the children to think of. She has put so much work and thought into the business and she will lose all that . . .'

'We have a joint account. She can draw anything she wants out of it and the shares we have bought from time to time are in her name. If the business fails, as it must do without her, she and the children can manage and with her capabilities, she can easily get a job, which she says she intends to do. She won't suffer in any way.'

His voice was bitter with frustration and anger, not for himself but for the woman he loved. Romaine had always realised the weakness in him, that he had the soul of an artist rather than the hard core of a business man, but no amount of strength could have availed him now.

'I'm sorry,' she said more gently. 'I don't think we can do anything but await events and hope this will resolve itself. I had better go back now. Don't come with me. We won't take any chance of being seen together again,' and she walked swiftly away from him and shut herself in her own room.

It took her only a few days to become quite sure that Gertrude was the source of the sinister rumours that spread rapidly by the grape-vine of village gossip. People stared at her curiously and looked away again before she could greet them in her usual friendly way, and once when she came face to face with Gertrude outside the village store, the girl, instead of avoiding her eyes, looked at her with studied insolence and triumph and Romaine had to brush past her to get into her car.

Marion had made no other move as yet, but she had not returned to her home. It was Lady Manning who gave her this information in all innocence.

'It's an extraordinary thing,' she remarked at dinner one night, 'but I hear that the Vannerys have split up, or at least that Mrs Vannery has taken the children and gone away, leaving that poor Mr Vannery alone. I heard about it at the Women's Institute. I was asked if I would take over the library until they could find someone to do it. I should not think anybody could have quarrelled with him. Such a hard-working and inoffensive little man.'

Sir Julius smiled.

'You are turning into a real countrywoman, my dear,' he said, 'taking such a keen interest in village gossip.'

'Well, you can't live in a village like Worbury and *not* be interested. You must have heard the talk, Romaine, visiting the houses as you do. What has happened? Do you know? It's nearly a week since she went, and according to Mrs Slater, Mrs Vannery called yesterday and took away trunks and all the children's toys and put them into store at Bigby's.'

'Mother, really! You *are* becoming a real old gossip. When I visit my patients, I am only concerned with them and not with idle talk about other people,' said

Romaine, with heightened colour.

Lady Manning laughed.

'Well, I suppose you're right. It hasn't really anything to do with us, though I had hoped Mrs Vannery would find me another girl to replace Gertrude. If she's not coming back, I shall have to put an advertisement in the local paper or something. You might do it for me when you go into the village, Romaine. By the way, I met that girl yesterday and she gave me a most peculiar look. One would have expected her to look somewhat ashamed of herself, but not at all! She almost looked as though I was the one who should feel ashamed. Really, these modern girls! I am very glad to have got rid of her. Are you going, Romaine?' as her daughter got up precipitately. 'Won't you stay for your coffee?'

'No, thank you, Mother. I've got some work to attend to.'

'Surely you haven't any more late calls to make, darling?'

'No, just some office work. Forms to fill in,' and she made her escape.

'I don't think Romaine's looking at all

well,' observed Lady Manning after she had gone. 'Do you think something's worrying her? It couldn't be that husband of hers again, could it?'

'I imagine that's all over and done with. She never mentions him, does she?' asked her husband.

'No, but you know what she is about keeping things to herself, and she never really wanted to divorce him, though it was the only thing to do. He would have been a constant source of worry to her. She ought never to have married him, of course. I only hope he never turns up again, but I suppose he's still rushing about with that motor-racing of his.'

'As a matter of fact, he isn't,' said Sir Julius, looking down at the coffee he was stirring.

'How do you know? Surely he hasn't contacted *you*?'

Lady Manning looked startled and affronted.

'Not intentionally, but I saw him the other day.'

'Where?'

'A client of mine has just bought a car from the firm he works for. Naturally I hadn't any idea I should see Jeffery, but when I went with my client to look it over, he was there.'

'Not Moller's?'

No, a place in the West End, quite a good firm and he seems to have a decent standing there, knows what he is talking about.'

'You mean you actually spoke to him?'

'Naturally, my dear, since he was actively concerned in selling the car to Madison, who obviously had no idea I had any — er — connection with Jeffrey. As a matter of fact, I took him along to my club for a drink.'

'Julius, how could you have done such a thing? After the way he treated Romaine, and the divorce and everything?'

'Well, as you know, I stood aside from the affair and left it to Romaine, to you and Romaine. It was her concern entirely what she did, but I always rather liked Jeffery. He was young and hot-headed and had no sense of responsibility, I know, but I felt that she was rather hard on him and I'm not sure sometimes that she doesn't think so too. He seems to have changed quite a bit, isn't racing any longer and has settled down to a decent job. Looks a lot older, too, and more serious about life.'

'Did you speak about Romaine?'

'Only a few words. He asked me how she was, and I said she was well and happy, which I don't think now was entirely the truth.'

'You haven't mentioned it to her?'

'No.'

'Then you won't, will you, Julius? The sooner she forgets the whole miserable business, the better.'

'I agree, of course, but — well, Romaine is faithful, you know. She has remained faithful to her career, and that and her husband have been the only two important things in her life.'

'You surely wouldn't like to see her married to him again, Julius?' she asked, shocked.

'I only want her happiness, my dear, as you do.'

'Well, it doesn't lie with Jeffrey Elster,' she retorted. 'Of that I am quite sure. It was a most unsuitable marriage for her in every way, and as for your saying you always *liked* him – well, of course, you men always stick together and see life from an entirely different stand-point. Yes, Annie, you may clear,' as the maid came in and put an end to the conversation.

A few days later the whole village was agog with delighted anticipation, for Mrs Vannery had returned to Worbury and bought a small house in the neighbourhood in which she had established herself and the children. There was no sign of a reconciliation between herself and her husband, who had engaged an elderly man to help with the books but was otherwise carrying on the business alone.

Romaine realised at once that the gossip which had begun to die down was revived with renewed interest by this development, and that the sympathy lay with the wife. She took up again the library work and other activities of the Women's Institute as if she had never left it, the two little girls returned to the village school, looking more scared than ever, keeping to themselves even more than they had done before and accompanied their mother, silent and withdrawn, to church. Marion got a job at the village stores, left vacant by the death of the owner's wife, Mrs Wenham, where her capabilities and her shrewd business instinct were invaluable. In such a position, she came into contact with everyone and as her manner did not suggest she had anything to be ashamed of in leaving her husband, all the village accepted that the break had been entirely his fault and behaved accordingly.

None of them, in their heart of hearts, really liked Marion Vannery and she was aware of it, but they respected and admired her.

Only when she was alone, the day's work behind her and the children in bed, did she drop her mask of cheerful complacency and face what she had done. She had no regrets and no remorse, feeling herself perfectly justified in the course she had taken. She was filled with an implacable hatred for Romaine Elster and had every intention of doing all she could to bring her to shame and ruin.

Harshly, and with no feeling that she had ever been at fault in her life, she surveyed her forty-five years of it and saw her long toil, the strenuous, unremitting effort, brought to nought by this mere girl, the daughter of titled, high-and-mighty parents, who had never had to work as she had done, never known what it was to go hungry so that those dependent on them might eat and have a roof over their heads.

The eldest of a large and straggling family, with an ailing mother worn out by too many childbirths, too many miscarriages, and a shiftless father who was more often out of a job than in one, she had early learned to accept the burden, to take charge of her destiny and to turn it from its purpose. At fourteen, a big, strong girl, unprepossessing in appearance because she had had neither the time nor the means to try to make herself more attractive, she had left school and taken charge of the family. The boys had to do equal work with the girls in keeping the home, a poor enough place, neat and spotless and she ruled them with a rod of iron, with her own two hands and a strong cane. It was of no consequence to her that they heartily disliked her and that even the frail and gradually helpless mother was afraid of her.

That mother occupied the one comparatively soft spot in her heart and was cared for harshly but devotedly by her eldest daughter until, before Marion was fifteen, she drifted thankfully out of life, regretted by none of them except secretly by the girl herself. Then she turned her attention to the father whose vagaries and drunken habits she had endured for the sake of her mother.

'Now you get to work, Joe Bence,' she told him after the funeral, 'or there's no place here for you. I've been to see Mr Alder and he's willing to take you on as a labourer, but only as long as you do a day's work every day and earn your money. And that money's mine, mine and the children's, and I want your wage packet every friday night before you've opened it or out you go. I'll give you back five shillings a week out of it and if you like to spend the lot on getting drunk in one evening, that's your look-out, only if you do get drunk don't come back here till you've sobered up or you'll find yourself with the key of the street. Sober – or out. And I can do it, mind you,' and he knew that, drunk, he would be no match for the power of her muscular arms.

'There's another thing too whilst we're at it,' she added. 'You can move out of the big bed where you've been hogging it with Ma all these years and go into the room with Bob and Johnny. The three girls can have your bed and I'll have the smallest room for myself. I'll have earned it by the time I've looked after you lot,' and though there was a good deal of grumbling and muttering about the new arrangements, that was how they stood.

Her father would have argued and resisted her attempt to get his wage packet each week, but she always managed to be at the pay office to snatch it from him and open it and dole out to him his five shillings a week.

'Five shillin' a week! Fat lot I can do on that!' he grumbled. 'It won't even pay for me baccy an' a pint, wot with the taxes an' all.'

'Well, who made the war that made the taxes? Not me. Five shillings is all you're going to get and that's that. I'd go out to work myself and earn a jolly sight more than you'll ever earn, but somebody's got to look after the house and the kids till they're big enough to fend for themselves.'

He was killed in a drunken brawl some months later, having stolen the money to get drunk on from his employer, and Mr Alder, who had come to respect her if not to like her, offered Marion a job in his office and took the eldest boy, just ready to leave school, into the brickmaking business which had given their father employment.

The second girl, almost fifteen, had been learning typewriting, but Marion soon put an end to that.

'That was all very well when *he* was alive and I had his money,' she said ruthlessly. 'Now I've got to go out to work and you must stop home and look after the house and the kids. There'll be time enough for that fancy stuff when they're off hand.'

'But Johnny's only five,' wailed Dinah.

'So what? He's got to be looked after, hasn't he? Do you think I want him and Jessie running the streets?'

'Why can't Florrie stay home if anybody's got to?'

'Because Florrie's only eleven and she's got to go to school. When she leaves, she can take over and you can do what you like but till then you're staying home and no more nonsense, and you'll keep the place clean and the kids tidy or you'll feel the weight of my hand,' using a threat which Dinah knew, in spite of her years, would be carried out.

So for three years Dinah ran the house under her sister's iron rule, and then it was Florrie and after her the youngest girl Jessie. All Marion's earnings went into the home. She kept nothing for herself save for the barest necessities of clothing, and these she made for herself and the children, not scorning to buy at the jumble sales anything which could be turned to good account for one or another. When Florrie was old enough to leave school and take over, she got Dinah a job and found the extra money herself to pay for

291

the typewriting lessons and never for a moment relaxed her iron grip on all of them.

And then came the Second World War and with it Ian Vannery.

Marion was twenty-nine when it started, and it broke up the family. Even Johnny, the youngest, had left school and was learning a trade, but at the earliest possible moment he managed to get into the Air Force. Dinah and Florrie had escaped Marion's rule by getting married, and Jessie joined the A.T.S. Bob, who had developed chest trouble and was too delicate to go into the forces, had gone to work on the land, and Marion was left alone.

There was not enough now to fill her capacity for hard work, as the brickmaking business had almost closed down and it no longer warranted the continuation of her job as the firm's secretary and bookkeeper. She was scornful of the amount and type of work which girls appeared at that time to be doing in the army, so she took a job at a grocery store where she did the work of two men, and at the same time became an air-raid warden.

She had kept on the little house in a London suburb which was subjected to constant and heavy bombing and it was one night when she was on duty that she first met Ian.

He was in the army, a reluctant but dutiful soldier, a private on leave but, caught up in the raid, he had worked all night beside Marion, clearing debris and helping in the rescue work. Towards morning, when there had been little more for her to do and she had been told to go off and get some sleep, he was still beside her, as grimy and tired as she was herself, and for the first time they took stock of each other and smiled.

He saw a rather gaunt figure in navy blue warden's uniform and white helmet, and she a rather scruffy figure, a little shorter than she was, in well-worn khaki with his 'tin hat' slipped sideways. Both had dirty faces.

'Thanks, soldier,' she said. 'You did a good job. You home on leave?'

'Yes, sort of. Got as far as this and found myself in the thick of it. You didn't do a bad job yourself! What are you going to do now? Can you get home all right?'

He was not the sort to make a pass at her, nor had any man ever ventured to make a pass, and she pulled a face.

'I'll have to,' she said. 'The place where I work got a direct hit earlier in the night and they've cordoned it off, so I can't go back there as I sometimes do. I shall have to get home.'

He put out a hand, quite unnecessarily, to help her over the rubble, which was a new experience for her.

'Where do you live?' he asked, and she told him and asked him the same question.

'Well – nowhere now, actually,' he said. 'My father and my sister were killed in one of the first raids, house wiped out and everything. My mother died some time ago so there's only me left. I was going to try for a bed at the Y.M.C.A., but I'll see you home first. That is if I may.'

She was eminently capable of looking after herself even if he had been the oncoming sort, which he obviously wasn't. In fact, she felt able to look after him rather than of being looked after. She had never had a boy friend and had never been seen home in her life.

'Well — all right, if you like,' she said rather ungraciously. 'I don't mind.'

That had been the beginning of it.

There was plenty of room in the house which had once held the whole family and when he had had a wash at the sink and she had made tea for them and opened a tin of corned beef, she offered him a room for the rest of the night. There was not much of the night left, and she felt it was the least she could do.

Since there was no point in going to work at the bombed shop in the morning, she allowed herself the rare luxury of an extra hour in bed, and when she came downstairs, she found that he had put the kettle on and laid the breakfast on the kitchen table for her.

'I'll be getting along now,' he said awkwardly. 'Thanks for the night's lodging.'

'Stay and have some breakfast anyway. There's not much. Only one egg in this week's quota, but I'll scramble it and put in some breadcrumbs and it'll do for two,' which, in spite of his protests, she did.

'I'd have thought that working in a grocer's shop, you'd be able to wangle a bit extra,' said Ian.

'Who, me? Not on your life. I keep an eye on the girls to see that they don't take a ha'porth more than their rations and I never do it myself. If everybody made do with what they're entitled to, we'd all get a bit more. No hanky-panky tricks under the counter for me. Have some more tea? I use the leaves twice and put a bit more in each time to eke it out. Have you got your own sugar?'

'No, but I've got my ration card,' producing it. 'You take it. I can manage.'

'As if I should! What's your name, by the way? Mine's Bence, Marion Bence.'

'Ian Vannery,' he said and anticipated her slightly derisive smile. 'It's rather a fancy name, but it's the only one I've got.'

'You can't help your name, can you? Take your ration card back — Ian. The breakfast's on me, but you can't have sugar in your second cup. I'm out of it for this week.'

'I could go and buy some and bring it back. I believe that on leave we get a bigger meat ration than you do, so I'll get you a chop or something for your dinner.'

'Not chops. They're all bone. You could get a bit of what they call stewing steak, though, and I'll do it up with some vegetables, and you can stay and have it with me if you like, as you haven't got anywhere particular to go. As a matter of fact, I've been thinking that you can have that room for the rest of your leave, if you like. It isn't much, but it's clean and there's no one here but me.'

'Well – if you'll let me pay for it ...' he stammered.

'Yes, you can do that. I won't charge you much,' and she rapidly worked out a price that was fair but not over-generous, and he accepted it gladly.

He did various jobs about the house for her, though he admitted that he was not very handy with tools, and when his leave was up, she knew that she was going to miss him. As the shop had not been able to open again yet, she was able to go to the pictures with him, insisting in paying for her own seat, and one fine afternoon they went to Kew Gardens and he revealed an astonishing interest in and knowledge of plants and flowers.

'Thank you for having me, Marion,' he said like a small boy after a party. 'I've enjoyed my leave, which is more than I can say of my last one, which was after the house was bombed and I had nowhere to go. Will you let me write to you?'

'Yes, if you like, and – you can come again if you want to, and if we're still alive.'

After he had gone, she found that he had been back and left a plant on the doorstep for her, a little hardy plant with blue flowers on it.

'Silly fool,' she grunted. 'As if I've got time to go messing about with flowers,' but she watered it and kept it alive until he came on his next leave.

Before he went back again, they were married.

No one, unless it were Ian himself, was more surprised about it than Marion, but the raids had increased in number and intensity and neither of them had friends and life itself, and the expectation of a future, was so uncertain that it seemed inevitable that they should try to create something permanent in a world where nothing seemed to be for more than an hour or a day.

Marriage seemed to have transformed Marion. It had given her restless energy new scope and direction and in the long periods apart from him she made endless plans for him and for their future, writing long businesslike letters to him about them, working steadily towards their end. He had been a mere boy at the outbreak of war and was only twenty-two now, his future only vaguely formed by the insurance office in which he had been working when he joined up. She had dismissed that without a second thought. It would never bring him to anything better than a clerk's job and her ambitions soared higher than that. To own one's own business, to be master and not man, that was the way to success, and no clerk was likely to own an insurance company, however long and hard he worked.

The grocer's shop had been patched up and reopened, its essential business given priority, but the blow of seeing the premises shattered and his stock destroyed had taken the heart out of its elderly proprietor and it was only Marion's indomitable energy which had made it possible for him to start again. It was she who harried the few inefficient builders into patching up shop and store, getting the necessary permits, replenishing the goods and getting it opened again in the midst of confusion.

'I'd never have done it without you, Miss Bence,' said the tired old man who had only been too glad to leave it all to her.

'Mrs Vannery,' she corrected him briskly, proud of the new status as a married woman. 'Just leave everything to me. I can manage,' which is what she did, and saw how easily she could acquire the business herself when Ian came home and she had a man to work with her. By settling some of the bills herself out of her salary, keeping meticulous accounts for them and living with the utmost parsimony, she already had a firm hand over it. She paid as small wages as she could to the girls on the staff, who could not change their jobs as they were in the 'essential work' class, and she knew that when the war ended, it would be impossible for the owner to find the money to repay her the debt which she was piling up. He would, in the end, have no alternative but to hand over what remained of the business to her. It was of no consequence to her that the old couple would be left with nothing to live on. That was their affair, and she had a supreme contempt for anyone who was not able to protect his own business.

But just after D-day, Ian was sent home. He had not been in the first wave of the assault nor even in the second, but he had broken in the succeeding turmoil and carnage and, though miraculously he had not been wounded, his nerve had gone completely and he was of no more use as a soldier.

He was treated for a few months in hospital and then given an honourable discharge, but he was found to have an infection of the lungs and was advised to do an open-air job for at least the first few years of civilian life. Otherwise it was feared that tuberculosis would develop.

Marion who had been his constant visitor at the hospital in Hampshire, met the blow valiantly. It was not his fault, though she had a secret contempt for the lack of fibre which had produced the result and he was miserably aware of it.

Theirs had been an inevitable coming together of two lonely people rather than a love-match. Marion had no soft side to her though they had lived since their marriage as husband and wife, there had been no transports of emotion, only a more or less business-like mating and this formed the pattern of their life together without providing a background of mutual love.

When she had taken him home to the house of which she had prudently let everything but their own bedroom and a share of the kitchen, they discussed their future, or rather Marion talked of it and Ian, still weak and nerveless concurred.

'What did you do before you went into the insurance office?' she asked.

'You can't go back there, of course, even if they would have you.'

'I was only seventeen when I went there.'

'But you must have left school before that?'

'I wanted to be a musician, to play the piano,' he admitted sheepishly.

'Playing the piano? For a living?'

She was incredulous and contemptuous.

'My father thought I ought to have a chance of doing what I really wanted to do so he sent me to a good teacher when I left school at sixteen, but I wasn't good enough,' he admitted humbly.

She gave a scornful snort.

'I should think not indeed! Wasting a whole year tinkling on a piano! I wonder your father didn't have more sense. What sort of life was that for a man? Then you went into that office?' her tone suggesting that an insurance clerk's job was not much better.

'Yes, but I didn't like it much. I should have stuck at it, though, if it hadn't been for the war. You see, I'm not much good at anything, and now, if I've got to work

303

in the open-air, I suppose I shall have to get a job on a farm.'

'And be a farm labourer all your life? We'll see about that. Of course it's no good thinking of taking over the shop any more, but I can get back the money I've put into it so we shall have something to start on.'

'I thought you said it would ruin the owner if you asked for it back?'

'That's his affair. He knew I was putting my money into it and that he would have to pay it back by letting me have the shop or in some other way. I'll see him about it. I've got my accounts, properly audited, and he can't get out of it. It's over three hundred pounds now. I've managed to live by letting these rooms and have scarcely touched my wages and he knows it. You leave it to me. I'll get the money from him and look round for something for you to do.'

She was ruthless in demanding the whole of the money back, with interest, though it meant selling the small business with its still patched-up premises and leaving the Pearces without enough to live on, and with the money in the bank, she searched the countryside for some proposition that promised a future. Finally, giving Ian only a perfunctory say in the matter, she bought a smallholding at Worbury, with a cottage on it, and was prudent enough to secure an option on adjoining land. She had to borrow from the bank, but the bank manager had a respect for her business acumen and made the loan possible, and when Ian got his small gratuity, put that in as well and established them as joint owners of what afterwards became Merridew Nurseries.

Ian's health improved under the new living conditions and he liked the work. Marion was the manager and had the business head, and he was content to leave that side of it to her. When the children came, she moved them out of the inadequate cottage into the substantial little house in which they had lived ever since, gradually taking up the option on the extra land and increasing the scope of the business until it had reached its present prosperous state.

As the years went by, Marion was completely satisfied with her life and what she had made of it, though ambition still drove her on. She was master of her own life and of Ian's and her children's. She had attained a high status in the village, was drawn into and consulted and referred to on all its activities and would almost have been 'the lady of the manor' had it not been for the owners of the big houses and the titles who were still considered by Worbury the important people, treated with great respect and given all the jobs, opening bazaars, appearing in state at village functions, which Marion ardently desired to do and felt herself quite capable of doing.

That was the only rub. Try as she might, she never gained access to the 'big houses' nor was considered as of sufficient importance to be admitted to even the outer edge of friendship with people like the Delmains, the Hartingtons or, later, the Mannings. It made her frustrated and angry to continue to be classed with the village people instead of amongst the great, and when the undreamed-of, golden opportunity came of lowering their pride by the discovery of Ian's 'affair' with Romaine Elster, she felt herself to be on the pinnacle of triumph.

That was how it was when she made that amazing discovery.

Chapter Eight

MARION VANNERY was satisfied with her life and its progress, apart from her inability to rise to further heights socially, but through the years Ian had gradually become aware of the lack in his life of personal happiness, of something above and beyond mere wordly success and the comparative prosperity which he had attained largely through his wife's ambition. They were not rich, but they wanted for nothing material according to their status and their capital, zealously hoarded, looked after and invested by Marion, had grown to sizeable proportions so that their future was assured. They had long paid off their debt to the bank and redeemed the mortgage on their good acreage of land. No money was wasted or spent unnecessarily. The children went to the village school, but were to go to a good, paying school in Greatborough for further education when they had gone beyond it, and in order to prepare them for it, Marion had rigidly controlled their associations with the village children and would not allow them to make any closer friendships than those of the school-room so that the house never rang with noisy chatter and laughter and the little girls crept in and out, mouse-like and silent, always on the watch for Marion to tell them not to do whatever they were doing, always, as her own brothers and sisters had been, afraid of her sharp tongue and heavy hand.

'I'm going to bring you up decent and well-behaved girls, not like the riff-raff in the village, even if I have to half murder you to do it!' was a frequent preliminary of hers to the production of the ever-handy cane and a whipping and Ian, if he were in the house, would rush out of it and shut himself in his shed so as not to hear the sound of the cane and the children's cries.

He dared not interfere. Any protest on his part would only have increased her anger and the severity of the punishment, as he had found out by experience, and he was glad that they were always sent to bed afterwards so that he would not have to see their pale, red-eyed faces.

He would try, by some secret little treat the next day, to show them that he had taken no part in the punishment, but they were afraid of accepting even the few sweets from his pocket and usually dodged away from his attempts to give the small gift in case their mother learned of it.

They grew up without love, product of a marriage without love, and as the years went by, he knew that he was hungering for it and had missed the best thing in life, and when he met Romaine and was admitted to her warm and uncritical friendship, felt her admiration for him and had the unfamiliar knowledge that he could give her pleasure, his reaction was inevitable.

And now, through linking her with the only other being in the world whom he truly loved, his daughter Gwen, he had brought this irretrievable disaster to her.

Romaine was first made surely aware of that disaster when one day, in the post-office, she met a little girl who had been her patient during the measles epidemic. The child made a dart for the door, but could not make her escape in time. Romaine had not even known she was trying to escape and spoke kindly to her.

'Why, Rosie, not at school?' she asked. 'Not another holiday?'

'No, doctor. I — I've been ill. Tonsillitis, the doctor said.'

'The doctor? What doctor? I thought you were my patient. Have you deserted me, Rosie?' trying to speak playfully, though there was a sudden constriction of her throat.

'It was Dr Heath. Mummy has changed us on to his panel,' said the child and ran out with a backward, half-frightened glance.

So it had started? There was no reason why anyone should not change from one doctor to another, and no doubt she would have formal notification in due course from Dr Heath, but she herself would not have accepted such a change from another doctor without at least private inquiries. If Dr Heath had done this, what had he been told?

And she had no defence. She could not take action against the insidious rumours unless and until Marion Vannery made a public statement which mentioned her name, and so far she had not done so. She was merely living apart from her husband for reasons which were for the moment merely speculative.

At last, when more of her patients had trickled away and Dr Heath had told her, with an amused smile, that 'evidently the Worbury inhabitants had decided that they did not like a woman doctor', in desperation she telephoned to Ian.

'It's Romaine,' she said, needlessly. He had warmed and then grown pale at the first sound of her voice. 'I must see you. Where can we meet? Not in Worbury, or Greatborough.

'Is Bournemouth too far away?'

'No. Perhaps at one of the big hotels? When could you manage it? Soon, please.

They arranged a day and approximate time and chose a hotel which at this time of the year would be full of visitors and they might meet there undetected. Romaine hated the need for secrecy, which she felt degraded them and gave their former friendship an unpleasant flavour, but Ian could not think of anything but the happiness of being with her again. He had avoided going to Glen House even for necessary consultations with Sir Julius. He was now working at a considerable distance from the house, and he had left the careful plans to his foreman to carry out so that his actual presence was necessary only for the routine inspection of the progress of the work.

He was already in the Bournemouth hotel, sitting in an inconspicuous corner of the lounge, when Romaine came in. His pulses quickened at sight of her trim figure, and he could not hide the gladness of his face as he rose to meet her.

They shook hands briefly and she took a chair with her back to the room.

'How are you, darling?' he asked in a low voice. 'I've been hungering and thirsting for sight and sound of you and I can hardly believe that you are here.'

'Please don't, Ian,' she said nervously. 'I only came because I had to talk to you for a few minutes. It's really better that we shouldn't meet at all. Have you seen Marion? I have heard that she is still away, but living in the village and working at Wenham's Stores. Naturally I've never gone in there since.'

'She hasn't come back to me and I haven't seen her or had any word from her, though she came back to the house once when I was out and took away her things and the children's. That was before she moved into Cedar Cottage.'

'Ian, what are you going to do about it? What is she going to do?' asked Romaine desperately.

'What can I do until she makes a move?'

'You must see her, ask her what she intends to do, if she means to do anything. We're innocent, Ian. Can't you make her believe that? You know that the whole village is talking about your separation and — my name is being associated with it. I am sure of it,' and she told him of the patients who had transferred to Dr Heath for no apparent reason.

'It's not as if I had failed them in any way as a doctor. They were quite satisfied with my treatment and I have worked very hard, as you know. There can't be any other reason than these — these spiteful and quite unfounded rumours, which could only have sprung from Marion. I think that girl Gertrude Maston would be too frightened to go on spreading them when she realised what effect they have already had.'

'I'm sorry, Romaine, desperately sorry. I'd rather have died than had this happen to you through me. Of course I'll see Marion if you want me to and think it would do any good, but you don't know her as I do. When she's angry, she's like a fiend and nothing can stop her from getting her own back when she thinks she has been wronged. It isn't that she loves me, but I belonged to her and she's furious at — at the thought of — someone taking her property.'

'But that's ridiculous, Ian. I haven't "taken" you, as you express it.'

Only his harassed, stricken face kept her from adding 'I don't want you.'

'I shan't get her to believe that,' he said moodily, 'though only you and I know that it's true.'

'Will you see her? Try to show her how awkward and impossible it is? Get her to come back to you? It's the only way, Ian, and you don't want to go on living as you are, or to lose your children, do you?'

'I don't want to live with her again,' said Ian with a sudden explosion of vehemence, 'and the children have never been allowed to be anything to me or I to them. Romaine, is it the only way? I'd do anything, go anywhere, be anything, if only you would go with me. I love you and I've never loved a woman before and never shall again. I'll work for you. I'll make good, and I still have money in the business. She can't take it all . . .'

The look on her face stopped at last his spate of words. It was not so much horror at what he said but complete incredulity. He knew that no such idea had ever entered her head.

'Ian,' she began shakily, not knowing

315

what to say that would not be too shattering and cruel, but he interrupted her.

'I know,' he said in a changed voice, all the eager light going from his face. 'I know. You need not say it. It's an impossible idea, isn't it? You don't care for me. You never could. That's it, isn't it?'

She leaned forward and laid a hand gently on his arm.

'Not in that way,' she said. 'Only as a friend, a very dear and trusted friend. Thank you for loving me, Ian, though I wish you didn't. It only makes you unhappy.'

'I'm not good enough for you, I know. I'm not even of your class . . .'

'Oh, Ian, not that. Don't bring that into it. It doesn't mean a thing to me. I like people for what they are and what they do, not for who they are, a mere accident of birth in which they had no say at all. I am proud of having won your love, though I have done nothing to deserve it, and who knows what might have happened if things had been different, if you had not been married or

316

– if I had not?'

'You're not married now, Romaine.'

'Not in the legal sense, no, but I have been, and my husband is still alive and . . .'

'And you're still in love with him?' he asked in a low, defeated voice as she paused.

'Perhaps. I don't know. I only know that he meant everything in the world to me and that when our marriage broke up, something in me broke as well and I don't think anything can mend it now. So you see, *dear* Ian, that even if I could do as you ask me to do and come away with you and eventually, I suppose, be able to marry you, I should have nothing to give you.'

'It would be enough for me to be with you, to love you and work for you.'

'But not for me, Ian.'

Her voice was gentle but inflexible, and he made a despairing gesture.

'I think I've known all the time that it was hopeless,' he said, 'but somehow, when you see the gates of heaven so near . . .'

She managed a smile but it was not

317

reflected on his own face.

'But not open even by so much as a crack,' she said, 'and even if we did manage to push them open, it wouldn't be heaven on the other side. I'm sorry, Ian, but that's how it is,' and, after a pause, 'You'll see Marion?'

'Yes, I'll see her,' he said dully, and they rose to go, his last hope gone. Now all that remained for him to do was to protect her if he could, even if that meant going back to Marion and taking up again a life which would be the sheer hell she could and would make it.

He let Romaine go first, watching her until the revolving door hid her from sight and then slumping in his chair in apathy. Life had nothing now to offer him.

He did not know how long he sat there, but finally he got up and went to the door, leaving the tea they had ordered untouched and putting a note down on the table which later made the waitress open her eyes in astonishment. He was incapable of counting out silver.

His mouth set in a line of misery, he drove back to Worbury and the cottage

318

where his wife and children lived.

Marion had just returned from the shop and was taking off her plain, serviceable hat and coat in the passage when she heard the car stop and went to open the door. Beyond her, in the little sitting-room, he could see the little girls with their heads bent over their homework. They looked up, wide-eyed and startled, when they saw him.

'You?' asked Marion harshly. 'What do you want?'

'I've got to talk to you, Marion.'

She shrugged her shoulders and turned to the children, leaving the door open for him.

'You can go to the recreation ground to play,' she said, 'but don't go on the swings and don't talk to anybody. I'll come and fetch you.'

They needed no second bidding, but hastily collected their books and put them in their satchels and scuttled out through the back door, not daring to glance again at their father.

'You can come in,' said Marion, going into the room they had vacated, 'though we've nothing to say to each other.'

'I want to know what you're going to do,' he blurted out without preamble.

'Why?'

'Because – because of Romaine.'

'Romaine? Oh, Dr Elster, of course,' she said with curling lip. 'I'm not doing anything about her – at the moment.'

'You are. You're spreading rumours, lies, about her. The village is buzzing and she's losing her patients because of it.'

'So you're still seeing her?' she asked, and he bit his lip with annoyance at the slip he had made which she had been quick to take advantage.

'We met today for the first time since you left Merridew.'

'Locking the stable door after the horse has been stolen?'

'Marion, this business is doing her a lot of harm and she is absolutely innocent, absolutely. The whole thing's so impossible. As if she would ever stoop – as if she could ever think anything of me . . .' floundered poor Ian, getting deeper and deeper into the mire.

'Out of her class, you mean? I agree. She was just amusing herself with you. You can't imagine that the *Mannings'* daughter would go in for a serious affair with a *nurseryman*? She just wanted a bit on the side whilst your wife was away.'

'I mean nothing to her, nothing at all,' he said with a growing realisation of his helplessness to defend her against this bitter, enraged woman.

'That's what I said. It wasn't very wise of her to have picked on a married man – and a patient of hers, was it?'

'I'm not her patient.'

'Oh, but you are. Remember when you had measles? She saw you then and prescribed for you and I paid her fee, which she took.'

'I don't see that that makes any difference.'

'Don't you? Ever heard of the British Medical Association? They don't look very kindly on doctors who have affairs with their patients. In fact, if they hear about it, she may be struck off the rolls. It won't be a matter of rumour either. I hadn't quite made up my mind what to do about you, Ian, but now I have. I shall apply for a Judicial Separation, naming her,' and she held up her head and gave him a jeering, triumphant smile.

'You haven't enough evidence!'

'Possibly. Possibly not. I may lose the case, but it's worth it.'

'You'd drag her into that?' he asked, dumbfounded and sick with fear. She had threatened it before, but he did not think she meant it.

'I don't think the Mannings would fancy it either, especially as she's been divorced once.'

'She was not to blame. She divorced her husband.'

'So they said. People of the Mannings' class usually arrange it that way, don't they? It looks better. It's a gentlemanly agreement. The fact is that she's had one husband and got rid of him, and now she proposes to take mine, or she'd probably have to if I divorced you. That's why I'm going for a Judicial Separation. Even if I win it, you still wouldn't be able to marry her.'

'She wouldn't marry me in any case.'

'So you've discussed it with her? Poor Ian. Did you ever imagine that she would? The Mannings' daughter?'

'You're doing this to spite them.'

'Why not? They're like the rest of their high-and-mighty set. They take notice of people like us only when we can be of use to them. "Oh Mrs Vannery, could you find me a maid?" "Would you bring me some of your lovely flowers and arrange them for my dinner-party? You do them so beautifully. I'll pay for them, of course." "Oh, Mrs Vannery, you know everyone in the village. Could you get me some extra helpers for my garden-party and supervise them yourself? You're so clever at that sort of thing."' Her mincing tones were meant to mimic Lady Manning's voice. 'But as for sitting at her dinner-table, or being a guest at her garden-party or being introduced to her friends, that's a different matter. Oh, I know that it's not only her. It's all her sort. But it just happens that I've got a chance of showing her up, she and her *lady doctor daughter*, and I'm going not going to miss it.'

'And to spite her, because we're not of her class and she doesn't count us amongst her personal friends, you'd ruin Romaine, who is perfectly innocent?'

He had listened to her furious diatribe in silence. He knew that, with rising prosperity, she had wanted to be recognised by people like the Mannings and admitted to their circle on terms of friendship and that her inability to bring that about had made her sore, but he had not imagined the venom she had been nourishing about it, not the triumph of her vengeance. He had never loved her, but now he hated her for the bitter, spiteful woman she was. It was not for his sake she was bent on doing this dastardly thing, but to humiliate one of the class that had spurned her.

'That's as may be,' she said. 'Why should a woman spend the night with another man when his wife is away, if not to have a bit of fun on the side? Innocent, my foot!'

'I've told you why she came. My daughter Gwen was in the house and ill and needed a doctor.'

'And where, pray, is this daughter of yours who appeared so miraculously and disappeared again? A likely tale! Only a fool would invent such a story and only a fool would believe it, and I'm no fool.

Produce the girl if you want me to believe it.'

'I can't. I don't know where she is.'

Marion gave a snort of mocking laughter.

'Most unfortunate! As if you ever had a daughter other than mine! You'd better think up a better tale than that — if you can.'

He was silent. If he could have produced Gwen, he would have been prepared to sacrifice even her to save Romaine, but he had no idea where she had gone nor where she might be hiding. She had vanished mysteriously and completely and he might never hear from her again.

In desperation, he changed his tactics.

'Marion, I know I've been a fool. I've treated you badly. I've admitted that I was in love with Romaine and nothing I can say will take that back, though she doesn't love me and never will. Can't you forgive me? I've been a good husband to you all these years and we've been — happy together, with the children and the nurseries and everything. We've got on and made a good job of it. Why should you want to break that up and lose everything you've worked for, for nothing? Come back, Marion. Or if you like, we'll sell the place and get another, get right away from here . . .'

'And start again?' she asked witheringly. 'Not on your life. I'm all right working for Wenham, and even if you gave up Merridew tomorrow, there's enough there to see the children through school at Greatborough and provide for me. I've seen to that! You can do what you like about leaving Worbury but I'm staying, and the girls are going to Greatborough. Joan's due to start there next year, but I may take them both away from the village school and send them to Hill House at once. As for going back to you, what do you think I'm made of, you've made your bed and you can lie in it – with Romaine Elster!'

His face was quite white, his eyes strained. He was, and looked, a desperate man.

'There's only one way out then,' he said in a muffled voice, and before she could guess his intent, he took a paper packet from his pocket and tipped the contents into his mouth and swallowed them.

Chapter Nine

ROMAINE was busy with her surgery hour when the telephone bell rang. The waiting-room was full, for by no means all of her patients had been kept away by the rumours about her connection with the Vannery's trouble.

'Excuse me a minute, Mrs Roper,' she said to the woman who had been pouring out her troubles into her sympathetic ear, and she picked up the receiver.

Her expression changed to one of startled dismay as she listened.

'But I can't come,' she said. 'Ring up Dr Heath — or the police for an ambulance to the hospital.'

'There's no time. He must have a doctor at once. You're a doctor, aren't you? Do you think I'd send for *you* if I didn't have to?'

Marion Vannery's voice was harsh

and imperative.

'But . . .'

'Don't you understand? Do you want him to die?'

Romaine gulped.

'All right. I'll come,' she said. 'What has he taken?'

'I don't know. Something he uses in the nursery. Arsenic probably.'

'Give him an emetic, salt and water or mustard,' and she put up the receiver and got up from her chair. Her face was white.

'I'm sorry, Mrs Roper. You'll have to go. Tell the others in the waiting-room, will you? It's an emergency call. If any of them want to wait, they can, but I may be a long time,' and she picked up her medical case, checked over its contents rapidly, added some things from her drug cupboard and ran out to her car, which she had left in the drive.

What could have induced Ian to do such a thing? What good could it do either of them if he were to die?

Marion said that he was at Cedar Cottage and she drove there rapidly, praying that she would be in time.

Heaven knew what complications would ensue for all of them if she weren't. The fool, she thought angrily, the utter fool!

Marion had got back to the house from the call-box at the corner of the road and had left the door standing open and Romaine went in quickly.

Ian was lying on the floor of the sitting-room, almost unconscious but writhing with pain and clutching his stomach.

'Where's the rest of the stuff he took?' she asked and when the half-empty packet was thrust into her hand, she sniffed it, ran her eye over the formula of the contents, and laid it down again.

'What have you given him?'

'Salt and water, but I had to go out to the phone and get back.'

Romaine mixed up a stronger emetic from bottles taken from her bag and between them she and Marion managed to force it down his throat to make him vomit the poision from his stomach.

'Have you got any olive oil?'

'I think so.'

'Give it me and then go out to the telephone again and ring up

Greatborough Hospital. Mention my name. Tell them to send an ambulance at once.'

Marion wasted no time. When she came back, Ian was still being sick but not violently, and consciousness was returning. He was still in great pain.

'Romaine?' he gasped. 'Forgive me, darling. It was – for you . . .'

'Yes, all right, Ian. Don't try to talk. Can you swallow some of this oil? It will ease the burning till we get you to the hospital.'

Marion stood erect, looking down at the man on the floor and at Romaine kneeling beside him. Her face expressed nothing. She could not have let him die, of course, but she did not care greatly if he did, except that it would rob her of her revenge.

'Don't – leave me – darling,' she heard him gasp. 'Stay – with me if I'm going – to die.'

'You're not going to die,' said Romaine firmly, 'but you're going to feel very ill. I'm going to help you and you can sit in the chair until the ambulance comes. Help me!' peremptorily to

Marion, who had not offered to do so.

Silently she obeyed, putting a strong arm beneath him and heaving him into the chair indicated. Her lip curled in disgust at the vomit on his jacket which had escaped the bowl Romaine had held for him. Romaine saw the look and spoke sharply.

'Get some warm water and clean him up a bit,' she said. 'There is no need for him to go to the hospital in that state. Then you'd better get a bag ready.'

'What with? He doesn't live here, you know. There's nothing here of his,' said Marion in a tone of studied insolence.

'Then you'd better go to his house and fetch them. I'll stay here with him and if necessary I'll go to the hospital with him. You can follow when you've collected what he needs, pyjamas, dressing-gown, slippers and his washing and shaving things.'

Her voice was coldly authoritive.

'I've got my children to look after. Besides, in the general ward they'll provide him with what he wants, won't they?'

'You'll put him in a private ward,

331

surely, Mrs Vannery?'

'And pay for him? Why should I. He took the stuff himself, didn't he? It's nothing to do with me. But if you want him to take his own things, why don't you go and get them? You know your way about the house.'

Her eyes, which had been staring at Romaine insolently, fell before the straight, clear gaze. The younger woman held herself with calm dignity and did not vouchsafe a reply, and a moment later the ambulance drew up and the men entered with their stretcher.

'One of you had better ride inside with him,' she said to them, 'and he will probably vomit again. Sit him up and let him get as much as he can away and keep him conscious if you can.'

He gave her an imploring look but she turned away from him and scribbled a note on his case for the hospital, giving it with the half-empty packet to the man. Neither she nor Marion went in the ambulance, which was driven away rapidly.

Then the two women faced each other in the disordered room, Romaine calm and ice-cold, Marion's anger increasing before the other's composed dignity.

'I suppose you know that all this is your fault?' she snapped.

'Mrs Vannery, why did your husband try to take his own life? May I suggest that it was because you had left him and refused to return? The police will have to be informed of the attempted suicide, of course, and it took place in your house.'

'You've got a nerve, haven't you? Yes, it was because I refused to go back to him, but you know why, don't you? If he killed himself, I couldn't take out an action against him and you'd get off scot free. All very fine and large if it had worked out, but it didn't, did it? I daresay it would have suited your purpose for him to die, but you had to save his life, Dr Elster. Funny that, wasn't it?' and she gave a short, mirthless laugh.

'This is the first time you have made any direct accusation against me, Mrs Vannery, and it is without any justification at all. If these rumours go on spreading in the village about me, I warn you that I shall take legal action against you for slander.'

'You will, will you? We'll see about that. And if there are rumours, who can prove that I started them? All I did was to leave my husband and take the children with me. What people speculate about my reasons are not my fault. They think what they like.'

Romaine managed to swallow her impotent anger without revealing it. Marion Vannery might be speaking the truth. At least no one could prove otherwise at the moment.

'Someone is spreading lies about me and your husband, Mrs Vannery, and you surely know him well enough to know that they cannot be true, whatever your opinion of me.'

'Ian's a man, and all men can be fools when a pretty girl comes along. Anyway, we'll see. When Ian is well enough, you'll both have a chance of having your say. I'm going for a Judicial Separation.'

'You haven't a hope of succeeding,' retorted Romaine hotly. 'There's not a shadow of evidence, as any reputable lawyer you go to will tell you.'

'Then I'll go to a shady one who

knows all the tricks. Some of them will do anything for money, and I've got money.'

'You'll be wasting it.'

'I don't think so, even if I lose the case. No one can prevent me from bringing it.'

'It's aimed at me rather than at Ian? Mrs Vannery, what have I ever done to you to make you feel so vindictive? I have always been friendly and pleasant.'

'Friendly? Pleasant? Yes, you have, haven't you? You and your fine folks and their stuck-up friends! Very pleasant and friendly when you can make use of us, but we're not good enough to be invited into your houses through the *front* door. "Go round to the back door and Cook will give you a cup of tea," or to my Joan and Connie, "Run along, little girls, and find your mother. You mustn't play here, you know, with our children. Here's sixpence for you." Yes, very friendly and pleasant! That's what the government pays *you* for, *Dr* Elster.'

Romaine almost reeled back from the viperish tongue and the bitter, spiteful face. She had no idea that people, Mrs

Vannery at any rate, thought of her or her parents and their friends like that. She would have said, unthinkingly perhaps, that in this day and age there were no class distinctions but evidently they were being kept alive by the very people who stood to benefit by their eradication. In a way, the woman was justified, she thought uncomfortably. Mrs Vannery would never have been shown in at the front door, nor had she presented herself at it on the few occasions on which she had called to see Lady Manning; nor would she have been invited to dinner and she was remembering an occasion on which there had been a children's tennis party at Glen House, and the Vannery children had come to wait for their mother, who was superintending in the background for tea on the lawn. They had stood apart, ready to dodge away behind the bushes, eyeing, wistfully perhaps, the little guests in their frilly white frocks and white shoes.

But who would have thought that people like Mrs Vannery, the villagers, plain country people who were always so smiling and polite, were hiding this bitter jealousy and resentment behind the smiles? Did they feel all like that, or was it only Marion Vannery?

And her class consciousness was so great that she was prepared to go to any lengths to strike back at one of them! It was absurd, unreasonable, but could it be true?

'I don't know what to say to you, Mrs Vannery,' she said at last, after a long, uncomfortable pause, 'except to assure you that there has been nothing, nothing at all, between your husband and me that could possibly justify your accusations. We are friends, that's all and surely that is an answer to your statement that people like − like us,' stumbling over the awkwardness of finding a word, 'do not make friends with − well, with people who earn their living in a different way.'

'Friends? Have you ever invited him to dinner, or me? You've sneaked him into that music-room of yours and even had the piano moved out of the drawing-room so that your mother's visitors shan't come upon him playing the piano and be shocked at it! Fancy the gardener in the drawing-room, playing the piano!'

Romaine flushed, knowing it to be the truth.

'It was more convenient to move the piano,' she said.

'Convenient? I'll say it was! And he's got his own piano to play on when he wants to waste his time like that.'

Romaine began to pack the things into her medical case with trembling fingers. This was a poisonous woman and she had her fangs, full of deadly venom, ready to strike at her and Ian, and there seemed nothing to do about it.

'I don't think we've any more to say to each other, Mrs Vannery,' she said, managing to keep her voice steady.

'If you have, you'll be able to say it in court. I wish you a very good evening, Dr Elster,' tauntingly.

'Good evening, Mrs Vannery,' said Romaine coldly, and got into her car and drove away.

There were still a few people waiting in her surgery, but she asked them to go away.

'There's nothing urgent, is there?' she

asked, running her eye over them. 'Is it another prescription you want, Mrs Smith? I'll give it to you. Perhaps the rest of you can come back tomorrow?'

She knew that the news of Ian's attempted suicide would be all over the village in the morning if not tonight. It was incredible how things became known almost as soon as they happened, but they always did.

Presently she rang up the hospital to make enquiries about Ian, received a satisfactory reply and then made her way slowly to the drawing-room where her parents sat watching a television programme, alone for once.

'Are you very much interested, or may I turn it off?' she asked. 'I've got something to tell you.'

She would not risk their hearing the story through any other lips but her own.

'No, dear, turn it off,' said Lady Manning. 'I can't make head or tail of the story. Too many people and these modern actresses always speak with their backs to the camera, or the microphone or whatever it is, and much too quickly.'

Romaine switched off the set and then

stood with her back to it. She looked white and tired.

'It's something rather bad,' she said. 'I'm afraid it's going to be a shock to you. Ian Vannery has just tried to commit suicide. I was sent for and I've got him into Greatborough Hospital. He's not going to die.'

'Vannery? Whatever did he do that for?' asked Sir Julius.

'Romaine, why are you telling us?' asked his wife, knowing from her daughter's face that there was something below the surface.

'Because he did it on my account, mistakenly of course, but – to save me,' said Romaine, and put out a hand to hold the back of a chair.

Sir Julius rose and went to her, drew her forward and pushed her gently into the chair.

'Better sit down, my dear,' he said, and went to the cabinet to pour out a brandy for her.

'To save *you*, Romaine?' asked Lady Manning, startled. 'But what has it to do with you?'

'Drink this, child, and then tell us

quietly,' said her father, putting the glass into her hand and standing over her until she had drunk it.

'Marion Vannery is threatening to take an action for Judicial Separation and naming me in it,' she said then in a tight, restrained voice. 'It isn't true. Of course it isn't true, but she may be able to make it appear so. He thought that by killing himself, he could save me.'

She saw her father's hand tighten round the glass he had taken from her and heard her mother's shocked exclamation and hated what this was doing to them. They had been so good to her, and this was how she was repaying them. She had a momentary sick longing to be back in her safe, happy childhood again, with no Jeff, no Ian. She had not appreciated that happiness until, feeling old and disillusioned, she had lost it.

'I can't believe it,' said her mother when she had recovered her power of speech. 'You – and *Vannery!*'

'You had better tell us how the whole thing came about, my dear,' put in her father's grave voice. 'Something must be done about it, of course, if it is true that

341

this woman can bring such an accusation against you, but tell us about it.'

'You don't believe she had justification, Father? Mother?' her eyes going beseechingly from one to the other.

'Of course we don't. It's impossible!' cried Lady Manning, and a quick look of relief and love flickered in her eyes as she felt the unchanging quality of their devotion.

Then, omitting nothing, seeking to minimise nothing, she gave them the bare bones of the story, ending up with the final disaster of Ian's attempted suicide.

When she had finished, her mother could find nothing to say, looking to her husband for a lead as she had always done in the bigger issues, trusting in his wisdom and guidance.

'Is it possible to prevent this case being brought to court?' he asked. 'I hesitate to suggest it, but can she be — bought off?' in a distasteful tone.

'I don't think so, though money means a lot to her. She has a grudge against you, against all our class, and she sees this as a marvellous opportunity of paying it off. I doubt if she really believes herself that there is any truth in it, but she doesn't love Ian and I don't think she really cares about breaking up the marriage.'

'But what cause have we ever given her?' asked Lady Manning. 'Why should she bear us such a grudge? I'm sure I've been particularly nice to her . . .'

'That's just the point,' said Romaine drearily. 'You've been much "nicer" to her than if she had been one of our friends and she resents it.'

'But why . . .' began Lady Manning, quite at a loss.

'I think I understand,' said Sir Julius. 'It's all part of the social revolution and the sort of inferiority complex from which people like Mrs Vannery still suffer. The more intelligent ones don't of course, but here in a village things move more slowly. Anyway, we need not go on analysing her motives. Let's rather consider what is to be done about it. I think you should go to a good lawyer, Romaine, so as to be prepared if she does do this dastardly thing. I don't think she's a hope of succeeding, by the way, but the damage will have been done to you and your career just by the bringing of the case. I'd better arrange in the morning for you to see Climson.'

Romaine looked gratefully at them. They might not be able to do anything to stop the catastrophe, but it was comforting to know that she had their love and trust and that they had never for a moment doubted her complete truthfulness.

'Thank you for believing me,' she said simply.

'Of course we believe you!' said Lady Manning. 'As if any such thing could possibly be true! Our daughter and – Vannery,' supreme disdain in her tone.

In spite of the gravity of the situation, Sir Julius smiled.

'You see, Lydia? That's the crux of the matter. If it had been someone else, Lord Hartington, for instance, we should not be so appalled. Well, now, I'm sure you're exhausted and worn out with all this, Romaine, so what about prescribing for yourself and having an early night? I only hope no one will call you up, decided to have a baby or anything. I suppose you could not leave your telephone off for once?'

'No, I must do my job — whilst it lasts,' said Romaine with a wintry smile, 'but I'll take your advice, Father, and go to bed.'

She called the hospital again in the morning and then, reluctantly but of necessity, went to Greatborough to see Ian, who had, after all, been sent there as her patient. After this, she need not go again.

She rang up Dr Heath first to explain what had happened. He had not heard about it and sounded amused. Romaine felt that he knew about the rumours connecting her name with Ian's and she was stiff and formal and very much on her dignity.

'I felt you should know as Mr Vannery is your patient,' she said. 'I was merely called in for emergency treatment as the only doctor actually living in Worbury, but if you would like to take it over ...'

'Not at all. Not at all, my dear Dr Elster. You carry on, though of course the hospital doctors are now responsible. After all, he's been your patient before, hasn't he?'

She let that pass.

'I will only make a routine visit, then, and leave the case with the hospital. They will want to see me, of course.'

'The police, too, if they've been notified,' commented Dr Heath with relish, and Romaine snapped back her receiver.

Because of the nature of the case and the inevitable visit of the police, Ian had been put in the small side-ward attached to the main ward, in which was only one bed. He still looked ill, but he was fully conscious now and reasonably comfortable.

He was surprised and embarrassed at seeing Romaine.

'As I attended you last night, I had to come and see you, though you are now out of my hands,' she said, having taken care to leave the door open in spite of the attendant nurse who had taken her to him. 'You're feeling better now, Mr Vannery?' taking the chart which the nurse offered her and studying it.

'Yes. I suppose it was silly of me?'

'Very silly. I hope you'll never do such

346

a thing again?'

'No, I promise you that,' he said humbly.

For a moment their eyes met, and in spite of herself and the watching nurse, her look was soft and compassionate. She was remembering that he had done it, however mistakenly, for her sake.

'You are, of course, in the hands of the doctors here now, you know.'

'You mean you won't be coming again?' he asked wistfully.

'No.' She turned to the nurse. I'll see the R.M.O. before I go. Please send him a message that I am here. Good-bye, Mr Vannery. I hope you'll soon get over the effects of what you did. You were fortunate that they were not more serious,' and without another look at him she went out, thankful to have the interview behind her.

But she was haunted by the look in his eyes, which was that of a faithful dog, wounded by an attempt to save the one beloved being and deserted by that being. 'Greater love hath no man than this', and, however foolishly and mistakenly, he had tried to give his life for hers. She

347

did not go to see him again in hospital, knowing that by this time her own connection with him must have reached it and that a personal visit would only make matters worse, but she could not get him out of her mind.

What lay in the future for him, deserted and alone? Had anyone ever loved her so selfishly and with so little return?

She had not believed that Marion Vannery would carry things as far as she had threatened to do, but soon after Ian had returned from the hospital, she heard from a lawyer who had a doubtful reputation in Greatborough that proceedings had been instituted by Mrs Vannery against her husband for Judicial Separation and that she would be named in the case. At her father's instance, she went to see her own solicitor, Mr Climson, who had told her that there was not the slightest chance of such a plea being successful.

'Only a very vindictive woman would bring such a case, Mrs Elster,' he said, 'but I am afraid nothing can prevent her from doing it if she is bent on it. After the case, assuming that it fails, you could possibly take one against her yourself for defamation of character . . .'

'Oh no. No, I couldn't do that. All the publicity – and there would be sure to be newspaper headlines – I couldn't bear any more,' said Romaine with a shudder. 'And whatever the result, the damage will have been done already. Mud sticks, and there will be plenty of people in the village who will believe that the successful factor has been my father's money and influence. After the case, I must just let it rest and accept the consequences.'

The case, when it was heard, roused enormous interest in the village, of course, and there were lively factions for and against Ian Vannery and Romaine Elster which made her every appearance as she went doggedly about her work a martyrdom. Her impulse was to give it up and sell the practice and move, with her parents, out of the district, but Sir Julius persuaded her not to do so.

'At this stage it could be taken as an admission of guilt,' he said. 'I know that it will mean sheer hell for you, but if you can bear it, I feel that you should be courageous enough to do so. I'll see Vannery and make sure that he is adequately represented in his defence.'

'He's proud and I don't think he would accept help and so sure that his innocence will prevail in any court of British justice,' said Romaine.

'Well, let us hope that he is justified in his belief. You've told me everything, my dear?'

'Everything, Father.'

He kissed her, a rare gesture with him.

'I believe you,' he said, and she returned the kiss gratefully.

As Mr Climson had assured them, the result of the case was a foregone conclusion, but Marion Vannery had succeeded in her object and left the court unruffled by her failure. Ian had refused the offer of help in his defence by Sir Julius but the evidence was so flimsy that it had not needed a highly-paid counsel to get the case refuted. Romaine, sick and white-faced from the ordeal, left the court with Sir Julius and Lady Manning, and her father was at least able to keep the case out of the London newspapers, though it was reported in as great detail as was allowable in the local papers.

'I shall give up the practice now, of course,' she said when they had reached home. 'I couldn't carry on with it. Dr Heath has stood by me in a way I shouldn't have expected of him and has been seeing a good many of my patients and I think perhaps he will manage to take them on until I can sell it.'

She was clearly exhausted and at the end of her tether, and there was now no need for her to continue her work, nor could she have done so.

Dr Heath, inexpressibly shocked by the vindictiveness of the case, had buried his animosity against a member of his own profession, and offered her all the help he could, not only by taking over her patients but also by finding her a purchaser for the practice, and in a few weeks she was free of her obligations.

When she had notified her patients of the final handing over of the practice to her successor, she was touched to tears by receiving a deputation from them and the presentation of a silver table-lighter. The sympathies of the village had swung in her direction, and many were the protests and lamentations, largely from the mothers to whose children she had given such unstinting care and attention.

But at last it was over, and after her final interview with the young and energetic woman who was taking the practice, there was nothing more for her to do and after dinner that night, Sir Julius spoke about the future.

'We did not want to distress you or add to your troubles through all this bad time, Romaine, but we know that you won't want to stay in Worbury so your mother and I have decided to sell Glen House.'

'But Father, you love it so much . . .'

'We love you a lot more, my dear, and we have not been here so long that it will be any wrench to leave it. Have you made any plans for the future?'

'No, except that I don't want to practice again. I may not feel that I even can,' said Romaine wearily. 'Perhaps it's cowardly after all my work and training to give it up, but − I should always be afraid that all this would follow me, and be looking at people for some sign that they knew. The thing is that at the moment I haven't any energy to do anything, but I don't want you to give up your home for me a second time. I've brought nothing but trouble on you in return for all your kindness.'

'Nonsense. None of it has been your fault. We've been thinking that it might be a good thing for you to go away with your mother for a bit, see fresh things, meet fresh people, make a new circle of friends, and then we can decide where we want to live. We're certainly not going to leave you alone.'

She gave them a wintry smile.

'And I don't feel that I want to be alone,' she said, 'but please put out of your mind, Mother, any new ideas of marriage. I've had enough complications of that sort to last me the rest of my life! I'd like to go away for a bit and though I don't want to stay in Worbury, I don't care where we live,' with inexpressible weariness of spirit.

Chapter Ten

ROMAINE and Ian had not met since the hearing of the case, but a few evenings before she was due to go away with her mother, Lady Manning having made all the arrangements in which Romaine had taken little or no interest, he rang her up.

'I've heard that Glen House is up for sale and that you are going away, Romaine. Will you see me before you go?'

Evidently no one could do anything in the village that was not discovered and talked about!

'Do you really want to see me, Ian?'

She did not want to meet him again. It could do her no good, and what good could it possibly do him? She was still haunted by that look in his eyes when she had left him in the hospital. They had not exchanged even once glance whilst the case was being heard, and her father had hurried her away afterwards.

'Please let me see you just this once,' he begged. 'It may be the last time we shall ever meet,' and against her better judgement, she agreed.

'I don't think you had better come here,' she said. 'I'll meet you tomorrow morning in Bournemouth, where we met before. About twelve?' but as soon as she had rung off she regretted her weak surrender to the plea in his voice.

The eager light in his eyes as she came to him in the hotel the next morning made her the more sure of the unwisdom of their meeting, but in spite of that she felt a small core of warmth in her heart. No woman could remain unmoved by such obvious devotion and he, as well as she, had suffered a good deal in the last few months.

'I haven't ordered anything,' he said. 'I wondered if you would have lunch with me somewhere. We could drive into the country, to some little inn. Will you, Romaine?'

She looked round hesitantly. There were very few people there, and she felt they were conspicuous.

'Yes, all right,' she agreed with some reluctance. 'You go first and I'll follow your car.'

Some miles away he pulled up at a

small country hotel where they were unlikely to be recognised, and he ordered lunch.

'It's so long since I've seen you,' he said, his eyes still filled with that warm eagerness.

'It would have been better if we hadn't met again,' she said, but her voice was gentle and regretful.

'I had to see you. I couldn't bear you to go out of my life like that, without being able to tell you how sorry I am for what I have done to you, and – without telling you that I love you, Romaine, and always shall.'

'Ian, please don't,' she said in a troubled voice.

'I must. Please let me. Please listen to me. You've given up your practice and you're going away. I've laid your whole life in ruins.'

'Yours as well,' she reminded him.

'Not really. It woke me up to the full realisation of how empty my life was and how much I have missed. For what it has done to me I'm not sorry. Only for what it has done to you. Life can never be the same for me as it was before I knew you and loved you. Even if I never see you again, I shall at least have known what it is to love a woman with all my heart. Nothing can take that away from me. Marion and I have never meant anything to each other. I know even if she were willing, I could never live with her again. I am going away from Worbury. I have seen her and we have come to what I suppose one might call an amicable arrangement,' with a wry smile. 'We are selling the nursery and dividing the proceeds. Marion has agreed to that. She realises that now there is no possibility of a reconciliation between us. She is to have the lion's share of the business because of the children, but there will still be a sizeable amount for me to make a new start on somewhere else, though I don't think I'm really cut out for running my own business. Marion was always the brains! I've had a good offer from Brood's in Somerset, to take charge of their landscape gardening, which would suit me much better than trying to start up on my own again.'

Romaine had listened to all this, had

watched his fine, sensitive face grow eager and heard the increasing enthusiasm in his voice, seen the pleading, hopeful expression in his eyes, and she was gradually beginning to understand why he was telling her.

When he paused, she made no reply and after that pause, he went on.

'Romaine, I think that when all this is settled, Marion could be persuaded to divorce me. She sees that everything is over between us and I have a feeling that she is vaguely ashamed of having brought that case. I don't mean that it would involve you. I know the ways and means and would, of course, employ them. Darling, you know what I am trying to say, don't you? You're my whole life, everything I could ever have dreamed of. If I am free – *when* I am free – can I have any hope that you will marry me?'

'I wish you hadn't asked me that, Ian,' she said in a troubled voice. 'I didn't realise that – that you might . . .'

'Now that it's more than remotely possible, may I come and ask you again?'

The idea was so surprising, her mind so confused, Ian's face and voice so hopeful, so charged with the love to which she had so long been a stranger, that she could not at first find words.

'I – I don't know what to say. I'm fond of you, Ian. We've been good friends, good companions, but . . .'

He stretched his hand across the table and covered hers with it. They were alone in the room.

'Don't finish that sentence, Romaine. I know what you were going to say, that you don't love me. But it will come, my darling. At least give me a chance, and yourself. You say yourself that we are good friends and companions, and what better basis is there for marriage? You're young, but you've known heart-break and disillusionment and you know what are the real values in life. Let me see you sometimes, write to you wherever you are. Will you let me do that?'

She hesitated.

'Ian dear, it would be so much better to forget me, to put all this behind you.'

'I could never do that. You'll let me write? Answer my letters occasionally?'

'I am going to travel with my mother for a bit, Italy first and then probably to the States.'

'Give me a poste restante address so that I can catch up with you now and then.'

'Well – write to me in Rome, at the Victoria, at the end of the week,' she said reluctantly. 'I think we'd better go now, if you don't mind, Ian.'

Why had she been so foolish as to encourage him by saying he might write? It would have been so much better, as she had said, if they both put this behind them and he forgot her. She had never imagined that any such position could arise, that Marion would in any circumstances set him free.

But as Ian's letters came, sometimes two or three at a time as she and her mother moved about from place to place, she found herself looking for them, disappointed if she did not find one. They were not love letters in the ordinary sense, though in each was some phrase to tell her that she was always paramount in his thoughts. He wrote of his own affairs, telling her of the successful sale of Merridew Nurseries and that Brood's were willing to wait for him until he had initiated the new owner into the details of the business. Then, as she began to answer his letters, which she had not done at first, he showed an interest in what she was doing and where she went and the people she met, of whom she wrote entertainingly.

He was becoming a part of her life, nearer to her by his letters than he had ever been and she began to think deeply of the new position that was developing between them. They were more than friends now and less than lovers. They might almost have been a happily married couple separated for a time and they wrote more freely and frankly of their thoughts as the friendship ripened.

Then (they were now in New York) he touched for the first time on their future.

'I hope to be free in a few weeks' time,' he wrote. 'How soon will you be in England again?'

She knew that the hiatus was nearly over and that she would have to make up her mind, one way or the other, as to what she was going to do about marrying him.

The thought was no longer such an incredible one. She knew that her parents would be opposed to it, but it was her life whose course she was deciding and, once convinced that her happiness lay with Ian, they would accept it. She was thirty and took so little interest in the various men she met, eminently eligible from her mother's point of view, that Lady Manning had given up hope of being able to influence her in that direction.

'Mother dear, I know you'd like me to marry again,' she said once to her laughingly, 'but really I'm not interested. I've never been a social butterfly and I couldn't start being one now. I'm just not cut out for that sort of life. In fact, I'm already getting tired of all this flitting about, the entertaining and the parties and so on, and Father must be missing you badly.'

'Well, he is, of course,' admitted Lady Manning. 'I wish you could find someone like him, darling, so steady and reliable and still in love with me after all these years,' with a tender smile for her absent husband whom she herself was missing more than she would have admitted to Romaine.

Romaine thought of that marriage, which was surely as perfect as any human relationship could be. Ian was like her father, she thought, steady and reliable and loving her with a love that would surely last all the years of his life. If she could not feel for him the wild tumult of the love she had once known with Jeff, did it really matter any more? There could be none of that tumult now between her father and mother, but they shared something better, more enduring and, parted for these few months, their only desire was to be together again.

Could she not attain that quiet happiness with Ian, with whom she had so much that was basic in common? And, remembering how on that one occasion in his arms he had been able to stir her senses and arouse her desires, would it be so impossible for him to reawaken in her some semblance of the love which could enrich and sweeten their shared life?

'Let's go home, Mother,' she said

suddenly, and that night she wrote to Ian and gave him the answer for which he had been waiting and hoping during these months apart.

You say that you will be free in a few weeks' time [she wrote]. *That means free for me, doesn't it? As you know, I've been uncertain in my mind about how we should make out in the future, you and I, and whether I can give you what you deserve and have the right to expect, but if, when things are finally at an end between you and Marion, you are still of the same mind, shall we meet and talk it over? I am not a child now or even very young and I no longer expect the heavens to open or the sun to shine all the time, and I don't think you do. But I am sincerely fond of you, Ian dear, and in your letter you have put so much of yourself, so much that I can admire and trust and, I think, love. It isn't much to go on, I know, but is it enough?*

I want you to think about that very deeply before we meet again. We are starting for home, by sea because my mother hates flying, and my father is meeting us for a holiday in Paris before we return to England, so it will be some weeks until we reach each other, by which time your divorce will probably have gone through. I'll let you know where you can write to me in Paris and meantime we shall, of course, keep this to ourselves.

She did not know how to end that letter. She wanted to be absolutely honest with Ian, and she could not say 'with love' when she knew it was not yet love she felt for him, so she just signed her name. He would understand. His understanding of her was one of the most endearing things about him. She could be herself with no pretences and no fear.

Her letter brought the most profound satisfaction and happiness to Ian who during all this time had scarcely dared to let himself hope for it though it was only for that end that he had been able to bring himself to face the humiliating conditions by which he could get his divorce.

Marion's change of attitude about it had been a surprise in spite of his vague hope that he might bring it about.

'We are never likely now to come together again, Ian, or to make anything of our marriage,' she had said brusquely when they had met to discuss the sale of the business. 'It was only the business that kept us together and since we both want to part with that, there's no point in trying to patch things up. I may have been a fool in bringing that case. I don't know. But since we've been apart, I've realised that we're better off and I don't want to start again. If you're fool enough to imagine that Romaine Elster will ever marry you, you can try. I'll divorce you if you give me grounds.'

'Not citing Romaine,' he said at once.

She gave a shrug.

'Any way you like. The whole thing's disgusting.'

It had dragged on and even now the case was not listed for hearing, and Romaine's letter sent him into a fever of expectation, but Marion would do nothing to hurry it, even if she could.

'It's of no consequence to me,' she said indifferently. 'Why should I trouble about it? You've got what you want. Let

366

the law take its course.'

He wondered if she were really as indifferent as she sounded, but he dared not press her further. It would, he thought bitterly, be just like her to call the whole thing off if she knew how ardently he longed for his freedom.

He had to content himself with writing long letters to Romaine, letters in which he had no longer to hide from her his love and longing. For the first time in his life he was writing love letters, and each one revealed to her the intensity of his happiness and his eager anticipation of their marriage. She had told him that her parents must not be told until his divorce was through and he was completely free, but his letters, which came daily to her once she was in Paris, could not, she knew, have escaped their knowledge though there was no mention of them.

She was restless and Ian had made her as impatient of the delay as he was himself. Having made her decision, she wanted to be irrevocably committed to it, to marry him and begin to rebuild her life with some purpose and design in it again. She wanted to see Ian again and yet, deep in her mind, was the fear she had, in her loneliness, let him assume more importance in her thoughts than really existed. She had little to distract her thoughts from him and no plans for the future. She felt that if she continued to practise her profession, she would always be dogged by the fear that her part in the hideous case brought against her, vindicated though she had been, might pursue her, so that she would never be free from it.

What had her life to offer her now, other than this marriage to a man who adored her, and of whom she was sincerely fond? No other man had aroused the least interest. She knew Ian intimately and could trust him never to alter nor to disappoint her. Sharing his life she would be tranquil and peacefully happy.

Her parents had taken a furnished flat in Paris for three months, assured that she was content to be there with them, renewing old friendships and making new ones. It was the first holiday Sir Julius had taken away from the business in which her brother was proving his worth, and after their months apart, he and his wife were enjoying being together again. They were in fact, as they said laughingly, spending a second honeymoon at the scene of their first one and they made sentimental journeys to various spots which held happy memories for them, Romaine assuring them that she had no wish to go with them but was perfectly content to be left alone to pursue her own acquaintances with a city full of charm and interest.

Their pleasure in each other's society and their enjoyment of a freedom from the business activities which had always been paramount to Sir Julius was pleasant to see, but inevitably she felt shut out and drawn the more closely towards thoughts of Ian.

As her letters grew almost unconsciously more affectionate, he revealed his ecstatic happiness in their now foreseeable, shared future, for which he was making plans, all of them for her happiness and comfort. Every line of the letters expressed his devotion to her. How could she not be happy in giving him such perfect happiness?

There came an afternoon when, after seeing her parents off to spend a few days out of Paris with some old friends, she decided to go again to the Louvre. The hours hung heavily on her hands and she felt that she had already seen, with her indefatigable mother, all the shops she would ever want to see for the rest of her life.

Inside the Louvre it was quiet and peaceful except for the few groups of tourists who were being shown round by an official guide and, managing to escape them, she found her way to the Mona Lisa, whose enigmatic smile never ceased to interest and intrigue her. What had lain behind those unfathomable eyes at that moment? Had she found the answer to the secret of life, or was she completely disillusioned by it?

She was standing in front of the picture, trying as so many people had to solve that riddle when a voice spoke softly behind her.

'Sharing her thoughts, whatever they are, Romaine?'

She turned sharply as if stung and stared at the speaker, unable to believe

370

her eyes. Her hand went instinctively to her throat to suppress the cry that rose in it, whilst every vestige of colour left her face.

'Surprised to see me? I saw you come in and I've been following you for quite a time, trying to make up my mind to speak. Here, come and sit down. Not going to faint or anything, are you?' and as she swayed on her feet, he put a hand beneath her elbow and guided her to a seat.

'Jeff,' she whispered, her voice a mere thread of sound.

'Himself,' he assured her with the old, jaunty smile which had always been able to turn the heart in her breast, which turned it now.

'I can't believe that it is really you,' she said chokily. 'What are you doing in Paris?'

'I brought a car over for a client. Just delivered it. A smashing affair. But never mind about that now. Have you had enough of this dreary place? Let's get out into the sunshine and have a *fin* somewhere and tell each other the story of our lives! Ready?'

As in a dream, she rose to her feet and went with him, his hand still tucked under her arm.

This could not be happening to her. She could not be here, in Paris, with Jeff.

He went on talking in his gay, inconsequent fashion but she did not listen to what he said, could not have answered him. He was Jeff, and she was with him again and nothing else mattered. She was incapable of coherent thought but knew that her whole being was flooded with the old, unforgettable happiness.

She had been in Paris with him before, only for a few days, but she had not forgotten anything and when he stopped before one of the pavement cafés, gay under its striped awning, she knew that he had not forgotten either. She threaded her way, still in a dream, to the table in a corner where they had sat before and he smiled and ordered from a passing waiter the drinks they had always had.

'Remember?' he asked softly as he took the chair opposite her, and suddenly the tears stung her eyes. It was too much to bear.

'I've never seen you cry before, Romaine.'

She blinked away the tears before they could fall.

'I'm not crying now,' she said.

'Could it be happiness?'

His voice was dangerously soft. There was a hint of the old mockery in it, but it did not quite ring true. There was an under-current of seriousness in it and she dared not meet his eyes for fear of what she might see in them.

She put her handbag on the table and he reached out for her hand and held it in his own, looking down at it and touched her wedding ring.

'Still mine?' he asked.

She nodded, unable to speak.

'You gave me one. Remember? It was too small for me but I wouldn't give it back to you even to have it altered. I've still got it. My talisman,' and he released her hand to take the ring from his pocket and lay it on the table.

He need not have done that, for she remembered it only too well, the signet ring in which, with the foolish sentimentality of those far-off days whose memory was so dangerously near again, she had had engraved the words 'My love for ever' with her initials.

'We were young and foolish,' she said. 'Nothing is for ever, is it?'

'Isn't it? No, perhaps not,' and as the waiter came with the drinks, he picked up the ring and slipped it into his pocket again.

The man gave them a friendly smile. They were obviously lovers, he thought, and all the world, particularly in Paris, loves a lover.

'You haven't married again, Romaine?'

'No,' and she flushed a little. 'Have you?'

'Of course not,' and her flush deepened at the implication of the words.

'You said you came to Paris to deliver a car,' she said, trying to get the conversation on to a normal basis – if anything could ever be normal between them. 'A racing car?'

'No, a Rolls-Bentley, very super, very lush, not to be trusted to Tom, Dick or Harry but only to Jeff,' with an impish smile. 'I'm doing respectable work now.

No more racing. That confounded accident, you know. Can't trust my arms to control a racing car at high speed any more, but not to worry. They're still good enough for every other purpose!' with another mischievous grin.

'I'm sorry. You must miss the racing,' she said primly.

'I did at first. Nearly drove me crazy. Then they let me have a go just to prove that I couldn't do it. I couldn't, so that was that. Now I'm with Mattison's, selling elegant, expensive models to the lordly sort who've never even heard of H.P. Doing quite well too. Believe it or not, I've settled down! But never mind about me. What about you, Romaine? What are you doing here? And for how long will you be doing it?'

She hesitated. She must tell him about Ian, of course, and that she was going to be married — and then, she thought, why should she? It could make no difference to her life now. They were just ships that were passing in the night and had hailed each other in passing.

'I'm here on holiday with my parents,' she said. 'I don't know how long we shall

375

be staying.'

'Not doctoring any more?'

'No. I – I gave it up. I don't suppose I shall ever practise again.'

'Isn't that a pity? You were always keen on it, and it really suited you better than marriage to the madman I was then. How did you come to fall in love with me, my sweet?'

His tone, light and speculating but with that undercurrent of seriousness in it, plucked at her heart-strings. How surely, how maddeningly, he had always been able to do that!

'You do all sorts of things when you're young and don't know much about life or what it can do to you,' she said, trying to make her voice sound casually amused. 'Why did you? Fall in love with me, I mean?'

'Don't you know? Didn't I remember to mention it from time to time? Careless of me! Suppose I remedy the omission – now, Romaine?'

There it was again, the wild music which only he had ever been able to evoke in her, setting all the strings jangling!

Resolutely she smiled.

'Rather late now to recall that old tune, isn't it? It's like trying to play jazz on a harp.'

He chuckled.

'Perhaps you're right. I never could play the harp. Tell me some more about yourself, where you've been living, what you've been doing to fill in the time.'

She ignored the implied suggestion that that was all she had been doing, just filling in the time until they should meet again.

'I've been living in Hampshire, in a small village. I had a practice there.'

'You, in a small village? It didn't work, I take it, since you are on an indefinite holiday?'

'No, it didn't – work. I gave it up.'

'Not been ill, have you? You're thinner, you know,' giving her a critical, appraising look which made her flush again and avoid his eyes.

'Meaning I'm an old hag?'

'Meaning that you're even more beautiful than I remembered,' he said softly, 'and I thought I'd remembered everything about you, the way you smile

377

and look sad at the same time, the curve of your cheek, the way that little bit of hair always got loose and twisted round your ear, your mouth – especially your mouth, my sweet.'

She rose precipitately, upsetting her drink which she had scarcely touched.

'This is quite ridiculous,' she said. 'We'd better go.'

Before she could pick up her handbag, he calmly appropriated it.

'You wouldn't get far without this, would you?'

'Please, Jeff,' she said, a note of desperation in her voice.

He smiled, shook his head, looked at their two saucers which showed the cost of their drinks and put some money down on the table.

'Where next?' he asked.

'I'm going home,' she said. 'Please let me, Jeff.'

'Not yet. I'm coming with you, at least as far as your door. Where is "home", by the way? You're not living in a hotel?'

'We've taken a furnished flat. I'm with my parents. Come if you must, but only as far as the door.'

There was nothing else she could do whilst he retained possession of her handbag. She could hardly struggle with him for it in a public place.

'Do we take a taxi or walk?'

'Walk.'

She would not have trusted him in a taxi with her and she hurried through the streets, feeling ridiculous but helpless.

'I observe that we're in training for the Olympic Games,' he said, easily accommodating his long stride to her shorter one, and in the end she laughed and had to slow down.

'You're really being quite absurd, Jeff,' she said, but he only smiled and when they had reached the block of flats and she stopped, he pushed open the swing door for her and waited for her to go in. The tiny hall held nothing but the gates of the lift and there was no *concierge*.

'What number?' he asked, pulling open the gates.

'Jeff, please leave me here. Please give me my bag,' she entreated him.

'Not yet. What number?' and she had to tell him, for two other people had followed them and were waiting for them to enter the lift, and they were alone in it again by the time it reached her floor.

He opened her bag, looked for the key and found it.

'Will they be in?' he asked.

'Probably,' she said desperately.

'Oh well, I'll take a chance on that. I don't think they'll mind. Your father won't, anyway. I saw him a few months ago. We had a drink at his club.'

She stared at him, stupified.

'You *saw* my father?'

'Yes, didn't he tell you? No, I suppose he wouldn't. Let sleeping dogs lie and all that.'

He had been fitting the key into the lock, and now he turned it and opened the door. The inner doors stood open. There was no sound in the flat. It had the unmistakable air of being empty but for them, and he grinned mischievously as he closed the door behind them.

'We're in luck,' he said. 'Not back yet,' and he went in at the open door of the sitting-room and put her bag down on the table.

'Please go now, Jeff,' she asked him,

but there was a quiver in her voice.

'Don't you think you owe us a drink, having upset yours without giving me time to have mine?' and she moved to a cupboard and opened it with that feeling of being caught in a trap.

'What will you have?' she asked, gulping down her panic.

He came behind her and put his arms round her and turned her to face him.

'This,' he said, and kissed her, holding her helpless until she ceased to struggle and stood there, her eyes closed, her whole being caught and held in the old, remembered joy, the ecstasy, the rapture of his arms about her and his lips compelling her own.

When he released her mouth, his arms still held her.

'I've wanted that from the first moment I saw you going into the Louvre,' he said in the soft voice of a lover. 'I've always wanted it, all the time we've been apart. You too, Romaine?'

'Oh yes — yes, Jeff!' and she swayed towards him again, her arms locked about him, her mouth warm and eager and passionate. She remembered nothing but that he was Jeff, her beloved, her husband, and that she was in his arms again.

'Are they coming back?' he whispered against her lips.

'No.'

She scarcely knew that she had spoken, but he laughed softly and slipped her coat from her shoulders, pushed her dress aside to kiss her throat and her neck and then she felt his fingers finding the zip at the back and pulling down the slide.

'Oh, Jeff – no,' she said weakly and put up her hand to stop him, but he laughed again and pushed it away.

'Why?' he asked. 'I've done it hundreds of times. Remember? Haven't I told you that I remember everything about you? There's nothing we don't know about each other, is there? And its been so long, my darling, so long! We're aching for each other, me for you and you for me.'

'Jeff, we can't – you mustn't . . .'

With a last despairing movement she tried to free herself and the frail satin straps over her shoulders broke beneath his questioning hands.

'And that isn't the first time either, is it?' he laughed and bent to kiss the smooth skin of shoulders and breast and she knew that she was lost, powerless to resist him and herself and the wild upsurge of desire which only he could rouse in her.

'My darling,' she whispered brokenly. 'My darling.'

★ ★ ★

It was quite dark in the room when Romaine woke with a confused sense of catastrophe and, automatically switching on the bedside light, saw Jeff's dark head on the pillow and his bare shoulder where her own head had lain.

She was shocked into full consciousness and crept out of the bed without waking him and, huddled in her dressing-gown, tried to make sense of what had happened. How could it possibly have happened? What madness had possessed her?

Then, looking almost fearfully at his sleeping face, she felt herself melting again with an unbearable tenderness for him, for Jeff, her husband in a way that no other man could ever be. She loved him. He held her for ever though she might never see him again, must never see him again. It could not bring them any real or enduring happiness, only these brief, wild moments of passion which meant nothing to Jeff. She despised herself for the ease with which he had been able to possess her again. She might tell herself that she loved him, but what was she to him? No more than an hour of excitement, a few days perhaps, at the most a few weeks, and then the torment of another betrayal, those same tortures to go through again, the same anguish and unhappiness.

And there was Ian.

The thought of his loving kindness, his tenderness which sought only her happiness, his faithful love which would be her guard for ever, swept over her in a stream of comfort. She had given him her promise and she was glad — glad! She must make Jeff understand that she had finished with him for ever, that there could never be another occasion like that of the last few hours.

She moved softly about the room but as she did so, his eyes opened and he looked at her and smiled, stretching out a hand.

'What are you doing up?' he asked. 'Come back to bed, darling,' his voice as lazy and contented as the purring of a cat.

She drew back so that he could not reach her.

'No, Jeff,' she said. 'I'm getting up, and you must go.'

'Why, my sweet? Your people won't be back tonight. You told me so. And even if they were, does it matter? I'm your husband.'

'Not now.'

'Well, it comes to the same thing. Let's get married again. It was all so silly when we love each other.'

'That's not what I want at all.'

'Then why did you let me make love to you? You did, you know. It was no one-sided affair, was it? Come on, sweet. Own up that you've never stopped loving me and wanting me any more than I've stopped loving and wanting you.'

She shivered and drew farther away from him.

'That isn't love. It's just sex, the biological urge.'

He chuckled.

'Are you suggesting that any man, given the same opportunity, would have had the same effect on you?'

'No, of course not.'

'Then if I am the only man who could give you — what was it you called it? the biological urge . . .'

She stopped him.

'All right. I'll admit it. Perhaps you are the only one. That doesn't make it love.'

He sat up, hunching his knees and pulling the bed-clothes about him, evidently prepared to have an interesting discussion with her.

'Now that's a point. What is the demarcation line between love and sex? I find it entertaining to discuss that with a doctor, who should know all about it.'

He was smiling at her, mocking her gaily, his mischievous eyes an invitation though his hands were now hugging his knees and not attempting to touch her.

386

'Oh, you're impossible!' she cried and snatched up her clothes and fled into the bathroom.

He tried the handle of the door.

'Darling, you've locked me out!' he complained, but she did not reply and when she came out, she was fully dressed.

'You can go in now. Then you must go,' she said briefly, not looking at him.

'Aren't we going to have breakfast first?'

'Breakfast at eight o'clock in the evening?'

It maddened her that she had to restrain an impulse to laugh.

'All right. Let's go out to dinner,' he said and vanished into the bathroom. She heard him singing tunelessly as he had always done.

What could she do? Now that she had been fool enough to bring him here, now that he seemed to have established something or other with her father, she would not be able to prevent him from coming again. He had told her that he was expected to stay in Paris for several days at the request of the client to whom he had delivered the car.

He sauntered back into her bedroom to finish his dressing, used her toilet water, borrowed her brush. It was fantastically like what it had always been and though she went into the sitting-room, he kept the door open so that he could talk to her.

'Where would you like to go for dinner? I'm quite well off. A change for me? I'm changed in lots of ways, you know. I've got a good job and I'm a respectable working man now. Sorry I haven't got my car here, but you'll like it when you see it. It's the latest Jag, a smasher.'

'I'm not likely to see it.'

'Of course you are. You're coming back to England with me.'

'I'm not, Jeff. Didn't you listen to anything I said?'

He came into the sitting-room, her clothes brush in his hand.

'Brush me down, darling, will you?' he asked, handing it to her, and automatically she took it from him and began to do so.

Then she threw the brush down, the

task unfinished.

'Jeff, it's no use. You've simply got to understand. I'm not going to England or anywhere else with you I'm never going to see you again. You asked me if I had married again. I haven't, but I'm going to, in a few months' time.'

'H'm. I see. Anybody I know?'

'No.'

'Tell me about him — poor chap.'

'Why do you say that?' she asked sharply.

'Because he'll be getting a raw deal since you love me.'

'I don't. I don't!'

He smiled disbelievingly, and then his face grew grave again.

'Well, let that pass. Going to tell me about him?'

'He's — he's sincere and fine and honest, a man to be trusted — and he loves me and always will,' she said, but how could she talk about Ian to Jeff? Even the memory of him was a pale wraith at this moment.

'In fact, except for the last part, everything that I'm not. You have omitted the most important part, which

389

is that you love him and always will.'

'I do, and I shall,' she said, and if she failed to hear the defiance in her voice, he did not. 'I mean to marry him, Jeff.'

'All right. Let's accept that, and I hope you'll be very happy with him. Now what about dinner? You probably know Paris better than I do, so you choose.'

She felt defeated and helpless. She lifted her hands and let them fall to her sides again.

'Jeff, you're impossible. What is one to do about you?'

'Just come out and have dinner with me. You surely can't refuse that to an old friend? Besides, you've got to eat somewhere and so have I. Why should we eat alone?'

'Well — tonight then, but it's for the last time and I must be mad to even agree to that,' she said crossly, and picked up her coat from the chair on which it had been lying and went past him swiftly and out into the corridor which connected the flats.

She was mad, of course. She must be and already, as she went towards the lift, she was regretting it, but it was too late. She knew him and that if she turned back now he would not hesitate to batter at the door until she opened it again.

But it was impossible to remain angry or be on bad terms with him, for as the evening progressed, he was at his most charming, entertaining her as he always had done by his outrageous tales and making her laugh. It was dangerous for her to be with him and she knew it. In its way it was almost as dangerous as it had been in the flat, for though he did not speak a word of love to her, his every look was a caress.

When he took her back, he stood inside the little hall with her and did not suggest even getting into the lift with her as she had been afraid he would do.

Instead he kissed her, gently and without passion.

'Thank you for having dinner with me, Romaine. May I telephone you tomorrow when I've contacted my client and found out whether he needs me or not? I made a note of your telephone number.'

'It's so much better not to, Jeff,' she

said but her voice lacked conviction.

She wished desperately that her parents would return or that Jeff would have to go back to London, but for two more days she saw him constantly and knew she had been deluding herself by trying to pretend to herself as much as to him that she was no longer in love with him. She knew that, whatever had happened in the past to separate them, he was and always would be the only man she could ever love, and on the second evening with him, when he told her he would have to go back in the morning, she could hide it no longer.

Her eyes were sad, her heart full of grief, and as they danced, she pressed herself closely to him and neither of them spoke until the music ended and their arms fell from each other reluctantly.

'Come with me tomorrow, Romaine.'

There was now no laughter in him, no mockery in his tenderness. He had changed in their two years apart, changed almost beyond recognition now that she had come to know this new Jeff. He could still be gay and full of fun, but he had grown up, was no longer the laughing Peter Pan she had never understood.

She shook her head.

'I can't, Jeff,' she said in a strangled voice.

'Because of this Ian?'

'Yes.'

'He will find someone else. You belong to me.'

'I haven't told you the whole of it. He is getting a divorce from his wife.'

'Not because of you, Romaine?'

He was startled and incredulous.

'No, not really. That is – we've done nothing wrong, Jeff. Please believe that. But – if I hadn't promised to marry him, he would not be getting free. He – he tried to take his own life because of me.'

'He's weak, Romaine. No man has any right to lay a burden like that on a woman. It's a kind of blackmail,' he said indignantly.

'It's not quite like that, Jeff. There's a longer story to it than that.'

'I'm waiting. I've got all the time there is,' he said grimly.

She shook her head.

'It's no use. I've made up my mind to

marry him. I've given him my promise
. . .'

'You gave it to me first, Romaine. No,
don't answer that, I know I broke it first
and that absolved you, and now we're in
this unholy mess. I know I broke up
your life once though, as you've said
yourself, sex isn't love and there was
only sex between me and Elinor and the
others. It was just that I was parted from
you . . .'

She made a weary gesture.

'Must we go into all that again, Jeff?
It's over now.'

'I know, but there's something I want
to tell you, and that is that in these two
years, ever since the divorce, I've never
had any other woman. Do you believe
that? You can, you know. It's perfectly
true. Somehow I always believed that we
should come together again, that we'd
had something wonderful between us
that some day we should find again. And
now we've found it and you won't take it
. . .'

'Can't take it, Jeff,' she said with a sad
finality in her voice.

'Well, have it your own way,

Romaine, but you can't believe that you're going to find happiness with anyone else.'

'Is one's own happiness to be the only object? It's no use, Jeff. Let me go now. Don't come with me and – please don't try to see me again. I can't bear any more,' and she went swiftly from him, threading her way between the tables and the dancers.

He watched her until she was out of sight.

Chapter Eleven

IAN VANNERY stared at the telegram which had been lying on his desk at Brood's since the morning. He looked at the time of delivery. Ten o'clock, but he had been out all day.

Its very curtness conveyed a sense of urgency.

Come. Marion.

He had written her a week ago, begging her to do what she could to speed up the divorce but she had not replied. And now this telegram had come.

He did not want to see her again, but if this was the only way, he must go.

He looked at his diary of work. What he had to do today could be put in hand without him and he had a free hand at Brood's. If he went now, tonight, he could be back later tomorrow. If Marion had sent for him so peremptorily, he would get an answer from her in no other way. He put from his mind the fear that she had changed her intentions towards the divorce. It had gone too far and since she had agreed to it with a certain hard finality, she would not alter her mind. That was not her way.

But on the journey from Somerset, the worry bit into his mind as to what had happened that she should want so urgently to see him.

It was late when he reached Worbury and the village was in darkness. The house too was in darkness. Evidently she had given him up, had not believed he would come that night but, going round to the back of the house, he saw a light burning in the room which he thought to be the one the two children shared and whilst he stood looking up at it uncertainly, the curtain was cautiously drawn aside and he saw Joan's face.

'Joan, it's me, Father,' he called.

He saw her turn to have a consultation with Connie, and then she pushed up the window.

'I'll come down and let you in,' she said, and he thought she looked and sounded frightened.

Presently the bolts on the back door rattled and both little girls stood there in their dressing-gowns and he went into the kitchen, which struck him at once as untidy, the supper things unwashed and their school books scattered about the table.

He kissed them. It was a long time since he had seen them and he felt a rush of affection for them and was touched when, quite unusually, they clung to him.

'Has anything happened?' he asked. 'Where's your mother.'

'In the hospital,' said Joan. 'They took

her away this morning. She said you would come but we've been waiting for you all day. We thought you weren't coming.'

'The hospital? Is she ill? Has there been an accident or something?'

'Not an accident. She's been ill and today they took her away and we're frightened. You won't go away again, Father?'

That was Connie, and she still clung to his hand.

'Not tonight, of course. Where is she?'

'In Greatborough Hospital.'

'And you don't know what's the matter?'

They shook their heads, standing close together and looking childishly forlorn.

'Well, go back to bed and I'll go out and telephone to the hospital,' he said. 'It's all right. I'm not going to leave you.'

It took him some time to get any satisfaction from the hospital.

Yes, Mrs Vannery had been admitted that morning, he was told when the Night Sister had been brought to speak to him, but it was against the rules of the hospital to give him any explicit information. She was in no immediate danger and was asleep and there was no need for him to go that night, but he could see one of the doctors in the morning.

After a restless night of worried conjecture, he saw the children off to school and drove into Greatborough. He was not permitted to see Marion, but when after a long wait he saw the doctor, the news about her stunned him.

Marion had been stricken down with polio.

'We can't tell yet how serious it is, but she is, of course, isolated and we shall know in a few days, Mr Vannery, but at the moment it is paralytic. This condition may improve but, as you probably know, it is serious and highly contagious. You may see your wife but not touch her or go too near her.'

When he was shown into the small ward, Marion's eyes were open and she was conscious but she could not move. Already, and so swiftly, she was completely paralysed and helpless.

'Sorry,' she managed to articulate with difficulty and that was all.

He was stricken with horror and pity for her and, at that moment, had no thought for himself nor what it might mean to him. It was beyond belief that this could be Marion, this helpless, immovable log.

'Marion – my dear . . .' he said in a strangled voice. 'Try – try not to worry. I'll stay, of course. The children . . .'

He could not go on, but he saw a look of relief in her eyes and knew that this was all he could do for her.

'You'd better go now, Mr Vannery,' said the nurse quietly. 'She must not be disturbed or have any emotional upset. You can see her again presently, this afternoon perhaps.'

He drove back to Worbury still filled with that horror which numbed him.

To see Marion, the strong, the capable, the utterly self-reliant like this!

He got on the telephone to Mr Brood, who did not even know he had a wife and family, but he was a kindly man and he asked no questions.

'Of course you must stay, Mr Vannery,' he said. 'I'll arrange for someone to take over your work for the time being and there's no question of the job being kept open for you, so don't worry about that. Keep me informed about your wife.'

The next few days were a nightmare. The little girls, capable since they had been brought up by Marion, looked after themselves and him and a kindly neighbour came in and out. He knew there must be lively talk in the village about Marion's illness and his sudden reappearance, but he met only sympathetic glances and many offers of help. Joan and Connie, after their first fright at finding themselves without their domineering and all-powerful mother, soon accepted the new conditions and even, as Ian was uncomfortably aware, became relaxed and at ease with them. They had not seen Marion and they found life far easier and more enjoyable under the lighter rule of the father whom they had never really known. They chattered and giggled, made the house untidy with the playthings and litter which had formerly been confined to their bedroom, and ran in and out with muddy shoes, unreproved. For the first time their house had become a home to them, and Ian was guiltily aware of it. They asked dutifully after their mother when he had been to the hospital, but he felt that they were not really concerned about her. There was a holiday spirit about and sometimes he came in to find the kitchen filled with their friends, who had never been welcome when Marion was there.

A specialist from London was called in and every known treatment given, but at last Ian was told the tragic truth. It was unlikely that Marion would ever walk again, though there was no reason why she should not live for many years.

He drove on to the moors and stopped the car and sat in it and faced the future.

He could not leave her. The divorce case was on the lists at last, but was deferred because of her illness. Now he knew that it would never be heard. Romaine and his happiness were lost to him for ever. Sitting alone, his arms across the wheel and his head bent on them, he passed through his Gethsemane. Then, grey-faced and stricken, he drove back to Worbury and, far into the night, wrote his letter to Romaine.

It followed her to London, to the hotel where the Mannings had taken temporary accommodation until they could find a house or flat to suit them.

She glanced at the envelope and put it into her bag to be read when she had gone to her room. It was some time since she had heard from him, and it was probably to tell her that the divorce had gone through at last. She was still determined to marry him and resolved to make him a good wife. She had not seen Jeff again and was not likely to do so. She tried not even to think about him. She bitterly regretted having seen him again and having shared with him that shattering experience which had told her the truth about herself and the love which she still held, immortal, in her heart.

Late that night she remembered Ian's letter and got out of bed to open the envelope, slowly and reluctantly.

It was not a long letter, though it had taken him hours to write it and in the end he had just told her, plainly and simply, what had happened and that he could not marry her.

I cannot leave her. You will understand that. You would not want me to do otherwise. I want you to know, my darling, that I have known for a long time, right from the first, I think, that you have never been able to feel for me as I do for you. That makes it easier for me to do this. I had hoped and believed that in the end I should be able to win your love. Now I know that it is not to be. Be happy, Romaine. Somewhere, with some other man, you will find your happiness, a greater happiness than I, with all my love, could give you. And don't think of me as just sacrificing myself to what we both know is my duty. I shall have my children, and Marion needs me and has never needed me before.

So it is good-bye, my beloved. God bless you and keep you and give you happiness. Ian.

Romaine pressed the paper to her lips and the tears came, the slow tears running down her cheeks unchecked. He had loved her. Perhaps she would never know such a love again, and the tears were for the love she had not been able to give.

What could she say to him in farewell that would not hurt him more?

In the end she wrote only a few lines, but knew he would not want her to say more. He would understand. He had always understood her better than anyone else had done, even to knowing that she had not loved him.

Ian put the letter with all the others, and burnt them, watching them as they were reduced to blackened ashes and finally to grey dust.

Good-bye, my love, my one love.

Then he went to the hospital to see Marion, as he had done every day.

He saw from her face that she knew she would never be well again. No one had told her, but she had said nothing when they had tried to buoy her up with false hopes and bright, insincere smiles. Her mind was unimpaired, her brain alert. She had always faced life with courage.

It did not fail her now.

But there was, for all her courage, a look of defeat in her eyes and, kneeling by the iron lung in which they had placed her, he answered that look with a voice that was strangely gentle.

'I shall never leave you, my dear,' he said.

Her eyes closed and she did not try to speak, but the slow, difficult tears, the first he had ever seen her shed, forced themselves between her closed lids.

After a time, she slept, and he went softly away.

★ ★ ★

It was weeks before Romaine could bring herself to contact Jeff again. Then the ache and the hunger for him would not be appeased.

He had told her where she could find him, though she had told him she never would.

'Put the address away somewhere, darling,' he had told her with nonchalant lightness. 'You never know.'

Now she found the scrap of paper,

tucked away in her handbag.

It was a flat at the top of an old house, with many stairs to climb. He had always liked to be 'on top of the world', even when they had had to live in that dreary house in a back street.

No one answered her knock, and as a last resort, she turned the handle. It was not locked and it yielded. That again was so like Jeff.

'If anybody wants anything of mine badly enough to steal it,' he had told her laughingly, 'let them have it.'

It was in darkness, and she switched on the lights and looked round curiously, almost with fear. This place held a part of his life in which she had no share, a part so remote from her as hers had been from his at Worbury. She had tried to turn back the clock, but the hands had gone on inexorably.

The flat was a bare little place, with probably someone else's furniture, adequate but without real comfort or brightness. There were no pictures, no ornaments, no flowers, no cushions – a place to exist in but not to *live* in as she understood the art of living. This was the sitting-room. Beyond it was the kitchen, a small bathroom, and (she went into this last and shrinkingly) the one bedroom. Everything was tidy and moderately clean, so, knowing Jeff, she knew that he employed a woman 'to do' for him, but there was no other trace of a woman's presence, no lingering perfume or drift of powder. She pulled open a drawer. It was, as things had always been, in indescribable confusion, socks, ties, underwear just thrown in together.

She smiled as she remembered his justification for that.

'But, darling, it's much more convenient than your way. Say I want a tie, or a particular pair of socks. All I have to do is to open the drawer, run my eye over the contents, see a bit of whatever I want sticking up, pull it out and Bob's your uncle, whereas you have to go through neat piles of things all on top of one another to find what you want!'

Automatically she began to put things in order, and at the back of the drawer she came upon one of her own nightdresses, a filmy crumpled thing which still bore the faint traces of her perfume, still, she imagined, the imprint of her body. No one else, she knew, had ever worn it. He must have carried it about as a reminder of her all this time, even on that last ill-fated trip to America, for she had not lived with him since.

It caught at her heart, and she folded it and placed it in the drawer again, switched off the light and went back to the sitting-room, which she left in darkness, drawing a chair to the window to sit looking out over the roof-tops of darkening London.

How long she sat there she did not know, but presently she heard his step on the stairs, taking them one at a time, not two as he had always come back to the home she shared with him, full of the small happenings of the day, eager for her feel of her body in his arms and their kiss.

The door of the sitting room stood open, and he paused at once, sensing the presence of another individual though he could not see her and she had not even switched on the light in the little lobby.

'Who's there?' he asked sharply.

'Me, Jeff. Romaine,' she said, with odd apprehension now that the moment had come.

She heard him catch his breath. He stood still in the doorway for a moment.

'Don't turn on the light,' she said. 'Not yet,' and his hand which had gone to the switch dropped again.

Dimly he could see her outline in the chair, but it was her voice which drew him to her, as it always had, as it always would.

'Romaine – Romaine ...' he whispered, and then he went down on the floor beside her, his head buried in her lap.

Her fingers touched his hair, running gently through its strong growth.

'Oh Jeff – my darling,' she said brokenly, and he lifted his head and her mouth came down to meet his.

HERMINA BLACK TITLES IN LARGE PRINT

DENISE ROBINS TITLES IN LARGE PRINT

A Love Like Ours

Sweet Cassandra

Mad Is The Heart

The Crash

Arrow In The Heart

The Untrodden Snow

The Strong Heart

Strange Rapture

Restless Heart

Love and Desire and Hate